Others Available by DK Holmberg

The Cloud Warrior Saga

Chased by Fire
Bound by Fire
Changed by Fire
Fortress of Fire
Forged in Fire

The Lost Garden

Keeper of the Forest
The Desolate Bond
Keeper of Light

Assassin's Sight:

The Painted Girl
The Durven
A Poisoned Deceit
A Forgotten Return

BOUND
BY FIRE

THE CLOUD WARRIOR SAGA
BOOK 2

ASH Publishing
dkholmberg.com

Bound by Fire

ISBN-13: 978-1511808378
ISBN-10: 1511808373

ASH Publishing
dkholmberg.com

BOUND BY FIRE

THE CLOUD WARRIOR SAGA
BOOK 2

CHAPTER 1

The Master Shaper

TANNEN MINDEN SAT AT A LONG, faded oak table, leaning forward as he waited for the instructor to arrive. Only a week in Ethea and already he longed for the forests of Galen around him. Had he been able to find Amia, he wouldn't have bothered coming to this lecture, but he struggled to find her the last few days and when he did, she seemed anxious. How much of the anxiety came from the strange and massive capital city and how much from losing everyone she knew?

After how the lisincend destroyed his home of Nor, he understood that anxiety well.

He rubbed his neck. The aching he'd felt since reaching the city throbbed with more intensity this morning. At first, he thought it the change in altitude—Nor sat much higher than Ethea—but now he wondered if it had to do with the connection he'd made while there. Could the distant sense he still had of the draasin be giving him the pain?

The girl at the end of the table glanced at him again. She had brown hair cut short and a thin face. A green dress several sizes too large draped over her. A thick book rested open on the table in front of her, but she kept looking up from it to him.

Another boy, built like a blacksmith, sat down the table. He kept his eyes fixed straight ahead, as if he feared looking around too much. Tan watched him, waiting for a crack in his focus, but none came. He wore a thick wool jacket dyed a dark blue and his hair was cut short. His skin was deeply tanned.

And then there was a man near the window. He stared out, fingers drumming across the stone as he stared through the opaque glass. He shifted from one foot to another, his boots the only part of him visible beneath the long gray cloak he wore. Even his head was covered, hiding his face.

As far as Tan knew, these were all students at the university. And he was older than each of them.

Since arriving in Ethea, Tan had seen people from all over the kingdoms. It had surprised him how different each style of dress was, and he hadn't been here long enough to know where each style came from. Amia might, since she was one of the Aeta, traders given the freedom to wander without concern for borders, if only he could find her.

Like usual, no one spoke. Tan had attended few classes since arriving in Ethea. When they had first reached Ethea, Roine encouraged him to attend as many as possible, especially those with an earth-sensing focus. He remained convinced Tan could become an earth shaper, but how would he ever even sense anything within the walls of the university? At least in Galen, the trees and grasses and life around him gave him something to sense. Here, all he sensed was the vast expanse of stone that comprised the university.

The girl looked up at him again. Tan frowned at her and she looked away, burying her face in her book once more.

He didn't want to be here. Not only this room, but in this city. This had always been his mother's dream for him, never his. If he had his choice, he would have remained in Galen, climbing the hills around Nor.

The man near the window stopped drumming his fingers on the window and turned to face them. The hood of his cloak fell down to his shoulders, revealing curly brown hair. "This is all who choose to attend?" His voice sounded low, thick and gravelly.

The girl pushed her book aside, closing it slowly. The thick boy turned to face Tan.

Now that Tan could see the man's face, he saw he was older—much older than Tan. Not a student, then. The man grunted and looked around the room, flinty eyes stopping on each of them before they settled on Tan, widening slightly as they did. His nostrils flared briefly as he sniffed.

"A waste of time," he muttered. He flicked his gaze to the boy. "You. Where in Ter are you from?"

The boy blinked and swallowed. "Keoth, sir."

The man grunted and the corners of his eyes twitched. "Keoth? Does that make you a farmer or quarryman?"

The boy's back stiffened slightly. He looked at the man, unblinking. "Farmer, sir."

The man sniffed, his nostrils flaring again. His eyes narrowed and he pursed his lips as if he might say something, but then he looked over to the girl. "And you. Where in Vatten are you from? Too slight to be a fisherman's daughter. A weaver?"

The girl glanced at her book and then looked up and past the man, nodding as she did.

3

The man shook his head, not bothering to hide his annoyance. "And then there's you," he said, turning to Tan. "You're too old to be a new student—" he regarded Tan's age with derision "—but I haven't seen you in other classes."

"I've only been—"

The man cut him off with a wave of the hand. "From your build, you could be from Ter or Vatten, but you don't have the right coloring. Your hair is too dark for Nara. That leaves Galen."

Tan nodded. The way he spoke of Galen put Tan on edge, his tone making it seem like he wished he could exclude Galen from the kingdoms. Already, he didn't like this man.

"Not many come from Galen anymore. Fewer will come now that Incendin attacks." The girl sucked in a quick breath and the man turned to her. "The rumors are true. Best not to hide from them. You empower them with your fear. Besides, there's no reason to fear Incendin here in the university. You're safest surrounded by our best shapers."

"But their shapers—" she started in a whisper.

"Are no different than me. Fire works no different than earth." As emphasis, the stone around the window peeled away briefly before folding back into place. Tan's ears popped as it did.

The boy's eyes widened, the most reaction Tan had seen from him. The girl smiled and pulled her book up to her chest, clutching it to herself.

"A skilled shaper can hold back the fire shapers of Incendin, and isn't that why you're here?"

The Master shaper dismissed Incendin's fire shapers so quickly, but Tan knew what they were capable of. He'd seen their destruction firsthand, had witnessed how they destroyed his home as if it were nothing. "It's not only fire shapers to fear."

The man's eyes narrowed slightly and a tight smile pulled at the corners of his mouth. "So, you *are* from Galen."

Tan nodded.

"Don't scare the others with stories. The truth can be awful on its own."

Had he not lost everyone he knew to those *stories*, Tan might have been more forgiving of the comment. Instead, other than Cobin and Bal, only Lins Alles survived and Tan had no interest in seeing him again, not after seeing him working *with* the lisincend. And he hadn't seen Cobin or Bal since reaching Ethea. For all Tan knew, they'd gone somewhere else, away from the danger of the capital. Knowing how Cobin was an earth senser, Tan would understand him not wanting to return to Ethea. Likely, he wanted to get as far from Incendin as possible to keep Bal safe, someplace like Ter, where there would be other earth sensers and where the threat of attack was minimal.

And Lins? If Tan saw him again, he didn't know *what* he would do. He'd spent years fearing his temper; now he wanted nothing more from him. After helping the lisincend, had he gone to Incendin? Or had he faded into obscurity within the kingdoms?

"You don't think we should fear Incendin? After what they did?" Tan asked.

The man sniffed again. He kept his hands in the pocket of his cloak and fixed Tan with a hard gaze. "Their attacks have grown stronger, it is true, but the barrier protects us from a more direct attack."

"The barrier didn't keep the lisincend from passing through. The barrier did nothing to stop my home from being destroyed."

Tan realized he'd raised his voice and took a calming breath.

The girl looked from him to the man standing at the front of the room. The smile faded from her face, and with it, all the color in her cheeks. Her wide blue eyes made her look younger than Bal.

The other boy simply stared at the man. He didn't look over at Tan, as if taking his eyes off the shaper at the front of the room would get him into some sort of trouble.

The man leaned forward, resting his hands on the table as he stared at Tan. A dark expression flashed across his eyes. "You speak of rumors as if they are true. Few enough know of the lisincend. I would like to know how you learned about them."

Tan shook his head. He should leave. There was nothing this man would teach him that he wanted to know, but he was new to the university and he owed it to his memory of his mother to at least try. "I've seen them."

The man laughed. "Then you would be dead. Instead, you sit here and argue with a Master of the university." He paused and started to turn before catching himself and turning back. "Had the lisincend attacked, there would be little to slow them until they reached Ethea."

"Only a warrior shaper," Tan answered.

And even Roine had almost not been enough. Had not the draasin—the great winged fire elemental—come when Tan called, what would have happened with Fur and the other lisincend? Tan wouldn't have survived, but more than that, they would have captured the artifact, the one thing that might be able to help the kingdoms push back Incendin.

"There no longer are any warriors," the man said. "So be glad you have not seen the lisincend."

"The ashes of my village would say otherwise. And if you need further convincing, seek out Roine. Ask him what happened to Nor."

Tan started to stand. He wasn't in the mood to listen to the Master anyway. He would have to come another time, perhaps find another earth shaper to learn from, though Roine said the Master instructing this class was more skilled than most.

"Why would one of the Athans have been in Galen?"

Tan sighed and looked up, wishing he were back in Galen, back beneath the trees and following some unknown trail as it wound into the mountains. At least there, he knew what to do. He could sense his way along, so he knew where he needed to go. In Ethea, surrounded by all these people that he didn't understand, he never felt fully sure of himself.

But if he could learn to be a shaper—an earth shaper like the Master—wouldn't he take that opportunity? It required his allegiance to the king, but shapers were gifted with much power, abilities he'd only glimpsed while traveling with Roine. How much better would it be if *he* could do some of the things he'd seen Roine do?

"Serving the king," Tan answered. "And protecting the kingdoms from Incendin. More than that, you'll have to ask him."

"And you claim you encountered one of the lisincend while with Roine?"

Tan nodded.

"Where is it now?"

"Two were killed. Fur might still be running back to Incendin." Or eaten. Tan hoped the draasin had caught him but suspected Fur might have been strong enough to escape and survive. If he did, how long did they have before Incendin sent more of the lisincend into the kingdoms?

If he dared embrace the connection with the draasin, he might learn, but doing so meant pain and fear. Regardless of how it had saved them, the great fire elemental was dangerous to Tan.

The Master shaper blinked. "You faced more than one of the lisincend?"

Tan nodded again.

The Master studied Tan for a moment, gray eyes seeming to stare through him before taking a shallow breath. Without another word, he turned to the door and hurried out, pulling the hood of his cloak back over his head as he went.

Tan frowned. What had just happened?

So much about Ethea was strange. The last time he'd seen him, Roine tried offering suggestions about the university and promised to help in any way he could, but as Athan, he had other responsibilities. Tan hadn't seen Roine since their second day in Ethea.

The thick boy got up slowly and made his way to the door after the Master. He left quietly, making his way down the narrow hall and out of sight.

Tan sighed and started to leave. A gentle tug at the sleeve of his jacket caused him to turn.

The girl stood looking up at him. She barely came to his shoulder. Up close, her short brown hair looked uneven and ragged, as if she'd cut it with a dull knife. One hand gripped a handful of fabric, holding her dress off the floor so she didn't trip. The other held a stack of books she somehow didn't spill as she pulled on his sleeve. A serious expression furrowed her brow.

"Is what you said true?" Her voice sounded less meek than when she'd spoken to the Master shaper.

Tan nodded.

"You saw one of these creatures?"

Tan stiffened. "That's what I said."

"You said it was Fur?"

Tan frowned. "You know of him?" The Master shaper had been right that few knew of the lisincend. At least in Galen, he hadn't heard of the lisincend before they attacked, and Galen shared a border with Incendin.

The girl swallowed, her head bobbing in a nod. "My grandfather—" She took a deep breath and met Tan's eyes. "My grandfather fought in the Incendin war. Barely survived. When I was younger—" Tan snorted and she frowned "—he wouldn't talk about it. I knew he lost friends during the war. But as he's gotten older, his mind started to wander. Sometimes he speaks about the nightmares he saw. Only one of them ever had a name. Fur." She shivered, as if a breeze suddenly gusted through the window. "Always said his name in a whisper, and usually after having too much wine. He's real?"

Tan understood the reaction. Nearly dying at the hands of the lisincend did that to him. "He's real. And as terrifying as your grandfather said."

The girl shook her head. "He never said much other than a name, but not much scared him. A water shaper—and strong, too—so anything of fire that frightening…"

Tan nodded, remembering the way Fur had nearly burned away the lake. Had the nymid—the water elementals at the heart of the lake—not been there, Fur might have been strong enough.

"You plan to study at the university?" she asked.

The sudden change took Tan aback. He nodded.

"You're older than most students," she commented. "You know, most come to the university when they learn they're sensers. If you can sense the elements, some learn to shape as well."

"I never wanted to come in the first place," Tan answered.

"Never wanted to come? Why wouldn't you want to come? Don't you care to learn if you can be a shaper?"

Tan took a deep breath before answering. He'd never cared before. Not that he didn't think the idea of shaping sounded impressive, just that he didn't want to commit to what came with it: service to the king like his father—and his mother, he reminded himself—bought by learning. Service that claimed his father's life fighting Incendin.

But he'd seen what the lisincend would do. He'd seen the lengths they went—the mindless destruction they inflicted. How could he refuse to help if he had the ability?

"There's more to it than wanting to be a shaper," he said.

She looked at him skeptically. "What more can there be? Either you want to learn or you don't. And if you're here, it means you have the ability to learn."

"How did he know you're from Vatten?" Tan asked, changing the subject. He didn't know this girl at all, and here she was, pressing him no differently than his mother had.

"How can you not know?"

He shrugged. "I can't tell where anyone is from."

She laughed, the sound smooth and light, betraying a cloud that came over her face. "You should probably learn, especially if you're going to stay here. Everyone is like that Master. Once they figure out where you're from…"

Tan sighed and glanced at the window. Another reason for him to wish he was out of Ethea and back in Galen. At least there, he understood how things worked. As long as he didn't upset the manor lord—or his son—he was fine.

Maybe he needed to find Amia and see if she would leave with him.

Finally, he shook his head. Standing here changed nothing. "I need to get going," he decided.

Tan started out of the room, and the girl trailed after him. She kept her dress bunched in one fist to keep it from dragging on the floor. The books were pressed against her chest. A single lantern lit the musty, narrow hall outside the room. Rough stone shifted with strange shadows. Even here, Tan had little sense of anything.

"So what are you?" the girl asked as they reached a stair leading down.

He paused and looked at her. "What do you mean?"

She sniffed. "Well, you're *here*, right? So what kind of senser are you?"

He nodded. "Earth senser."

"From Galen?"

He nodded again.

The girl frowned for a moment and then shrugged. "I'm a water shaper. Pretty common in Vatten, you know."

He didn't know but didn't say anything as he continued down the stairs. At the bottom, a door led out into a wide courtyard. Grass and a few trees grew tidily here, though the center of the courtyard was cleared. There, stones were set in a circular pattern.

The girl said something but Tan missed it. Pressure built in his ears, the sensation familiar to him. Someone performed a shaping nearby, and a powerful one at that.

The sudden rumble of thunder followed by a loud crack of lightning made him take a quick step back. Tan had felt this shaping before.

When it cleared, Roine stood at the center of the clearing. Dried blood smeared on the top of his brow from an open wound and he held a slender sword clutched in his hand. He took a deep breath and then collapsed.

CHAPTER 2

A Warrior and a Return

ROINE LAY UNMOVING, splayed across the circular stones, his face turned toward the sky. Tan rushed over and knelt next to him. Roine breathed slowly, the sword resting next to him with the tip pointing to his leg. When Tan reached to move it, the girl grabbed his arm.

"Don't! You can't touch a sword like that."

Tan turned and looked up at her. The worry on her face made her look older than she'd looked in the small classroom. There, she'd seemed younger than Bal. "A sword like what?"

She nodded toward Roine. "I never thought to see one. I didn't think any warriors still lived."

"This is Roine, the king's Athan." As he said it, he realized how little the answer explained. Roine was much more than only the king's Athan. He was Theondar the cloud warrior, gifted with the ability to shape all the elements, and thought dead for decades.

The girl crouched next to him and set the stack of books carefully on the ground. She reached toward the silver band around Roine's finger that marked him as Athan. "One of the Athan. Of course, they'd be warriors." She looked up at Tan. "Do you think they're all warriors?"

He shrugged. "I only know Roine. And why can't I touch his sword?"

She stood and kicked it away from Roine, keeping the tip away from his leg. The silver sword clattered against the stones. Markings, like those that had been on the golden box Roine had used to find the artifact hidden in the mountains, worked along the surface and glinted in the cloudy light.

"A warrior's sword. Only those able to shape all the elements can carry a sword like that. To anyone else, protections worked in the blade would be dangerous." She paused, eyeing the sword. "My grandfather told me how an Incendin shaper tried taking one from a fallen warrior."

Tan looked down at the sword, thinking of how Roine had given it to him to wear before he'd gone to fight Lacertin. What would have happened had he actually tried to use the sword? "What happened to him?"

She shook her head. "Grandfather never actually said. Only that the Incendin shaper wouldn't be touching anything anytime soon."

Tan suppressed a shiver. He'd never tried to use the sword after Roine gave it to him, but what if he had? What would have happened to him?

Had Roine known what might happen?

Tan touched Roine on the shoulder. His chest rose steadily, but blood continued to pool from the wound on his forehead. The scent of ash and char radiated from him. His face seemed paler than when Tan had seen him a few days ago.

"Roine!" He tried shaking him, but Roine didn't move. "Theondar!"

He hissed the name silently, but the girl still heard him and looked over at him. Theondar, the name of a warrior long thought dead, one of the last great warriors of the kingdoms. Tan hadn't known him as Theondar when they first met, but his mother had. She'd known him when she had come to the university. Now she was gone and it seemed there was so much he would like to know about her.

Roine grunted and then blinked slowly. He turned and looked up at Tan. He sniffed softly and let out a long breath. "Careful how you use that name. Especially here, Tannen."

Tan swallowed. Roine said his name much like his mother used to say it. "What happened?"

Roine pushed himself away from the stones, standing slowly. Tan expected them to be singed by the burst of lightning Roine used to travel, but they were unmarked. "A minor skirmish. Nothing more."

"You went to Incendin."

Roine tilted his head and nodded once. "After what happened with Lacertin—"

At the mention of the name Lacertin, the girl sucked in a quick breath.

Roine looked past Tan and at the girl as if finally seeing her. His eyes hardened, his face darkening quickly. Roine's sword seemed to jump into his hand. "Who are you?"

Tan looked over at her. Again, she seemed small, as if the dress she wore swallowed her. "Elle Vaywand," she said quickly.

Roine took a step forward and winced, closing his eyes for a moment. "Vatten?"

She nodded.

"Weavers?"

She nodded again.

"How do you know Tan?"

The flurry of questions caught Tan off guard. Not just that Roine had appeared in the courtyard, but the way he questioned her. "I don't know her. We met earlier today."

Elle nodded. "Master Ferran's class." She had grabbed her books again and cradled them against her chest, clutching them tightly. Her long dress dumped around her on the ground.

Roine shoved his sword into its sheath and rubbed his fingers over his temple for a moment. Pressure built in Tan's ears. The bleeding slowed. "Ferran?" He looked at Tan. "He would be good for you to learn from. A strong earth shaper. You would do well to listen to him."

"I'm not sure he cares too much for me."

Roine grunted. "Ferran doesn't care too much for anyone. But he's skilled, and that's what matters. He's as likely as anyone to draw your sensing into shaping." Roine turned to Elle. "Why were you in Ferran's class?"

She blinked before answering. "My grandfather told me to learn as much as I can about each of the elements."

Roine frowned. "Grandfather?" His brow furrowed as he considered something. "Elton Vaywand?"

Her lips tightened and she nodded.

"I knew him. Powerful water shaper."

Elle swallowed but didn't say anything.

"What happened to you?" Tan asked. "Why were you in Incendin?"

Roine considered Elle a moment before answering. "In the caverns, there was something Lacertin said. The king asked me to investigate, so I went."

"By yourself?"

Roine shot Tan a look. "I've been by myself a long time, Tannen. Most of the time, actually. This is the first I've been back to Ethea in years."

"What did you find?"

Roine shook his head once. "Not much. Incendin is quiet, and that worries me. This side of the barrier is not. A village claiming their crops were burned. Charred cattle near the border. So far, no people lost." He glanced at Tan. "Which we'll have to discuss later."

The draasin. Tan didn't know where they were, but the remnants of the connection tugged at the back of his mind. Like an itch, it irritated him. He still worked on learning how to ignore it.

"Then how were you hurt?"

Roine shook his head. He nodded toward the far end of the courtyard and started walking. Tan and Elle followed alongside. With each step, Roine seemed stronger. Blood oozed from the wound on his head, but less than it had. "Stupid. After I crossed the barrier, I made my way along the Incendin border and got too lax. A pack nearly caught me."

Elle gasped again.

Tan glanced at her. She seemed to know quite a bit about Incendin. How much of it was from stories her grandfather told her, and how much from her studies? Could he learn more about Incendin here? If he had to face the lisincend again, he would need to know what worked against them in the past.

And then there were other things he'd like to understand better. The nymid and how he could speak to them. The draasin and what it meant that he could talk to them as well. And if he could speak to two of the great elementals, could he speak to others? Would golud or ara answer him?

Pain pulsed in his head and he rubbed it.

"Barely escaped. By that time, I'd learned enough to return," Roine went on.

"What's happening with Incendin?"

With Roine gone, Tan hadn't learned anything more about Incendin. Or about the artifact they'd risked so much to bring to Ethea. As far as Tan knew, Roine had given it to the king. From there, he had no idea.

"Nothing. The barrier holds."

They reached a high stone archway at the edge of the courtyard. A dirt path led away from the arch until it reached a low wrought iron wall. Beyond that, the city opened up, spreading away from the university.

Master Ferran crouched against the wall, watching them. The cloak he wore in class covered all parts of him, leaving only his face exposed. A curious expression pinched his lips as he studied Roine, as if trying to determine if what Tan had told him was true.

Roine nodded to him, an amused smile parting his lips.

Master Ferran nodded back and then stood, moving slowly into the city.

"The barrier didn't keep the lisincend out the last time," Tan reminded him.

Roine stared after Master Ferran before shaking his head. "And Lacertin is to blame. It was never meant to keep our shapers from crossing, and certainly not Lacertin."

Tan frowned, wondering what Roine meant.

"Only those of Incendin, those twisted by whatever they did to create the lisincend, and the hounds are excluded by the barrier. Their regular fire shapers might be able to cross, though they never have." Roine nodded toward the city. "I will find you later, Tannen. There is much we have to discuss. For now, mend fences with Ferran. It's important you learn whatever you can."

With that, Roine hurried away, leaving Tan standing next to Elle, wondering what to do.

He turned, considering returning to the classrooms. There would be another lecture today, though it would be with a different Master shaper—not an earth shaper. Today was Master Ferran's day, but he hadn't given much of a lecture. Partly that had been Tan's fault, but there seemed something angry about Ferran.

"How do you know him?"

Tan turned to look at Elle. She watched Roine as he passed through the gate to the university and beyond until he disappeared completely from view. Only then did she shake her head, her short hair bobbing slightly, and turn back to face Tan.

"Chance," Tan answered. "He came to my village looking for something." Or someone. Tan hadn't known at the time Roine sought his mother—a powerful wind shaper he knew as Zephra—only learning later what his mother had been. "I helped him find it."

The answer seemed vague enough.

Too vague for Elle. She frowned at him and pulled her arms more tightly around her books. "That's all you have to say about it?"

Tan shrugged. "What more do you want to know?"

She laughed as she followed him back into the courtyard.

A few other students stood near the trees off to the side. None dared get too close to the stone circle, but it didn't matter. Tan didn't know any of the other students. Being close wouldn't help him recognize anyone. Not when he only knew Elle and Amia.

"You traveled with one of the king's Athans. And a warrior, at that! You really have to ask what more I'd want to know?"

Tan hesitated. "You sound like it was something exciting, like a story in one of your books." He pointed to the books she clutched tightly in her hands. "I nearly died traveling with him. Had it not been for—" he caught himself before revealing too much about the elementals "—what Roine did, I *would* have died."

"It must have been pretty important to get Incendin's attention. And to have the lisincend attempt a border crossing."

Tan looked over at her and frowned.

Elle only shrugged. "The border has held for the last twenty years, keeping the Incendin shapers away. The border is the one thing my grandfather would talk about, and he spoke with pride of that shaping. Without it, the Incendin war would have continued and others would have died." She looked down at her books. "And I'm not reading any stories. I'm not a child." Her petulant voice nearly put lie to her statement.

"Then what are you reading?" Tan only wanted to change the subject, to talk about anything other than how they found the artifact. Roine hadn't wanted many people to know about it; as far as Tan knew, only the king had been informed.

Her eyes narrowed and she shook her head. "You wouldn't care."

Tan laughed. The way she said it reminded him so much of Bal. Hopefully, she and Cobin had made it safely out of the mountains, away from the hounds and the lisincend. Hopefully, they had found a quiet place to settle where Cobin could let Bal grow up, away from the threat of Incendin, and where he could raise his sheep and farm in peace.

"Why wouldn't I care?"

"I saw the way you looked at them. You're just like most people who come to the university. They don't think the archives hold much value. Everyone wants to become a shaper, so they follow the masters around."

"Like most people? You can't have been here long either."

She glared at him and tried to pull herself up straighter. "I've been here nearly a year. I came after my grandfather…" She trailed off and looked away, trying to hide it as she wiped a tear out of the corner of her eye.

Tan recognized the defiance in her, the desire to be someone more than what she was. It was different than how he'd felt in the year after his father had died. Then, all Tan wanted was familiarity, to spend his days as he would have were his father still there, doing anything to remind him of the man he'd lost. It wasn't until he'd gone with Roine, when he'd decided to help Amia and her people, trying to rescue them from the lisincend, that he finally began to forget what had happened. It was when he realized there were things worth fighting and dying for.

"I'm sorry. I didn't mean to offend you." He pointed toward the books. The way she clutched them to her chest told him that whatever she was reading was important to her. "What are you reading about?"

She bit her lip, as if trying to determine whether she'd answer him. Finally, she pulled the books away from her and showed him the cover.

Tan leaned closer and looked at the cover of the topmost book. Worked in leather dyed a deep blue with the shape of some symbol etched into the leather, he recognized the lettering around the symbol as the ancient language. He'd seen it on the golden box Roine used as a key to find the artifact and the lettering around the cavern where they'd finally found it. The symbol itself looked familiar, though Tan didn't know why.

"What is it?" he asked. "I don't read the ancient language."

She snorted. "Grandfather always told me there weren't many who did. Most felt it unnecessary." She laughed. "He always sorta clung to the old ways."

"Old ways?"

Elle tapped the front of the book. "I'm a water senser like my grandfather." She said it with a hint of pride. "He wasn't able to help me shape but told me if I learned about the udilm, it might help me learn to shape."

"This book teaches you how to speak to the elementals?"

If that were possible, why didn't more people reach out to them?

The nymid seemed willing to work with him. Had it not been for them, he would have died. Amia would have remained trapped by the lisincend. And without the draasin, the lisincend would have captured them both.

"I don't think it works quite like that," she said. Her eyes lingered on the cover. The finger of her other hand traced the outline of the symbol, running around it. "I don't think you can learn to speak to them. Either you do or not. My grandfather said the ability to speak to the elementals has been lost over time. Some still can, but there aren't many." She looked back at the book. "I never learned if he could. Some of the things he said… the way he spoke made me wonder if he'd spoken to the udilm. Might be why he went away after the war."

"My parents did, too. It changed them."

Elle nodded. "Most said my grandfather was a different person before he returned. I never knew him any other way. And now he's gone. And with him, anything he might have been able to teach me. Even if he could speak to udilm, that wouldn't help me become a shaper." She sighed and met Tan's eyes. "But if I can read about the elementals, try to understand how the ancient shapers were once connected to them, maybe it will help me learn to shape."

"Does the library have any books on golud?" If Elle were right—if the elementals could help teach shaping—could the earth elemental teach him to shape?

Tan had another reason to learn about the elementals, one more pressing than merely learning to shape. If there was something about golud, maybe he could learn more about the draasin before the gnawing sense in the back of his mind overwhelmed him.

She nodded. "There are many books on elementals. At least, ara, golud, and udilm. Some on the lesser elementals, too."

"None about fire elementals?"

She shook her head. "I don't know. Probably. The Masters restrict quite a few books. Anything dealing with fire shaping is restricted."

"Aren't there fire shapers at the university?"

Elle nodded. "We have fire shapers. But they're treated differently. That's part of the reason the Masters are so particular about teaching. Why did you think Master Ferran made a point of determining where we were from?"

Tan grunted and shook his head. Her explanation made more sense than what he'd considered. "I thought he was simply being rude."

Elle laughed. "Oh, he was. But most of the Masters are like that. Even your Athan friend did it."

Tan had noticed. It wasn't quite as obvious as what Ferran had done, but he'd treated Elle much the same.

"Why are you so interested in fire shapers anyway? You said you're an earth senser. Still not sure how an earth senser comes from Galen."

"My father was an earth senser." Tan wondered if his father—like his mother—had been more than he seemed. Could his father have been a shaper, too? Had that been how they met? But if that was the case, why hadn't his father shown him?

"You lost him fighting Incendin?" She waited for Tan to nod. "Then you lost your home to the lisincend. No wonder you want to know about fire shaping."

Tan didn't argue. That was part of the reason he wondered about the fire elementals, but not all of it. He needed to understand fire to understand the draasin. Roine hadn't known much about them and what he did know didn't fit with what Tan had experienced.

Of course, the great fire elementals hadn't been seen for over a thousand years before Tan released them to the world. Now he needed to better understand what he'd done.

Would the archives have anything about the draasin? And if they did, could he learn anything from it?

"Master Nass is speaking tomorrow," Elle suggested. "Maybe you could go and listen? Will I see you there?"

Tan shrugged. "I don't know. I need to understand earth sensing better than I do."

Elle shuffled through the books she held before holding one out to him. It was long and slender and covered in forest green. "Here. This one deals with golud and shapers who could speak to them. You'll need to translate it, but…" She smiled as he took it from her. "Make sure you return it to the library. The archivists have been a little… touchy… with me lately."

Tan looked at her quizzically. "Touchy?"

She only shrugged.

"Are you sure?"

Elle laughed. "I already read through it. Not much I can learn about earth shaping, but I think understanding the elementals is helpful. I'm probably the only one."

"*I* think you're right. We could learn much from them."

Elle smiled at the comment and glanced down at her books.

Tan thought of how the nymid had healed him, how they'd gifted him with their armor, the shirt he still wore beneath his jacket. It had been that armor that saved Amia. How much could shapers learn if they could speak to elementals? How much could he learn about earth shaping if he could speak to the great earth elemental?

Before she left, Elle stuck her hand out toward Tan. The long sleeve of her dress hung down her arm, falling past the end of her fingers. She pulled it back and waited.

Tan shook it carefully, feeling awkward.

"Glad to meet you, Tannen. I—" she looked around the courtyard, her eyes stopping on a pair of kids still younger than Tan sitting near the tree and talking. "—I don't have many friends here."

"Tan," he corrected. "My mother called me Tannen."

Elle shook his hand again, then turned, hurrying through the nearest door of the university.

Tan stared after Elle, still not certain what to make of her.

CHAPTER 3

A Lost Language

FIRELIGHT DANCED IN THE HEARTH of the small room had Roine secured for Tan, reflecting off Amia's golden hair. The slatted walls around them caught strange shadows. Not for the first time, Tan wished the room had a window, but in this part of the city, rooms were expensive enough. Roine hoped he would move to the university once acclimated to the city, but Tan still felt reluctant to do so. At least here, enough separated him that he could leave if he wanted. Once he committed to a room, he admitted he was staying.

Tired as he was, the pain in his head throbbed more steadily. As it did, he felt the pull of the draasin, as if he could close his eyes and speak to him, but doing that meant opening himself to the dangers of the draasin. The last time he'd spoken to him, the power of his voice had nearly destroyed him.

Amia stared at the fire and didn't turn to face him. A few streamers of smoke drifted away from the hearth. She held a steaming mug of birchbark tea in her hands but hadn't taken a sip since she'd poured it.

Her anxiety came through the shaped bond between them, the one she'd accidently placed upon him as he tried rescuing her from the lisincend. Through it, he could tell something was wrong.

"You're quiet."

Amia turned and met his eyes. She smiled. The thin band of silver that marked her as Daughter of the Aeta shimmered in the firelight, reminding him of the pool of silvery spirit she'd walked through to retrieve the artifact. They hadn't spoken of that time since, but the memory of her naked and walking through the liquid—liquid she claimed was a part of the Great Mother herself—burned into his mind.

"As are you."

Tan sniffed and leaned forward. The movement exacerbated the pain in his head. He rubbed his neck, but it made little difference.

The book Elle had given him lay next to him, unopened. The thick green cover felt as if woven from dried leaves. A symbol—another he recognized from Roine's golden box—worked across the cover. Letters in the ancient language scrawled across the top. He'd flipped through the book at first, but it was written in the ancient language.

"Roine returned today," Tan started. "I saw him at the university. He was injured."

Amia frowned a moment. "Injured?"

Tan nodded. "He returned to Incendin. Said the king sent him."

She let out a slow breath and turned to him. Pressure built behind his ears for a moment. Amia was a spirit shaper, but why would she shape him now? The bond formed—accidentally, he still believed—gave them both a way of understanding what the other was thinking. In spite of that bond, Amia remained distant.

"You haven't seen him much since arriving here," she said. She lifted her mug to her mouth and inhaled the steam rising from it. One hand went to the silver band at her neck and touched it.

Tan felt a hint of uncertainty as she did. "Not much," he agreed.

"You expected him to help ease the transition?"

Tan shrugged. He hadn't known what to expect. At least he had Amia. Without her, he'd feel completely isolated. When he first arrived, he thought he might look for Cobin, but likely he took Bal someplace safe after they escaped the lisincend in Velminth. There wasn't anything for them to return to in Galen now that Nor was destroyed. The only other person to survive the attack on Nor was Lins Alles; Tan hoped he never saw him again.

"He's Athan to the king. I know he has other responsibilities."

She leaned over and touched his hand. A wave of relaxation washed over him with the contact. He took her hand and held it. More than a shaped bond had formed between them during the time they'd gone searching for the artifact. She might have directed him to help her, but he would have helped even without the silent command.

"You spoke to the nymid. You released the draasin. I don't think the artifact could have been retrieved if not for that."

Tan sighed. Maybe she was right, but even that troubled him. "I wonder what would have happened had we *not* helped him. Would the lisincend manage to get past the protections? They wouldn't have been able to drop the warding at the cave entrance if we hadn't gone there first." And they wouldn't have gotten past the pillars formed from the great elementals. Had they not freed the draasin, would the artifact have been in any danger?

Maybe the lisincend would have eventually managed to destroy enough of the pillars to reach the artifact. Even then, they would have to get past the pool or spirit; Amia thought only one blessed by the Mother—a spirit shaper—would be able to survive that.

Amia shook her head. "The warding wouldn't have slowed Lacertin. Think about how he entered the cavern. Think about how persistent Fur was once he realized where to find the artifact."

"But would he have come so close without us guiding him?" Tan shook his head. "I can't help but think there was more to what happened we simply don't understand."

Amia turned back to the fire. "There's always more we don't understand."

A flicker of uncertainty surged through their bond. Tan didn't know if she tried to shield it from him and failed or if she *wanted* him to know what she felt. Either way, the sensation was disconcerting.

He slid forward on the wooden chair, shifting so he could reach her. Warmth from the hearth pushed upon him, the smoke from the oak logs reminding him of home. Not his time staying in the manor house but before, when his father still lived and they had their small house on the edge of the village. There, his father would build a cozy fire and they would all sit around it as night fell, talking. He would tell stories—tales Tan now knew they'd lived through—while his mother sat quietly, simply watching. Most nights, her eyes would be closed shortly after his father started talking, as if asleep. Tan now wondered if she sat back, remembering the times his father spoke about.

Amia met his eyes and sighed, then glanced at the book. "What is that?"

Tan watched her for another moment, wondering what bothered her, then pulled the book out and handed it over.

Amia took it carefully. One finger traced the symbol on the cover. "Golud," she whispered. "Conversations with golud." She looked up at him. "Where did you find this?"

"It was given to me."

"Given?"

He shrugged. "Lent might be a better word. A girl I met in the session with Master Ferran let me borrow it. She had another like it, bound in leather." And a third, Tan remembered. Elle must have had books on all the great elementals except the draasin.

"You can borrow books like this?" Amia asked.

Tan shrugged again. "I don't know. She said some were restricted, but others you could borrow. She thought that learning from the elementals might help her learn to shape."

"Who is she?"

Tan shook his head. "A student. Said she's been here a year but doesn't look old enough. Her name is Elle Vaywand. Says she's a water senser from Vatten."

Amia frowned a moment and flipped open the book. Her eyes worked along the text. "This is written in the ancient language."

Tan nodded. "I know. I can't read it."

Amia smiled at him. "I can."

He nodded. "I hoped you would say that."

"Do you want me to read it to you?"

Tan shook his head. "I want you to teach me how to read it."

If he could learn the ancient language, he might be able to comprehend more about the elementals. And if he could reach the restricted archives, he might be able to understand more about the draasin. Maybe then, he could get rid of the nagging pain in his head. Maybe then, he could be free of the connection.

Amia closed the book as Tan shook his head. "I don't see the patterns."

She smiled and patted his hand. "You've only been at it a few hours."

"How long did it take you to begin understanding the ancient language?"

Amia leaned back in the chair. The flames in the hearth had faded, leaving only glowing coals. A chill came to the air, less than there would be outside, but enough that Tan and Amia crowded together for warmth. Neither minded.

She flipped a strand of her golden hair off her shoulder and touched the surface of the book, her long finger tracing the pattern of golud on the woven cover, made of an inverted triangle with a swirling loop coming off one edge. "Mother began teaching me at an early age." As she spoke of her mother, her voice came out in a whisper and she took a shuddering breath. "Knowledge of the ancient language was felt important to the people." She looked down at her hands. "I never fully understood why. For most, it is a dead language. Like so many things, she said I would learn why later."

Tan touched her hand. "I'm sorry."

She shook her head. "I'm the one who should be sorry. You've never blamed me, but you should. If we hadn't come from Incendin with hounds trailing us, your home would still be there. You wouldn't have to be..." She took a deep breath and looked up, as if forcing herself to meet his eyes. "You wouldn't have to be here with me."

"And if I had been faster, more of your people might have survived." Tan shook his head. "I don't blame you for what happened to Nor. You left Incendin seeking safety. How were you to know the barrier wouldn't hold?"

Amia swallowed. "I think Mother knew."

Tan frowned. "How? The barrier has stood for nearly two decades. Why would it suddenly start to fall?"

"I don't know. So much of our time in Incendin doesn't make any sense to me. We shouldn't have been traveling that deep in Incendin in the first place. Usually, when we visit Incendin, we stay near the borders, among the outer cities. Still dangerous, but we can find trade. For the most part, my people were left alone. No others travel into Incendin other than the Aeta."

Tan wished he knew more about Incendin, but what he did know frightened him. Any place that welcomed creatures like the lisincend must be a terrible place. "Why did the Mother bring you deeper into Incendin?"

She shook her head. "It was dangerous. We all knew it at the time, but she thought we could reach Isha. None of my people had ever visited the city, but the Mother said she knew a safe way to reach it without crossing through the blasted lands."

Tan sat silent, holding Amia's hand.

"We had only been a day into the desert when we heard the hounds. All knew their call immediately. Mother thought they were still far out across the rocks, the dry air carrying their howls to us. The sound haunted us day and night as it drew closer." She shivered. "The third day, we had to turn back. At first, it was only a single hound. Our men managed to stop it, but we knew others would come. We heard them calling." She brought her legs up, tucking her arms around them. "We reached an ancient road Hosh—" her voice choked up as she said his name "—knew of and took it. The trail was difficult, winding up the rocky mountains, but when we came through, when I *felt* it as we passed through the barrier, we all thought we were safe."

"That's when I saw you," Tan said.

Amia nodded. "I remember seeing you standing in the woods. Your smile seemed so out of place with how we all felt. We thought we were safe," she said again. Her eyes went distant as she looked toward the hearth and she swallowed tightly. "And then when Zephra met us at the edge of the village and told us we weren't welcome…" She sighed.

"I thought the Mother might finally break down. She didn't. Not until we were captured."

They had never spoken of what happened after the lisincend captured the Aeta. Tan remembered the destruction of the wagons, nothing but splinters of wood remaining. Everything charred. He'd thought everyone dead.

"If she knew the risks, why did the Mother bring you into Incendin?"

Amia shook her head. "We are a wandering people, driven by trade. What better than to trade exotic goods made in the heart of Incendin?"

Tan watched her as she spoke and heard the hint of bitterness in her words. "You think there was more to it than that."

Amia looked over at the fading coals. "I wish I had the chance to understand. Why did she push us so deep into the blasted lands when trading along the borders had always been profitable? There are so few of our people willing to cross the border into Incendin, it makes those of us who do that much more successful."

Tan leaned back in the wooden chair and waited for Amia to say more. When she didn't, he reached his hand across the distance and touched her arm. They sat silently for a while.

"Will you try to find another family of Aeta?" Tan asked after a while.

Amia didn't look up when she answered. "I have no need." She didn't elaborate.

Instead, she took a deep breath and reached for the book again. She turned the cover and flipped to the next chapter, resting her finger beneath the first line. "We should continue reading."

Tan shook his head. "Not tonight. I'm tired and—"

Amia smiled at him, but it seemed forced. "I think you might be right about learning from the elementals. If you could understand golud, you might be able to intentionally shape."

"Intentionally?"

Amia laughed softly. "When I first learned of my ability, I had little control. Shapings would happen without any intent. I suspect the same happens with other shapers."

Tan wondered if that were possible. What would accidental shapings look like for him? What had they looked like for Amia?

"But you were young when you first learned. I'm not sure I'll ever learn to shape at my age."

Amia laughed. As she did, the darkness that had seemed to hang around her faded. "At your age? You're not some old man attempting his first shaping."

"No, but you should see the students that have come to the university. Most are five or six years younger than me. The girl who gave me that book couldn't have been more than Bal's age! And that's still older than you were when you learned to shape." Tan shook his head. "I know I'm an earth senser, but I'm still not convinced I'll be able to learn shaping."

"Yet you have already done more than most of the Masters at the university," Amia suggested.

Tan snorted. "What? Survive a lisincend attack?"

"So a few things more than most Masters." Amia smiled. "You spoke with the nymid. You saved the draasin. How many people can claim the ability to speak to even one of the great elementals, and here you've spoken to two."

"It still hasn't helped me learn to shape any faster. I'm an earth senser but haven't managed to speak to the earth elemental. Even when I knew golud was in the cavern, I couldn't speak to it."

Amia smiled. "There are many shapers who never speak to the elementals. Why do you think you need to before you perform a shaping?"

Tan shrugged. Did it have to do with his age? He hadn't considered himself old—he'd not even left home before the lisincend destroyed it— but here at the university where everyone was so much younger than him, he couldn't help but feel like he didn't belong. Speaking to the earth elemental would make it easier for him. It might even help him understand what he could do with shaping—if anything.

Amia touched his hand. His ears popped as she shaped him and with it came a sense of relaxation. There was no command, nothing other than a slight surge in the bond between them. Through it, an understanding of her washed through him, a connection like he'd never shared with anyone before, closer than he'd even felt with his parents.

And through the bond, he could tell Amia felt the same.

"I never knew there was a spirit elemental until we reached the cavern," she said. "I'm still not sure whether that was an elemental or a part of the Great Mother herself. Either way, I've only ever spoken to her, never heard her speak back to me. But if you are determined to understand golud, then study until you can read on your own. Until then, I will read to you."

She shifted so that she could lean close to him and started reading.

In spite of the closeness, or perhaps because of the shaped bond between them, Tan felt a sense of uncertainty from her. He didn't know what, but something bothered Amia.

CHAPTER 4

Shapings

ROINE KNOCKED EARLY the next morning. Tan pulled the door open, eyes still thick with sleep. He rubbed them as he pulled on a shirt, wishing the room had a window. How long had he been sleeping? It felt like barely an hour, but the fire had faded to nothing and the room was cold. He and Amia had stayed up late into the night as she read the book to him. The book was written in a strange style, making it seem like actual conversations with golud. From what he remembered of golud in the cave as they secured the artifact, the elemental was a slow and heavy thing.

Now Amia had left. He wasn't surprised; she needed less sleep than him. He remembered her nudging him as she left and kissing him gently on the cheek. But how long ago had that been?

And then there had been the dreams. Tan had visions of the ground far below and tinted in orange and reds, as if seeing them through a colored lens. Waking had felt as if he were tearing himself away from something deep and primal.

Roine eyed him strangely as he opened the door, looking over Tan's shoulder and into the room. He wore a loose-fitting jacket of dark green with black pants. His graying hair stood wildly on his head. "Ah… Tan? Am I interrupting?"

Tan shook his head. "Only my sleep."

"I didn't think you'd be here but when I couldn't find you at the university…"

Tan rubbed his eyes again, pressing against them and hoping to push back the pain in his head. "What time is it?"

Roine laughed and pushed past Tan and into the room. He took a seat in one of the chairs and looked around, his eyes finally settling on the borrowed book resting on the table. "Noon," he said softly. He leaned forward and picked up the book, setting it on his lap as he flipped through the first few pages, shaking his head as he did. "Where did you get this?"

Tan closed the door. How had he slept so long?

Roine watched him as he rubbed the back of his neck.

He wished Amia were still here. He always felt the nagging ache of the draasin more acutely when she was gone. Or maybe the sense of the bond helped him forget about the draasin while she was nearby. With her gone, he felt as if he could track along the connection to the draasin and practically *see* them hunting, only he was too scared to actually do it. The last time he spoke to the draasin, the connection had nearly destroyed him.

"The girl you met. Elle."

Roine frowned. "Where did she get this book?"

Tan shrugged. "She said she got it from the archives. She had a couple of books. This one was about golud."

"I see that. But how would she have known? And why would the archivists allow her to take it?"

Tan shrugged again. "She said her grandfather taught her," he said to the first question. "And I don't know about the archivists. Maybe they knew her?"

Roine's face looked troubled. "The archivists can be touchy about such things. I'm surprised she has this. And Elton?" He shook his head, frowning. "Elton was never much of a scholar when he was here…"

Tan rubbed his neck again. The aching seemed worse today. He tried pushing away the sense of the draasin, keeping it in the back of his mind, but the effort wore on him. And now he'd slept too late and probably missed Master Nass speaking about fire shaping.

Roine watched him.

"You still feel it, don't you?"

Tan looked away. "I have headaches. Probably slept wrong."

Roine set the book down and stood. He took a deep breath and let it out slowly. "I warned you what might happen if we released them."

Tan laughed bitterly. "You don't know what would have happened if we hadn't."

Roine made his way around the chairs and stood next to him. Pressure built behind his ears; Tan wondered what Roine shaped. As a warrior, he could shape all of the elements—all except spirit, though Roine claimed the ancient shapers once could even shape spirit. Tan had seen him work with water, earth, and wind. Never with fire.

"I haven't shared what we did with the king. After the Incendin attack on Galen, he has other things to worry about. But I've been tracking them."

Tan turned and looked at Roine.

"The draasin. Once they were freed, someone needed to follow them. And the king…" He shook his head. "He doesn't—or didn't—need this on his plate, too. With Incendin attacking, there's already too much for him to worry about. He doesn't need to fear ancient elementals long thought dead."

"They won't hunt man. Amia made it—"

"How long do you really think her shaping will hold?" Roine interrupted. "Do you really think her so powerful as to influence an *elemental*? She couldn't even shape Fur. Why should the draasin be any different?"

Tan swallowed. Why hadn't he considered that before?

He'd been there when Amia tried shaping the lisincend. When she'd tried—and failed—to save her mother and the remainders of her people. The shaping had seemed to work at first, but the lisincend recognized what she did and ignored it.

Why should the draasin be any different?

Except—they weren't twisted, not like the lisincend. The draasin were a natural part of the world, however dangerous they might be. And they suffered. Tan had felt their suffering. Worse, had they not released the draasin, Tan might not have survived.

"I felt the shaping take," he said. "I don't know what else to tell you."

Roine snorted. "Then you know where they are?"

Tan shook his head. It was something he feared. If he traced along the connection, what would he find? Would the draasin surge through and overwhelm him again? Without Amia to protect him, he didn't know if he would be able to survive. The draasin had practically torn his mind. "I don't know where they are."

"That should worry you. It does me." He sighed. "I know they've left Galen. I told you about the charred cattle. Other livestock lost."

"Any people?"

Roine sniffed. "No. So far, there are not."

"Then they still obey the shaping."

38

Roine laughed. "You speak of the shaping as if it is something that can contain them. These are wild creatures, one of the most powerful that ever lived. They will find a way around anything that restrains them."

Tan shook his head. The draasin hadn't been able to escape the lake. The nymid held them, trapped within the place of convergence, a place of much power. And they had suffered. Regardless of what Roine said, releasing them had been right.

"Is this why you came? To harass me about them again? There's nothing we can do about it now."

Roine glanced back toward the hearth, his eyes again lingering on the borrowed book. "No—I didn't come here to talk to you about the draasin, but we're going to have to do something about them sooner or later. If they mate—"

"Mate?" He hadn't considered that.

Roine nodded. "We released three draasin. I think the little one might have been a female. Perhaps even two of them." Roine watched him, frowning. "You don't know?"

"I only spoke to one."

Roine's brow furrowed. "And the nymid? How many of them did you speak to?"

Tan shrugged. "There didn't seem to be any particular nymid. Maybe at first." He remembered the face the nymid made in the water as it swam around him. "But when they helped me rescue Amia from the lisincend, it was different nymid."

"And with the river?"

Tan nodded. "Different."

Roine tapped his chin. "Why would you speak to only one of the draasin, then?"

Tan laughed. "You're asking *me* about the elementals? You're the Master shaper and you're the one who's studied at the university."

39

Roine snorted. "I think you mistake me for an archivist. My expertise is in shaping. And other things." He trailed off as he said the last.

Tan sighed and shook his head. "I don't know what happened that let me speak to the nymid, let alone the draasin. And I didn't really try to speak to the others. The one I talked to practically ripped my mind apart."

"Hmm." Roine took a deep breath and rubbed a hand through his hair. "Regardless, they are dangerous. But we have more immediate dangers to attend to now."

"Incendin?"

Roine nodded. "After the convergence, the lisincend were pushed back. Two were killed. But not Fur?"

"I don't know. The draasin chased him, hunting him."

Roine closed his eyes and let out a soft breath. "I wish we knew if they caught him."

"Why?"

"Because there is a secret to the shaping—to the creation of lisincend. I think Fur alone knows that secret. After what happened, I think he will move quickly to create more lisincend."

Tan shivered at the idea. Three lisincend had destroyed his home, had captured Velminth, and wiped out all of Amia's family. How much destruction would even more lisincend cause?

"Can the barrier keep them back?"

Roine took a deep breath. "Once I would have said yes. That was before I knew about Lacertin. Now... now, I don't know. Our shapers have weakened over the years. Without enough shapers, the barrier will eventually fall. We need to be ready."

It was the reason Roine had searched for the artifact in the first place. He thought the device would help with shapers. Ancient scholars anticipated such a need, but Roine had been unable to use it.

"And that's why the king has sent you to Incendin?"

"Not entirely. I need to know how many shapers Incendin has. Even in the war, we never had an accurate count of their shapers. We knew roughly how many lisincend there were, especially as they were so blasted hard to kill. But fire shapers?" He shook his head. "We never learned if the lisincend represented most of their shapers or if there were more."

"What have you learned?"

Roine stuffed his hands into his pockets and sniffed. "There are more. At least a dozen fire shapers near the border. That says nothing about how many are deeper in Incendin. And then the hounds. Too many to count. If they can cross the barrier, it won't matter how many lisincend they send. The hounds alone are deadly." Roine looked at him. "That's why I'm here. Why I need you."

Tan swallowed, wishing he knew nothing about Incendin or their attacks or how deadly the lisincend could be. All he'd wanted was to live in Nor and wander the mountains around his home. Now he'd been pulled into something he could barely understand and felt powerless to stop. He might be a senser, but he hadn't learned to shape, if he ever could.

"What do you need from me?" he asked.

"It's not what I need from you," Roine answered.

Tan frowned, already dreading what Roine would say next.

"The king. You helped find the artifact. Without you, we might not have succeeded. For all that and more, he would like to meet you."

They walked toward the palace in silence. The sun was out and shone brightly overhead. In spite of the bright day, a pall pressed on him. Roine glanced at him occasionally but stayed silent as they made their way toward the heart of the city.

They passed dozens of people in varying dress, and Tan tried not to gape. People outside the university were even more diverse than within the stone walls. The closer to the palace they got, the more uniform the clothing became, as if the city itself had a style. For the most part, Roine's dress fit in. The men wore heavy jackets and loose-fitting pants while the women wore long dresses. Some carried umbrellas to block the sun. Thick, gold jewelry adorned necks of women while many of the men wore bold rings with bright stones on them.

And then they reached a wall surrounding the palace.

The wall stretched high overhead, circling the palace grounds. Guards were stationed periodically, each carrying heavy crossbows they pointed away from the palace. Gleaming helms were marked by the now-familiar symbols of the elementals. Another pair of guards was stationed at the gate to the palace. Neither was armed. Shapers.

Roine nodded to them.

The guards ignored Roine but stared at Tan.

The nearest man wore simple leather armor dyed a rich black. Shapes branded into the leather were hard to make out. The man was thickly muscled and wore a heavy beard. Long, black hair hung to his shoulders. Dark, untrusting eyes stared at Tan.

Tan suspected the man was an earth shaper.

The other man was stick thin and short. He bobbed from foot to foot, sending dust swirling. His shirt and pants were both tight, but his head and face were kept clean-shaven. A smirk spread across his face as he studied Tan.

A wind shaper.

The wind shaper stretched out his hand. Pressure built in Tan's ears and then something pushed against him, holding him back.

Roine glared at the thin man. "He's with me, Alan."

Alan's smirk widened. "You know the rules, Roine." He spoke with a soft voice, but it carried easily, as if shaped on the wind. "Everyone must be checked."

Tan was amazed by the man's ability. Had his mother been so skilled?

And if she had, why had she stopped?

Roine faced the man. More pressure built behind Tan's ears and he wondered at the strength of Roine's shaping and what he would do. But then Roine let it out like a soft breath and the pressure eased.

"Check him, then. See if Zephra's son plans to harm the king. I think you'll find him empty-handed."

Alan's head jerked toward Roine at the remark. "Zephra's son?" He looked at Tan and eyed him carefully. "But she's been gone—"

"In Galen since the war. And where do you think I found him?"

The smirk faded from Alan's face. "And is he—"

Roine's eyes tightened. "He is Zephra's son. What do you think?"

The large man next to Alan grunted. The sound rumbled out of him. "Let him pass, Alan," the man said. "I never knew Zephra, but I studied with Grethan. Last I saw him, he spoke highly of his son."

Alan's shaping dissipated, fading to nothingness. "Does Zephra plan to return?"

Tan forced himself to swallow the emotions that came to him as they spoke of his mother. All his life, he'd known her as Ephra. All his life, she'd been nothing more than his mother. But to these men—to Roine—she was something more. A powerful wind shaper.

Tan wished he would have known her as they knew her.

He looked at the large man, wondering when he might have seen Tan's father. Had this man seen him when he went off to fight Incendin? Would he know more about what had happened? Tan had heard little about the fight other than his father would not return.

"Zephra is gone," Roine said.

Alan blinked. Wind whipped across the ground briefly and then faded. Tan almost heard a soft lament within the wind, but that must have been his imagination.

"Then she has rejoined the Grethan in the afterlife," the large man said. He grabbed Alan and pulled him to the side.

When Tan hurried after Roine, the large man nodded to him.

Past the gate, the palace gardens opened before him, a lush expanse of grass and trees and flowers. The scents mingled together. Roine took them down a path beneath arching oak trees that filtered the light. Birds chirped from high branches. Squirrels scurried and chipped. Finally, he let out a breath. If he closed his eyes, he could almost imagine he was back in Galen.

Roine chuckled. "I figured you'd appreciate this path."

Tan blinked and looked at him. "Why this route?"

"The courtyard is divided into quarters, each representative of one of the kingdoms. This, as you've likely gathered, is Galen."

The air had the same earthy scent he remembered from Galen. The only thing missing was the steep rocky climb and the steady gusting of wind through the branches. And his friends and parents.

"The other sections aren't like this?"

Roine shook his head. "I imagine your young friend Elle would prefer to stroll alongside the lake representing Vatten. Your father once would have liked the open plains representing Ter." Roine shrugged. "Even Nara is represented, though we have fewer and fewer people come from there."

They reached an intersection along the path and Roine turned. Tan sensed the pathway through the trees. He could practically close his eyes and find the way. Near the end of the path, a void blocked his senses, preventing him from going further.

He frowned.

"You sense it, don't you?" Roine asked.

"What is it?"

He motioned ahead of them. "That's the palace. Like the barrier that protects the border with Incendin, there are protections built overtop the palace to prevent access. Only a few shapers are allowed within." He tapped the silver ring on his finger.

"Only the Athan?"

Roine nodded. "This grants my access. Without it, I would be no more able to enter it than…" He trailed off, shaking his head. "I almost said no more able to enter than Incendin can cross our border, but we've learned that's not entirely right, haven't we?"

"What if I were a shaper?" Would the barrier around the palace tell him if he could learn to shape? If he could pass, did it mean he wasn't meant to become a shaper, that he'd have to be content sensing only?

Roine smiled, as if reading his thoughts. "It doesn't work like that. Only those who have demonstrated shaping are prevented access. Besides, you travel with me so could pass through anyway. This ring—" he tapped it softly "—creates a sort of bubble that allows me to pass through the barrier."

"Would it work on the barrier between the kingdoms and Incendin?"

Roine shook his head. "A good question, but that's a different type of barrier. Shapers hold that barrier in place. They can feel subtle changes trying to pass through."

"How did the lisincend get through? What did Lacertin do to let them across?"

Roine's face clouded. "I don't know. I still haven't learned how he managed that."

The trees ended as they reached the end of the path. In front of them, the massive white stone palace rose high overhead. Sunlight practically gleamed off the sides of the stone, making it almost seem to glow. Four spires surrounded a taller central spire that rose high overhead, looking overtop the kingdoms.

The king would be within the palace. Without his order, Tan's father might still live.

And without the lisincend, his mother might still live.

Tan sighed, pushing away his anger. Nothing he could do would change the past. All he could do now was work for his future, whatever it might be.

Roine clapped him on the shoulder. "Are you ready?"

Tan took a deep breath. "Ready for what?"

Roine grunted out a laugh. "For what? You get to meet the king. Not many sensers your age can claim to do so."

Tan only shrugged. "I'm as ready as I can be."

Roine studied him. He paused before starting forward. "Listen, Tan. I know you feel like you've lost everything. And you've lost more than most. But remember, Althem is our king."

Tan sighed and nodded. Something about the way Roine spoke made him frown, almost as if Roine were trying to convince himself as much as Tan.

CHAPTER 5

The Value of Shaping

THEY MADE THEIR WAY INTO THE PALACE. The floor looked to be made of slick marble, but Tan had no difficulty with his footing as they walked through the halls. Portraits lined the walls and it took only a moment for Tan to realize they were the faces of long-dead kings. Most portraits had symbols marked in one of the corners.

"They were shapers," he said aloud, finally recognizing the symbols.

Roine followed Tan's attention and nodded. "Most have been. Shaping is in the royal bloodline."

Tan looked at the pictures. There were shared features among them—the same prominent jaw, a distinctive nose, the dark coloring of their skin—but nothing that would declare them as shapers. "Any warriors?"

Roine grunted and pointed to one of the nearest portraits. It was no larger than the other nearby paintings. A gilded frame surrounded it, making it more ornate than the others nearby. Symbols marked each corner. "Ilton the First. He was the last warrior to sit the throne."

"And does the current king?"

Roine smiled. "I think he has some talent in shaping."

Tan turned and eyed Roine. "Think?"

Roine shrugged. "He keeps his ability hidden, but most suspect he has some modest shaping ability."

"Why would he hide it?"

They stopped further along the hall and Roine pointed at another portrait. This was larger than most, though set into a simple wooden frame. The man had a long, pointed nose and close-cropped hair. Pale blue eyes stared out at him, looking as if they could see the entire hall. Tan noted that no symbols marked the corners.

"This was King Weston."

Tan's eyes widened. Roine smiled.

"You've heard of him then?"

"My father spoke of him. He said he kept the kingdoms intact while fighting a war with Rens."

Tan recalled the night his father had told him of King Weston. The evening had been particularly gusty, even for Galen, and the fire in the hearth only barely pressed back the cold. His mother stooped over the kettle hanging near the fire, slowly stirring her stew. His father whittled on a piece of wood, turning the thick hunk of shapeless wood into a fantastic figure of a wide woodsman. Many nights were the same, but that one had been special. It was the night his father helped him realize shaping alone wasn't the key to power.

He let out a pent-up breath. Thinking of his father wouldn't bring him back. And it did nothing to curb his anger at the king for what had happened. Had the king not sent him toward the border with Incendin, his father might still live.

Only to die like his mother in Nor.

Roine watched him for a moment before nodding. "Rens. What would become Incendin. Yes, King Weston managed to keep the kingdoms intact as Rens worked to steal the eastern border. Nara once stretched much farther east, spilling into what we now know as Incendin. Rens claimed their people and Nara shared a common lineage, that they only sought to protect the bloodline." Roine shook his head. "Weston recognized what they intended. How they sought to claim shapers. He was the reason the university grew to what it is today. Before King Weston, it was a place for scholars, where only the privileged could study. He made it so any could come, drawing shapers from all over the kingdoms who would learn from other shapers, expanding their knowledge. He is widely known as a skilled soldier and wise leader. But he was no shaper."

Tan stared at the picture. The commitment made by his parents to the kingdoms went back farther than the king. It went back generations. And they had done what countless before them had done by coming to Ethea to learn.

He wondered if that was the point Roine was trying to make. That he shouldn't blame the king for what happened to his parents. Or did he have a different intent? With Roine, Tan was never certain. "You're saying the king wants to be judged on how he rules without needing to shape?"

Roine shrugged. "I'm saying a man can be great whether he shapes or not. Shaping does not make one man better than another, nor does it make one king a better ruler than another."

They paused near the end of the hall and Roine tilted his head at the door. He gripped Tan's shoulder and squeezed. It reminded Tan of what his father would do before they went hunting. And the way he'd said farewell before leaving for the war. Tan had never seen him again.

"Althem may not be a shaper—or a warrior—but he is your king," Roine reminded him.

Tan couldn't help but note the familiar way Roine said the king's name. As he did, he remembered what his mother had said about the long-dead princess and Theondar—the name Roine had once gone by—and the connection they shared. Of course, Roine would be close to the king.

"What will he ask of me?"

Roine shook his head. "I don't know. You have already done so much."

Then he turned from the door and pushed it open.

The room on the other side of the door was incredibly ornate. A latticework of gold worked around the walls. Massive pale marble pillars rose through the room. Decorative sculptures were worked into the pillars, most in the shapes of elementals. Tan noted the draasin as they swooped around one of the pillars, hot fire breathing from their lungs.

A massive chair—the throne—stood empty at the end of the room.

Roine approached it and slowed. "I thought he would be here—"

As he spoke, a hidden door opened and a thin man made his way through it, hurrying toward the throne. He was dressed no differently than Roine, wearing a rich navy jacket and deep black pants. Polished boots echoed off the stone. His gray eyes shone as he neared.

It was the nose and jaw that gave him away.

Tan recognized the resemblance to the portraits he'd seen in the hall outside the throne room. Other than that, only his decorative short sword, the hilt covered with bright jewels, looked in any way kingly or regal.

Another man walked alongside him, hovering slightly behind. He was thin and had thick, silvery hair slicked back over his head.

Piercing blue eyes scanned everything around him, pausing on Roine for a moment before turning to Tan. Something about the intensity of his gaze made the ache in Tan's neck and head pulse.

Like Roine, the man wore a slender band of silver on his finger. An Athan—one of the few direct servants to the king.

Roine watched him and nodded respectfully.

The king's mouth tightened when he reached Roine, and he nodded. He remained standing, looking up at Tan. "You are Tannen Minden."

His voice was sharp and he spoke it as a statement rather than a question.

Tan wondered if he was expected to bow or kneel or show some other sort of gesture. Living away from Ethea made him naïve to the customs of the capital. In Galen—and Nor, particularly—he had only to worry about the manor lord. Lord Lins had been of low enough station that Tan had not had to bow to him.

"Yes, sire," he said. He tipped his head, bending at the waist.

The king watched him, the tight expression on his lips relaxing into a smile. "I thought you instructed him better, Roine. Why did you want me to meet with him again?"

Roine blinked. "He's had as much instruction as the lisincend would allow. Unfortunately, Fur did not accommodate the needs of his training."

Tan frowned. His training? Roine had done nothing to train him. They'd spent their time searching for the artifact, barely able to stay alive.

"And you tell me Fur is not a danger." The other Athan spoke slowly, his voice infused with a strange accent that strangely reminded Tan of the Aeta.

Roine shook his head, looking over at the other Athan. "Fur is always a danger, Jishun. Until we know for certain he's been destroyed, we need to be careful. I've warned you what will happen if they create more lisincend."

The king waived his hand, interrupting the two. "The shaping is dangerous. The reports from Incendin have always said nearly half die in the process."

Roine snorted. "It is the half who survive we should fear."

The king looked at Roine with amusement. "You still think the barrier so weak that Incendin can cross?"

"The barrier is not weak—"

The king cut him off. "Had it not been for my father, the shapers would never have created the barrier."

Roine's eyes narrowed. "And it was his favored warrior who first thought of the barrier."

Jishun smiled. Darkness flashed in his eyes. "Lacertin? You still fear him after all this time?"

"I had not thought of him in over a decade. But then he attacked me as we claimed the artifact." Roine took a quick breath. "So yes, I think we should fear him."

"You said you've seen no sign of him since then," the king said.

"And I have not."

"Then why should we fear him? If he's hidden for nearly ten years, what makes you think he won't hide for another ten?" Jishun asked. He stood next to the king, leaning slightly toward him.

Tan thought he felt pressure building behind his ears, the sense of a shaping growing, and looked to Roine, but it didn't seem to be him.

"He knows we found the artifact. And if it's what we think—"

Jishun shot a look at Tan and shook his head, cutting Roine short.

Tan waited. What did they think the artifact did? Roine explained that it was a source of power, some way for the power of the ancient shapers to return, but he hadn't managed to make it work. What did they know?

Roine looked at the king, ignoring the other Athan. "Tannen nearly died more than once trying to reach the artifact, Althem. I think he can be included in this conversation."

Tan blinked. Had Roine just *chastised* the king?

Jishun leaned forward toward Roine. "And yet he has barely joined the university and is not a shaper. If knowledge leaks out… if it reaches Incendin—"

"What more can Incendin learn? That we found the artifact? Fur or Lacertin will tell them that more quickly than rumor from the university. Or that we haven't managed to successfully use the artifact?" Jishun glared at Roine as he spoke. "That might be more interesting to Incendin, but even that won't surprise them. And where does it leave us?"

The king laughed bitterly, waving a hand between his Athan. "No closer than we were to understanding."

Tan looked from Roine to the king. They spoke as if he weren't even there. "Understanding what?" he asked.

The king turned and studied him with an unreadable expression in his dark gray eyes.

Roine breathed heavily. "The kingdom is near a crisis, one our scholars have been unable to solve."

"Shapers?" Tan asked.

Roine nodded. "Yes. Shapers. Once the pride of the kingdoms, the source of our strength and power. Shapers kept our borders safe, but now…"

Tan didn't need Roine to finish. Most knew the numbers of shapers dwindled, if not why. "I know there aren't warriors like we once had," he looked at Roine, who only shrugged, "but I thought the university still had plenty of shapers."

He thought about what he'd seen while at the university. Tan hadn't been in Ethea long enough to understand how many shapers there were. Most of what he'd seen were sensers, people like him, and most too young to serve the kingdoms.

"As I said," the king spoke, turning to Roine, "he has barely joined the university."

Roine looked at Tan for a long moment, studying him as if trying to decide something. Finally, he took a deep breath. "Tannen has proven himself adept. He might not have mastered shaping yet, but his ability extends beyond that."

The king frowned.

Tan's heart paused.

Roine looked from the Jishun to the king. "Tannen speaks to them."

The king turned and leveled his gaze on Tan again. This time, it carried the weight of his station. Tan nearly bowed beneath it.

"Which one?"

Roine took a quick breath. "The nymid," he began. "At Tan's request, they aided me when I fought Fur. They helped him rescue the girl. And they released the protections around the artifact."

Tan didn't know what to be more surprised about—that Roine hadn't shared with the king how he'd spoken to the nymid before now or that he said nothing about the draasin.

"The nymid? They are one of the lesser elementals," Jishun said. "Many speak to the lesser elementals."

Roine shook his head. "I felt the same until I witnessed what they accomplished. At least at that place—the place of convergence—the nymid were the equal of the udilm." He smiled at Jishun without any warmth. "Perhaps the archives are mistaken, Jishun."

The king turned and began pacing, walking around the massive throne, tapping the long finger of his left hand on his chin. Tan noted he wore a slender silver band on his finger much like the one Roine and Jishun wore. Did that allow him to pass through the barrier around the palace, or was there another reason for the ring?

After he circled the chair twice, the king stopped and looked up at Roine, meeting his eyes. "You say he's an earth senser, like his father."

Roine nodded.

"Yet he speaks to the nymid."

Roine nodded again. "Not just the nymid."

Tan realized Roine was making a point of not looking at him.

The king's eyes narrowed and he looked from Roine to Tan. "He speaks to another elemental?"

"He does."

Jishun turned to Tan, who felt the Athan's gaze was almost heavier than the king's. "Which one?"

Roine did look over now. He met Tan's eyes. "The draasin."

The king blinked and then shook his head. "The draasin? They have been gone for—"

"Centuries," Roine finished. "Hunted to extinction. Or so we thought."

Jishun turned to Roine. "He claims to speak to the nymid and you believe him. And then he claims to speak to the draasin? Roine, I thought you better than that."

"The nymid saved his life. All our lives, really. And I saw the draasin."

The king shivered. "You—you *saw* one?"

Roine nodded. "The ancients had trapped them in the ice. They used them to fuel the protections around the artifact. Had he not spoken to them—had Amia not shaped it—we would not have succeeded in securing the artifact."

Jishun's eyes widened briefly at the mention of Amia shaping the draasin.

55

Silence settled around them for long moments. Finally, the king looked over at Tan. An interested fire came to his eyes. "What was it like? The draasin? What was it like when you spoke to it?"

Tan thought about the way the elemental had filled his mind, how he'd feared losing himself in the enormity of the creature. Could he explain to the king what he felt about the draasin, how they were a necessary—though dangerous—part of the world?

Or would the king feel the same fear Roine did?

Roine answered, preventing Tan from needing to. "The creatures were enormous. And terrifying."

"Where are they now?"

Roine shook his head. "I don't know."

The king breathed out slowly. "They must be observed. There are reasons the ancient shapers hunted the draasin. How many did we lose to those beasts?"

Roine snorted. "You know as well as I do that I'm no scholar, Althem."

"Creatures from a time when we had hundreds of warriors, some whose sole purpose was hunting draasin." He took a shuddering breath. "I remember learning how they would tear through the shapers, killing more than any lisincend ever did." He fixed Tan with a hard expression. "And you've loosed them upon the kingdoms."

"There are but three—"

"For now."

"For now," Roine agreed.

"If they show signs of a threat…"

Roine nodded. "I have been monitoring them."

Jishun's eyes narrowed. "You said they were shaped?"

Roine nodded. "The archivists were right about the Aeta."

Jishun's lips pulled into a thin line. "They are shapers."

Roine nodded.

"I fail to see how that helped with the draasin," Jishun said.

Tan interrupted, annoyed with how they spoke around him. He couldn't believe Roine would share Amia's ability to shape so openly. That was her secret to share. And he *knew* the draasin would not harm man. He had felt the shaping take hold and settle around them.

"You fail to see it because you can't speak to them," Tan said. "If you could, you would know the draasin will not hunt man."

Jishun snorted softly. "You think one Aeta managed to do what countless warriors have tried."

Tan shrugged. "I don't know what countless warriors tried. Maybe they never tried a spirit shaping on the elementals—"

"Because it would not work."

Tan shook his head. "It *did* work."

"How—"

The king cut Jishun off. "And if they attack in spite of what he claims? What will you do?"

Jishun looked from Roine to the king. His eyes narrowed as if he heard something no one else could hear. "I must see what I can discover about the draasin. If you will excuse me?"

The king waved a hand and Jishun disappeared through a hidden door.

"Will you do what is needed, then?"

A pained look spread across Roine's face. "I have always served the kingdoms."

The king snorted. "You have always served as you see fit, Theondar. As far as most know, you are Roine, merely one of my Athan."

Tan wondered how Roine would react to mention of his past. The one time they'd spoken about it, Roine had made it clear he was no longer Theondar. Theondar had been a warrior for the kingdoms, a man of arrogance matched only by his skill. Roine… Roine meant *tainted* in the ancient language, but Tan had never learned why Roine considered himself tainted.

Roine glanced at Tan. "There are benefits to remaining hidden."

"Lacertin knows you still live."

"Lacertin never believed I was gone."

The king shook his head. "If it comes to it… if I need a warrior…"

Roine took a long breath and nodded.

"All those years we sought the artifact, and now look what you've found. Not just the artifact, but also a long lost great elemental. And him." He motioned to Tan. "An earth senser who speaks to fire and water."

Roine looked over. "You understand my interest."

Tan did not, but remained silent.

"Has he shown any signs of shaping?"

Roine glanced at him. His mouth tightened. "There have been signs."

The king rubbed his chin, eyes distant as if lost in thought. "Earth? It would make sense, given his father."

Roine shook his head.

"Water? Did the nymid teach him their shaping?"

Roine shook his head again.

"Not fire. The draasin do not teach. That is not the way of their kind. They command and destroy."

Roine held Tan's gaze. "Not fire," Roine agreed. "It was wind he shaped."

CHAPTER 6

Possibilities

TAN SHOOK HIS HEAD. "I can't…" He looked from Roine to the king. How could Roine say something like that? "I haven't shaped the wind. My mother was the wind shaper."

The king nodded. "Zephra served well. She willingly went to Galen, Grethan with her, and served. Such power… without them, the barrier would have fallen long ago." The king looked at Roine. "What type of shaping did you witness?"

"None I saw."

Tan's heart loosened in his chest. If Roine had seen him shaping—even unintentionally—wouldn't he have said something?

"But there was a time while climbing where Amia—the Aeta girl with us—" the king nodded "—slipped from the rocks. A shaping lifted her. It was not one I crafted."

He turned and looked at Tan.

Tan remembered what happened. He had nearly lost Amia that day. She'd slipped, almost falling back to the brutal shore below. A gust of wind caught her and lifted her. Tan couldn't deny the wind had been shaped; he felt the pressure building as it happened: pressure he now recognized as shapings.

But he hadn't done it.

Though if what Roine said were true, if he *had* managed a wind shaping, what would it mean?

"So he is an earth senser, speaks to the water and fire elementals, and you think he shaped wind." The king came around the throne and stood in front of Tan. He looked up at him, tapping his finger on his chin. "How long has it been?"

Roine sighed. "Too long."

"Yet he's almost too old to learn. Did Zephra know?"

"I think she suspected. I believe she tried sending him to Ethea for several years, but he did not wish to come."

The king turned and looked at him. "You understand what we're talking about?"

Tan blinked. They finally noticed him again! "Roine thinks I could be a warrior."

The king nodded. "There has not been a warrior since before you were born. None of our shapers show any talent." He nodded toward Roine. "I sent him for the artifact, but he might have returned with something nearly as important, especially since the artifact does not seem to be effective."

Tan shook his head. "I'm not even a shaper. Even if Roine is right and I shaped wind—" the idea seemed nearly impossible, but Tan couldn't escape the logic to it "—I can't even shape earth, and I'm an earth senser. What makes you think I can learn to shape well enough to be a warrior?" He couldn't believe he was even having this argument, and with the king!

The king motioned him to walk and they moved away from the throne. He led them to the nearest pillar. There, on the surface of the marble, was a depiction of a man sitting on the shore of the ocean, waves crashing against rocks. A face appeared in the water.

"You know what this is?" the king asked.

"Probably udilm," Tan answered.

The king nodded. "And this represents one of our earliest shapers speaking to udilm. The great elemental is responding, answering the call." The king touched the surface of the pillar, tracing the outline of the face in the water. "But if you look carefully, you will see something more. You will see the man is listening."

Tan frowned but studied the sculpting. As he did, he saw what the king meant, how the shaper leaned toward the face in the waves, his head tipped to the side. This was not a shaper commanding the elemental, this was a shaper listening—learning from—the elemental.

"Years ago, when the kingdoms had many warriors, scholars debated whether shapers who could speak to the elementals were more skilled than those who couldn't." He laughed softly. "Now we don't even have the opportunity to have such a debate. We have no warriors and few speak to the elementals. I cannot help but think they are related."

Tan looked at the pillar again and circled around it. He noted how the face of udilm reminded him of the face he'd seen of the nymid. Perhaps udilm and nymid were more closely related than the scholars thought, or perhaps they simply took on a similar form for shapers.

The king led him to the next pillar. Wind whipped through, carrying the shaper. Ara was depicted as lithe and light, barely more corporeal than the wind itself. They moved on to the next pillar, one where golud stood like a massive boulder, unmoving. A broad shaper stood alongside, huge arms flexing as the shaper worked to lift golud.

"You see how they once worked together?" he asked, motioning to the pillars.

Tan nodded, but as he did, he looked away from the king, eyes settling on the stone pillar where the draasin were sculpted in the marble. In the relief, even from where he stood, he saw the almost arrogant way the draasin stared at the shaper standing on the ground, as if the shaper knelt before the draasin. Tan took a step toward the carving. As he did, the image seemed to shift, casting the shaper in a different light, leaving the draasin looking like it flew away from the shaper, as if chased.

He shook his head and sighed, rubbing his neck. They were hunters, powerful and swift, but they were intelligent as well. Whatever relationship the shaper would have could not be one of subservience or dominance. Either would fail. The draasin, more than even the nymid, needed a partnership, one of mutual respect.

"What can I do?" Tan asked. "Would you have me speak to the nymid and find out if they know what happened?"

The king pursed his lips. "I cannot ask of you what the best scholars have failed to learn." He grunted. "You are still untrained. Uneducated. But if Incendin continues to push, we will need strength." He turned to Tan. "Warriors thought forgotten will return. Already Lacertin has shown himself." He glanced at Roine. "And though he fights it, Theondar must return."

Roine's mouth tightened, but he said nothing.

The king shook his head. "A war is coming, one we may no longer have the resources to fight. Without the shapers we once had, Incendin may find the kingdoms easier to attack." He paused, as if seeing the question on Tan's face. "Oh, we still have shapers, but even this generation of shapers has changed, weaker than the one before it. So for you to appear—someone with the potential to become not just a shaper, but a warrior—" He shook his head. "I need you to learn what you can. Discover your strength as you learn to shape. And then…" He shook his head again. "Then you might be of use."

The king started away and Tan frowned. Was that it? The entire reason Roine brought him to see the king was to be told to study more?

"Wait—"

The king paused and turned to face Tan. He watched him with a hard expression.

"Is that the only reason you brought me here?"

The king frowned. "You question your king?"

Tan swallowed. He needed to be careful. "I only question why Roine brought me to you."

The king smiled, though it looked more like a sneer. "It was your reward."

"Reward?"

The king nodded. "You helped my Athan. Without your help, he would not have succeeded in securing the artifact. For that, you were granted the opportunity to meet your king. That is your reward."

With that, the king continued back out of the throne room, disappearing behind a hidden door.

Tan stood for a moment, rubbing the back of his neck, before turning to Roine.

Roine watched him, an unreadable expression on his face. "You don't care for your reward?"

Tan considered his answer for a moment before replying. "I don't care for my king."

Roine surprised him by laughing. "It doesn't matter if you care for him. Only that you obey."

Tan blinked; the answer surprised him. From what he'd seen of Roine—and the stories he'd heard of Theondar—it was unlikely that he always followed his orders. "So you will obey? Will Theondar really return?"

Pain lined Roine's eyes. Tan knew little about what Roine had lost, about what prompted him to abandon who he once was and take up the name Roine, but he knew what Roine had said. Theondar was gone.

"I don't know if he can," Roine said softly.

Tan opened his mouth to say something, to remind Roine of how he'd battled Lacertin and survived, but closed it when he saw the expression on his face. "What now? Do you really think I could become a warrior?"

Roine nodded toward the wide double doors they'd come in through and led Tan out of the throne room. They made their way silently, only the steady echoes of their boots across the stone disturbing the quiet. Tan glanced one more time at the pillar depicting the draasin. From this angle, the shapers on the relief appeared to be glaring at the draasin.

Even the ancients had an uncomfortable alliance with the draasin, and they had shapers of spirit. What made Tan think he could do anything differently than them? What made him believe he could control the draasin any better?

Except it wasn't about control.

They reached the doors and Roine shaped them open. He paused back in the hall and turned to Tan, his eyes drifting past the portraits of kings. "When I first met you, I learned you were a skilled earth senser," Roine said. He moved down the hall, occasionally looking up as he did. "Zephra said you were much like your father." He took a deep breath and shook his head. "It is unfortunate she didn't escape the Incendin attack. Much has been kept from you."

Tan looked back at Roine, his mind racing with what he was hearing. His mother kept the fact that she was a wind shaper from him for reasons Tan had never learned. If she'd kept that from him—something important about her past—it made sense that she'd keep other things from him as well.

Could there be more he didn't know about his father?

The king hinted at more, Tan suddenly realized.

He swallowed, a dizzying sense coming over him. "He was a shaper, wasn't he?"

Roine took a deep breath and nodded. "Zephra was powerful and proud. Strong-headed. Only another, equally strong, could be her match."

His father being an earth shaper made a twisted sort of sense. He always seemed so at ease in the woods, never afraid, even when tracking the massive mountain wolves.

Tan shook his head. "Why? Why didn't they tell me?"

"I don't know. I suspect they wanted to protect you somehow."

"But we lived in Nor… we lived so near the border!"

"And they served their part. They powered the barrier. That was the price of leaving Ethea."

Was that why his mother wanted him to come to the university? Had she wanted him to learn to shape to relieve her of her duty? "What happens now that they're gone?"

"Others have replaced them. When Grethan—" Roine tried offering a comforting smile. "When your father was called to the border, another took his place protecting the barrier. It might be why Incendin targeted Nor and Velminth."

Tan looked away. The long hall stretched in front of him. Marble and silver gilding and rows of portraits, all seeming so unnecessary. He hadn't noticed before, but lanterns hung on walls like those he'd seen in the cavern. Soft light glowed from them.

"And because both my parents were shapers…"

Tan didn't finish. He couldn't finish.

Roine touched his shoulder. "Your parents were skilled, and that makes it more likely you could be a shaper, but it doesn't guarantee anything."

They stepped back out of the palace. Bright sunlight shone overhead. Roine nodded toward the grove of trees. "You know you're an earth senser. That has never been hidden from you, though you seem to have some doubts as to your strength. Strong sensers often learn to shape. Not always, but usually."

Tan nodded. "But I've never shown enough strength to be a shaper," he argued.

Roine laughed softly. "Perhaps compared to your father. Grethan… well, Grethan was an incredible earth shaper. A Master. Were it not for your mother, I suspect he would have remained at the university." Roine nodded toward the section of the palace courtyard where tall grasses grew. "And if not Ethea, he would have returned to Ter, to work the land as his parents did. But your mother—" a wistful tone came to his voice "—she was something more than a Master. Her control of the wind was exquisite, almost as if she were one of the elementals herself." Roine smiled. "She steered your father toward Galen. She wanted to leave the university but saw a need to still serve."

"You knew them."

Roine swallowed. "I knew them."

During the time they spent searching for the artifact, Tan had learned Roine knew his mother, but he hadn't known how well. Roine spoke of her with remembered fondness. They were friends.

"And I know your mother cared for you. Had she known you could speak to the nymid, she would have seen what you could become. Had that been it, had you only spoken to the nymid, I could have believed you were merely meant to be an earth shaper. I recognized your sensing strength early in our journey. But then you spoke to the draasin." Roine sighed. "Earth. Water. Fire. Too many elements to be only a shaper. I thought your strength was in earth, but when Amia nearly fell and the wind caught her, I realized I was wrong." He looked Tan in the eyes. "There must have been other times where you accidentally summoned the wind?"

Tan started shaking his head, but stopped. There *had* been another time. When the hounds chased him. He'd been stuck in the trees, trapped, saved only by the sudden return of the steady winds of Galen.

Could that have been him?

"I see there might be." He chuckled softly. "For me, it started with a single element. I was a reasonable wind senser, but when I learned to shape…" He shook his head. "I realized I could sense other elements. Water. Earth. Fire last." He shrugged. "Probably why that's always been weakest for me. Not spirit. No warriors were spirit shapers."

"I—I'm not even a shaper."

"But you are. If you've summoned the wind, you've shaped it. Wind shaping is difficult and hard to master. Most of what's done with wind is done in broad strokes, over wide spaces, though men like Alan have some finer skill. Most don't. It's what made your mother so unique. She could shape the most delicate shapings of wind, so subtle you barely knew she did them."

Tan heard the respect in his voice.

"You were already an earth senser. The nymid, I think, awoke the water sensing."

"And the draasin?"

Roine shrugged. "Probably the same. You aren't a warrior, Tannen, but you *can* be. And the first the kingdoms have found in a generation. Incendin has waited, growing stronger while the kingdoms have become weaker. And now they've attacked. What happened in Galen will occur in other parts of the kingdoms. You *saw* what Fur could do. The kingdoms will need anyone who can shape to withstand them."

"Why me?"

Tan hated the way the question sounded, but he'd lost everything—everyone—only to realize he might have some precious ability. And the only people who might have been able to guide him through it were gone.

Roine looked to the sky, as if the sun overhead could grant answers. "Why any of us? Who knows why one of us is chosen and another not? Only the Great Mother and she doesn't speak to me."

They stood overlooking the courtyard where each region of the kingdoms was represented. He had spent years resisting his mother pushing him to come to Ethea. Now he was here... and she was gone. Times like this, he missed her most. There was so much about his parents he didn't know—would never know. All because of the artifact.

He turned to Roine, and looked over at him. "What is the artifact?"

Roine hesitated. He glanced up at the palace and nodded slowly, as if deciding. "To be honest, we don't know," he started, turning back to Tan. "It was supposed to be a source of power, but I begin to think it something else."

"Why?"

Roine shook his head. "The way we found it. The way the elementals were tied to it. I don't think that's a coincidence."

"You think the artifact does something to the elementals?"

Roine shrugged. "I don't know. The archivists study such things more than I do. Jishun thinks that when activated, it lets someone speak to elementals who might not otherwise be able to."

Tan frowned. "Then why all the protections around it?"

Roine nodded. "That was my question. If it was only about speaking to elementals, I don't think the ancient warriors would have put so much effort into its protection."

"What else could it be used for?"

A troubled look crossed Roine's face, but he shook his head. "It probably doesn't matter since none of us know how to use it anyway. Regardless of what it does, at least we kept it from Incendin. Had they acquired it—had Lacertin acquired it—there's no telling what would have happened."

They reached the end of the palace courtyard. Roine stopped and nodded to Tan. "I haven't been as available as I'd like. I hope that changes soon. I know you have questions and I'd like to help you learn the answers."

He patted Tan on the shoulder and turned back to the palace, leaving Tan standing and staring at the courtyard. He pressed out with his sensing ability, reaching through the trees and the grasses and the water, to feel everything around him as his father once taught him.

Suddenly, he felt so very alone.

CHAPTER 7

Past, Present, and Future

BOOKS STACKED ACROSS THE LARGE TABLE in this section of the archives. Dust piled atop most of them, practically seeping from the bindings. Shielded lanterns cast thin light across the table. Tan wished for a shapers lamp like were found in the palace or in the cavern, but those were reserved for only the wealthy. He would have to make the lantern work.

The archives were dark but dry. The air held little hint of moisture—likely shaped out—but carried a musty scent. Shelves worked in rows around the archives, most with newer texts, not the more ancient works he sought. Other than the lanterns, the archives were a dark, windowless place. Tan had the sense the archivists preferred it that way.

He dragged it down the table, creating a trail in the thick dust as he did. How was it so few people used this space anymore? The stone walls created an oppressive feel, and the dusty air had an unused quality to it, but otherwise he felt cozy. As if all he needed was a hearth with a fire and he would be reminded of home. Even the chair, with its wide slats and comfortable seat, felt like home.

Tan leaned over the book on the table, straining at the words. He'd asked the archivist for whatever records about the ancient language that might be helpful for learning the basics. After looking at him askance, the man had brought these from some hidden depths. Now, he moved around the perimeter of the archives, glancing at Tan, ostensibly checking the oil in the lanterns.

Pain lanced through his head, different than it had been before and growing more intense the longer he remained in the archives. He blinked, wishing to sleep, but what the king had said to him kept him searching. Were he to become a shaper, he needed to understand the connection to the elementals and to learn whether the connection to the draasin was the reason for his pain.

Tan sighed. His breath stirred up a cloud of dust and he covered his mouth to keep from breathing it in. This book had been little use. He turned to the next.

"You can't learn the ancient language entirely through books."

Tan looked up to see the archivist watching him. He leaned on the table, peering at the book Tan studied.

"Need someone able to speak *Ishthin* to learn it. There aren't many who still remember."

Amia did, but Tan hadn't been able to find her after leaving Roine. Other than returning to his room, he didn't know what else to do.

"Can you speak the ancient language?" Tan asked.

The archivist laughed softly. "Not as well as some. The older archivists read it as if they were born to the language. I'm still learning. Many of our oldest texts are written in *Ishthin*."

Tan looked at the book open on the table. Written much like the one Elle had lent him, strange characters filled the page, none of which he recognized. Try as she might, Amia hadn't managed to teach him to read it. He struggled enough reading the common tongue. Had he focused as his mother suggested, he might be more literate, but there were always trees to climb, hills to explore. Sitting in dusty archives had never appealed to him before now.

"How long did it take to learn?"

Amia had learned from a very young age, but would the archivist or would he have learned like Tan needed to learn, drudging through books older than him in order to understand the language?

The archivist shook his head. "Learning *Ishthin* takes a lifetime. There is much nuance to the language we no longer have the experience to appreciate." He looked around and nodded toward a thin man with a stooped back and spectacles making his way through the door to the back of the archives. "In time, I may acquire the same mastery our senior archivists have, but until then…" He shrugged. "Until then, I serve here."

Tan sighed. "So it's pointless?"

The archivist chuckled. "Not pointless. Merely challenging." He studied Tan a moment. "You would learn *Ishthin*? The archives interest you?"

He nodded. "Part of the archives interest me," he admitted. As friendly as this man seemed, he didn't want to tell him *why* he searched. What would happen if he admitted interest in the draasin?

The archivist tapped the books next to Tan. "To some, *Ishthin* comes easy. It is like shaping that way, or how some used to speak to the elementals. To others, the ancient language will never be mastered. You can't know unless you try."

Tan looked at the stack of books. Symbols worked around the top of the book much like the book about golud. And just like that book, he could make out nothing on the page. "Trying isn't getting me very far."

The archivist shrugged again. "Then maybe your strength lies elsewhere." He hesitated and nodded toward where the other archivist had disappeared. "I should go. Master Yulan has returned from his research. He's been gone for months and when he returns, he gathers the archivists together." He wiped his hands on his robe. "Let me know if I can help find anything else."

The archivist moved toward the back door. Tan sighed, pulling the next book over to him. A soft shuffling came from the end of the room and he turned.

Standing near the end of the table, Elle watched him. She wore what appeared to be a man's shirt and pants, both a few sizes too large. Short hair was pinned away from her forehead. She clutched two books to her chest, much like the last time Tan saw her.

"What are you doing here?"

Tan blinked. "You lent me a book on golud. How else am I to learn to read it?"

Elle glanced around nervously and took an uncertain step toward the table. "You actually intend to read it?" she asked in a hushed voice.

Tan laughed. "Isn't that why you lent it to me?"

Elle pulled a chair out from the other side of the table and took a seat. She set the books she held atop the table. Only the rough edges of the pages were visible. "You think the elementals could help you learn shaping?"

He let out a slow breath. If he could return the place of convergence, would the nymid help him learn shaping? If he truly could be a warrior, that meant he had the potential to be a water shaper. The nymid had been most concerned about Amia, doing what they did to help save her, but hadn't they kept Tan alive, too?

And the draasin...would it help him learn fire shaping? He had the sense it would laugh if he asked. Approaching the draasin would take a different tact.

"I think it might work better than anything else I'd tried."

Elle looked at the books Tan had spread in front of him. She touched them, tracing her finger across the binding. "What are these?"

Tan shook his head. "Trying to learn *Ishthin*. I didn't have a grandfather like yours able to teach me."

"And I didn't have parents to shield me," Elle said.

Tan noted the touch of resentment in her voice and sighed. "I'm sorry. You've been friendly with me. Not everyone I've met in Ethea has been."

Elle laughed, and Tan frowned. "Not many at the university are friendly," she said. "When you're here for long enough, you begin to see that. Either they want to use you or they fear you might be better than them."

"I'm not much to fear. I'm only a senser—"

"Who's friendly with one of the Athan. And Roine, at that." Elle shook her head. "You'll find most would think that's reason enough to fear you without even knowing you." She laughed again. "And then you challenge Master Ferran while he's giving his talk, making claims of seeing lisincend—and surviving—while in Galen." A smile split her lips, making her look slightly older than she did otherwise. "No, there's no reason to fear you!"

Tan looked at his hands, eyes drifting over to the books stacked there. Only the archivist hadn't seemed annoyed by him. But if everyone in the university felt that way, no one would teach the new shapers.

But then Tan thought about what Roine said. If he could become a warrior, others in the university *would* have reason for jealousy. There hadn't been a warrior since Roine's time, and even then, they were rare.

"I didn't mean—"

Elle pushed a book at him and smiled. "I know you didn't. You're too new here to mean anything." She leaned atop the books she'd carried into the archives, covering them with her arms. "If you think to learn *Ishthin*, you need someone who speaks it. You can't learn it from books, at least not well."

"That's what he said." Tan motioned toward the archivist standing near a darkened doorway.

Elle looked over at him and her eyes narrowed. "Him? He's the one I convinced to let me into the restricted archives. Now, if only I can get him to help me reach the lower archives…"

"What do you think to learn?"

Elle shook her head, pushing a strand of loose hair back behind her. "There's much not known about the elementals, but what *is* known is recorded in these archives. If I only had answers."

"Answers?"

Elle shook her head and turned away.

"Answers to what?" Tan pressed.

"It doesn't matter."

He thought about what he knew of the elementals, which was limited to the nymid and the draasin. But if the archives contained more information, could he better understand why he was able to speak to them and what that meant for his ability to learn shaping? Could he really learn to shape the elements, not simply speak to the great elementals? It seemed impossible to believe he could ever have the arcane skills Roine possessed, but if he had already shaped the wind—controlled it to save Amia—and could sense earth, what other answer was there?

The stooped man with the spectacles came back through the door and stared at them.

Elle turned quickly, pulling her books against her. "I should go," she said.

She stood and hurried from the archives. The old archivist watched her.

Strangely, pressure built behind Tan's ears.

Tan sat back in his chair back in his room, staring blankly. An oil lantern, one with impure oil leaving a sooty smoke streaming from it, burned on a table nearby. Tan felt tempted to quench it, but that would plunge the room into full darkness, and he wasn't quite ready for sleep.

Amia hadn't returned.

As he sat there, head throbbing since leaving the archives, he thought about Elle. The young girl amused him, but there was no questioning that she might be smarter than him. She could read the ancient language for one, but more than that, she had a level of experience with shapers Tan had not yet acquired. The few weeks spent around Roine would not make up for the years missed with his parents.

He sighed. How could they have been shapers but not tell him?

If only his mother were still in Nor, then he could go to her and ask why she'd kept so much from him. But at least she'd told him about herself. Tan had to learn about his father from Roine.

His eyes flickered closed and he rested his head against the chair.

As he sighed, the throbbing at the back of his neck bothered him. He rubbed at it, pushing back against the draasin. If only he could get the pain to go away.

Leave me alone.

It had been so long since he'd spoken to the elementals and he didn't mean to send anything, but the wave of fatigue washing over him told him he'd sent it.

Tan breathed slowly, letting sleep pull at him. The throbbing in his neck didn't change.

Then, suddenly, he heard a soft laughter in the back of his mind, growing stronger.

Little Warrior. You speak again.

Tan didn't open his eyes. What had he done, sending a communication to the draasin? Now that it spoke to him, he could no more shut it off than he could dam the Gherash River running through northern Galen.

The draasin laughed again.

You needn't fear us, Little Warrior. You are too far from me to bother hunting.

This time, Tan laughed. *Where do you hunt?*

Roine claimed the draasin still prowled Galen. Could he determine if that were true?

An image flickered into his mind. Sand and rock and stunted trees flashed across his mind, the vision blurred and streaked with orange and red. It took Tan a moment to realize he saw as if through draasin eyes, eyes as different to his as the draasin were to him. The vision reminded him of the strange dream he'd had.

He did not recognize the terrain, but it wasn't Galen.

Did you catch Twisted Fire? Tan used the nymid term for the lisincend, uncertain whether the draasin would understand.

He sensed irritation.

That one is strong. A note of respect simmered within the comment. *He is injured and will not hunt well again. But I did not capture him.*

Fur escaped. At least one question was answered. *And you... are you well?*

The draasin laughed again, the sound practically booming through his mind. Otherwise, the draasin did not tear at his mind as it had the last time. He wondered if it was distance or something the draasin did.

Your kind trapped the draasin for centuries and now you wonder if we are well? You are a curious one.

Tan thought of the relief at the palace, the relationship with the draasin depicted there, with either the shapers leading the draasin or the draasin chasing the shapers. Did it have to be that way? Could he forge a balance with them? Did it need to be one or the other?

I was not the one to trap you beneath the ice.

There came a pause, as if the draasin listened. Or perhaps it was distracted and ignored Tan. For long moments, the draasin said nothing.

Tan let out a sigh. He'd been careless. Roine was right—he didn't know enough about the draasin to communicate with them. From what Tan could tell, his mind wasn't strong enough to withstand them. What would happen if the draasin tried to overpower him?

Laughter echoed in his mind. The draasin had not gone.

Little Warrior. You are young, but not as weak as you believe. You seek to bend the earth when you should chase the flames.

Tan swallowed. The draasin had said something like that when he'd freed them from the ice though he didn't know what it meant at the time. He wasn't the warrior the draasin believed.

I'm an earth senser but I can't shape it.

Laughter again. This time stronger, closer. Did the draasin *come* for him?

You speak to the nymid. You speak to draasin. Few of your kind have ever bothered.

Tan felt as if his heart paused. *Could you help?*

As he said it, he realized the mistake. He could not ask the draasin.

Help? Teach so you can trap us again? Irritation came through the connection. *Already you have placed walls around us we never had before. Why should we help?*

The walls must be Amia's shaping. Then they still held.

Not walls, but protections so you don't harm people.

Laughter again. This time darker and with a hint of malice. *We have seen your people. We have seen how you harm each other. We have been hunted, chased, and killed, no differently than we hunt. That is how the Mother made us and how it will always be.*

Tan shook his head. He would not win an argument with the draasin. The creature was ancient—centuries old—and had experienced far more than Tan would ever know.

And he sensed that.

Through the connection, he sensed vast understanding and knowledge, a view of the world foreign to him—greater than him— that he simply could not grasp. To the draasin, his kind was transient, nothing more than a mote of passing time. The draasin were elementals, part of the fabric of the land. They had been trapped—abused—by the other elementals, forced into service. And they were still angry.

I am sorry.

There came another pause.

And then the pain in the back of his mind twinged briefly before receding.

Silence.

Tan opened his eyes. The draasin had severed the connection. If he thought about it hard enough, he could tell it was still there, deep at the back of his mind, but he didn't have the sense that he needed to push it away as he had before. He was left with the memory of the pain, little more.

Rather than relief that the connection was gone, Tan felt something akin to disappointment. If Roine were right—if he had the potential to become a warrior—he would need whatever advantage he had to learn about shaping. And the draasin were his advantage.

Tan turned and stared at the cold hearth, wondering where the draasin had gone. Not Galen as Roine thought, but no place he had ever seen either, but he might not even be able to recognize something as familiar as Nor when seen through the draasin's eyes.

He sighed again. If Roine were right, he needed to do whatever he could to learn how to shape. That meant the university and classes, but he hadn't particularly cared for any of the classes he'd attended so far. What he needed was a way to reach the restricted archives, a way to gain access to some of the hidden texts the archivists stored. If he could find them, he might be able to learn how the ancient shapers used their connection to the elementals in their shaping. Maybe then he could learn to shape.

But if Roine were right, then the draasin were dangerous. Too powerful to exist, at least as far as the ancient shapers were concerned, shapers who knew more about the draasin than Tan had learned. The same shapers he sought to learn from by accessing the archives. And if they felt the draasin were too dangerous to freely roam, why did he think he knew better?

But there was that glimpse of what he'd sensed through the connection. A glimpse of what it meant to be one of the draasin, the way they were a part of the world, a part that had been missing—trapped in ice within the place of convergence—for so long that memories of the draasin had faded, leaving little more than records in a musty archive.

Tan closed his eyes. As he drifted toward sleep, he decided it didn't matter. The draasin were free. Amia had shaped the restrictions preventing them from hunting man. And as far as he could tell, the restrictions held.

The draasin would not—and with what Amia had done, could not—harm anyone.

His neck throbbed again but different than before, sharper and with more intensity since leaving the archives. He rubbed it, but it did nothing to change the pain.

CHAPTER 8

Heat and Fire

A WEEK PASSED WHEN THE EXPLOSION came. Tan was sitting in another class at the university at the time, forcing his attention, determined to learn what he could about shaping. So far, it was not going well.

The speaker—Master Nystin, a thin, elderly wind shaper—spoke about how to use the currents in the air to capture the wind and pull it into a shaping, describing the shaping as something delicate and light, a mere touch of a shaping. Everything he spoke about sounded so impossible. The few people sitting in the class nodded. Most were likely wind sensers hoping to learn something that might allow them to become shapers. None were close to his age, though one—a boy who looked much like the kid from Keoth he'd seen in Master Ferran's class—looked close.

As he spoke, Master Nystin glanced at him. Every so often, he would frown and purse his lips, almost as if recognizing Tan. Had he known Zephra as well?

A series of narrow windows lined the wall of the classroom. Tan stared through the thick glass, part of him wishing he hadn't bothered coming to the class. He wasn't even a wind senser; what was there for him to learn here?

As Master Nystin spoke, a cool breeze flicked around the room. Tan suspected it was shaped. The building pressure behind his ears told him it must be. The old master swirled the wind around the room, barely rustling the papers on the teachers' lectern. Roine had mentioned how difficult shapers found it to finely control the wind; what must his mother's shapings have been like?

The breeze grew warmer and drier. Tan looked away from the window to Master Nystin, but he saw no sign the master did anything different. The way the wind felt reminded him of how Galen had been in the days before the lisincend attacked.

And then a distant explosion thundered.

Master Nystin turned toward the window. His eyes went distant and wide, the pressure of his shaping building behind Tan's ears, and then he hurried from the room, scurrying much faster than Tan would have expected for a man his age.

The others sat in the room for a moment, too stunned to say anything.

Another explosion came, louder than the last.

Heat surged through the air. Tan's skin tingled with it.

He had known heat like this before. The lisincend.

Could they have reached the university? Would they really dare attack Ethea with all the shapers here?

The idea seemed impossible, but what other explanation was there?

The others in the room hurried to the door. Tan followed, too uncertain to say anything. As they made their way through the dark corridors, a few of the other masters hurried out from behind closed doors, racing away from the university.

Tan followed the other students into the courtyard.

The air was still and hot, stagnant with the scent of ash and char. Dozens of students stood around, most in small groups, speaking softly to each other. Tan looked around for a familiar face but found no one. The only person at the university he really knew was Elle, and he hadn't seen her since leaving the archives nearly a week ago.

Thick clouds smeared across the gray sky, almost oppressive.

Tan turned as someone came running up behind him.

Roine ran toward the stone circle in the center of the courtyard. Dressed in a thick green jacket and pants, he held his sword unsheathed in his hand. His eyes were hard and intent. He barely nodded at Tan as he passed.

Once he reached the center of the stone, a massive bolt of lightning streaked from the sky, striking him. Roine disappeared in the flash of light.

The murmuring of voices started shortly after that.

"Who was that?"

"I don't know. Is he one of the Masters?"

"I haven't seen a shaper do that before."

"No shaper can."

Tan considered telling them how Roine was not merely a shaper, but decided against it.

Something tugged at his jacket, and he turned.

Elle looked at him, today wearing a dress that seemed a size too small. It clung to her tiny frame. Her short, brown hair hung limply against her head. Her dark eyes flickered around the courtyard before settling on Tan.

"Where did Theondar go?"

Tan raised a finger to his lips and pulled her to the side until they reached a corner between buildings. "That's not his name."

Elle frowned. "You called him that when he appeared the last time."

He'd hoped she hadn't heard him. "He doesn't go by that name anymore."

She shrugged. "Whatever his name is. Where did he go?"

Elle seemed unconcerned that a warrior long thought dead still lived. "I don't know. Off to learn about the explosions."

"What do you think it was?"

Tan shook his head. "I don't know."

He didn't want to think it could actually be Incendin attacking, not this close to Ethea, but what else made sense? The heat and stillness of the air were so much like what he'd felt when the hounds crossed the barrier.

But how would they have reached Ethea already? How would they have crossed the barrier?

Unless the barrier had grown too weak to hold them back.

"You think it's Incendin."

Tan shook his head. "I told you. I don't know what it is."

But he could try to find out. He closed his eyes and tried a sensing, pushing it out from him. His sensing washed over the city, over thousands of people living and moving within the city, and then farther, out beyond the edge of Ethea, to the small farms on the edges. Beyond those farms were open plains. Trees dotted there, but not as many as in Galen. Small animals moved, but nothing seemed out of the ordinary.

There wasn't a definite answer. And he sensed no evidence of Incendin, nothing that seemed out of the ordinary.

What had caused the explosion?

Elle watched him. "You really don't know, do you?"

Tan shook his head.

"What did you sense?"

He frowned. "How did you know I sensed anything?"

Elle sniffed. "I'm a water senser. It attunes me to things like that. I can feel it when people are shaping around me."

"But I didn't shape anything."

Elle shrugged. "Then you're a strong senser, but I don't usually know when someone is only sensing." She looked back toward the stone circle at the center of the courtyard. "What do you think it was, then? Something big enough to get an Athan's attention."

"He probably thought it was an Incendin shaper like I did."

"Incendin can't reach Ethea. They have to get through the barrier—" Tan shot her a look, reminding her of what had happened in Nor "—and then make it here without being detected. They wouldn't risk that."

"Unless they searched for something valuable," Tan said, realizing a reason Incendin might risk coming to Ethea. If they really wanted to get the artifact, they might risk the kingdom's shapers.

He leaned against the wall, wondering how many lisincend it would take to overwhelm Ethea and the king's shapers, when another crack of lightning streaked from the sky, striking the center of the circle of stones.

Everyone in the courtyard fell silent.

As the flash faded, Roine stepped away from the circle. He looked around the courtyard, his eyes dark and hard, until they settled on Tan, and then he pointed.

Tan blinked, hurrying over toward Roine. Elle followed without asking permission.

"What did you find?" he asked. "Was it the—" he turned, checking to make certain none of the other students were too close "—the lisincend?"

Roine shook his head. "You know the barrier keeps the lisincend out of the kingdoms."

"Not entirely."

Roine grunted. He started walking toward the archway leading away from the university. Tan followed along. "Not entirely, but the barrier still holds. Thank the Great Mother we still have enough shapers for that."

"Then what caused the explosion?"

Roine paused long enough to look from Tan to Elle. "Fire caused the explosion."

"Fire?" Elle asked.

Roine breathed out. "The kind not seen in the kingdoms in nearly a thousand years."

Tan swallowed. When he'd spoken to the draasin, they had been far from the kingdoms. Or had they? Would he have known? The draasin had severed the connection between them, had muted it so that Tan barely felt it, but surely he would have known had the draasin attacked?

"They couldn't..." he started, looking over at Elle.

Roine's eyes hardened, if it were possible for stone to get harder. "Are you certain? Can you be sure her shaping held?" He shook his head and started off again. Tan had to run to keep up. "I warned you, Tannen. What you did was dangerous. We had no way of knowing what would happen and now... now they've attacked near the capital."

"But the shaping—"

"You really think a shaping can contain one of the elementals?"

Elle's eyes widened. "A fire elemental? That's what you're talking about, isn't it? But they're not found in this part of the kingdoms, and when they are, they're so weak, they can't do more than burn the hair off a seal!"

Tan stared at Roine. "The shaping holds."

"You can be so certain?"

"Yes."

The corners of Roine's eyes wrinkled slightly and he shook his head. "I wish I could believe that, but I've seen the devastation left after their passing. And now it's more than only livestock. This time, an entire farm was scorched. Nothing remains of the farmer or his flock."

Scorched, not completely destroyed. Not like what the lisincend did to Nor.

Maybe Roine was right. Maybe it wasn't the lisincend. It still didn't make much sense. He'd just spoken to the draasin the day before and they hadn't been near Ethea then.

Tan let out a frustrated sigh. He didn't know, though, and that was the problem. Maybe they *had* attacked.

Another thought troubled him, one he had no answer to. If Amia could shape the draasin, what prevented another from doing the same?

But there weren't spirit shapers other than the Aeta. And they would have no reason to shape the draasin.

Roine continued away from the university. Tan hurried after him, weaving past the people crowding along the street. Most had a somber air, quiet and subdued, as if the explosions affected the entire city.

"What are you going to do?" Tan asked.

Roine looked over and shook his head. "I warned the king this might happen."

"Roine?"

He slowed his steps and turned to face Tan. "Incendin will continue to attack. We can't worry about an elemental attack catching us unaware."

"Roine?" Tan said again.

"I'm sorry, Tannen. I'm afraid I will be sent to hunt the draasin."

Somewhere next to him, Elle gasped.

CHAPTER 9

Chasing Fire

TAN LEANED OVER THE TABLE in the archives, frustrated that he had come back here, frustrated that Amia had not been more helpful in teaching him. He stared at the book spread in front of him. He still hadn't managed to learn anything more than what Amia taught him the first night she tried helping him learn the ancient language, but he kept at it, especially now with what Roine intended. Tan needed to understand everything he could about the draasin before Roine went after them. If only Roine would tell him when he planned to go.

He pushed back from the table and let his eyes drift closed. The dim lantern strained his eyes, giving him a different sort of headache than he had from his connection to the draasin. The longer he studied in the archives, the more his head pounded. Worse, it didn't matter that he'd been trying to understand the archives; nothing in the ones given to him by the archivist had anything to do with the draasin.

And he needed to know.

Could the draasin have attacked a farm near Ethea? Tan thought he would know if they had, that his connection with them would grant him awareness, but he'd felt nothing.

Draasin!

He sent the request with as much strength as he could. And then he waited.

For a moment, he felt a slight fluttering in the back of his mind, but Tan wondered if that were more imagined than real. The sensation faded, slipping back into nothingness, almost as if something blocked it.

Tan leaned against the chair, breathing slowly. Even the single effort of trying to speak to the draasin left him tired. How had it been so easy before?

As he sat there, he felt another sense within his mind and he opened his eyes, smiling.

Amia stood watching him. Her golden hair was looped atop her head. The silver band at her neck caught the dim light of the lantern, illuminating the top half of her simple white dress. Her eyes drifted to the stack of books on the table and she shook her head.

"You think to learn *Ishthin* by reading about it?" she asked, grabbing the topmost book.

Tan hadn't managed to read anything in the book. The archivist claimed it served as a primer, a way to learn the language once a few key words were identified, but Tan hadn't managed that much. Deciphering even a few words of the language seemed beyond him.

"I'd like to learn it somehow, but I think I'm too dense to really understand."

Amia set the book down and took a seat next to him. She set her hand on the table, and he took it. A wave of relaxation washed through him as he held her hand and the shaped connection between them, the one formed out of fear of the lisincend, surged in his mind.

"You might be dense about some things, but probably not about *Ishthin*. It is difficult to master. That's why my people are taught it from such an early age."

He shook his head. "The archivist seems to think it might take a lifetime to learn."

Amia laughed softly. "A lifetime to learn nuance, perhaps, but that's not what this book intends to teach." She tapped the primer lightly. "Why are you suddenly so interested? It can't be about the book on golud. The conversations written there were too dry to be of any use."

"Not golud."

Amia studied him, her lips pursed out slightly as she did, and then her eyes widened. "The draasin?" she whispered.

He nodded. "Didn't you hear the explosion today?"

Amia's eyes darkened for a moment. "I felt it."

"You felt it?"

She nodded.

To Amia, saying she felt it amounted to the same as sensing something.

As he looked at her, Tan noticed the troubled look on her face. What would she have sensed that would bother her so much? And what would she have sensed through all the noise of the people within Ethea?

"What is it?"

She shook her head. "Probably nothing."

He could tell she kept something from him, but not what. At times, he had been almost convinced the bond would let them share thoughts. If it would, what would he find if he shared her thoughts now?

He touched Amia's arms, and his fingers slid down to reach hers. "What is it?"

She turned to him. "I was in the city earlier today. Roine left some coins and after…" She took a breath. "After what happened, I needed clothes. I wandered to the east. Another shop owner told me about shops where prices were more manageable."

Tan smiled. Likely the shop keep hadn't intended to share such knowledge with Amia, but she was blessed by the Great Mother, gifted with the ability to sense and shape spirit. The ability to sense spirit is what gave the Aeta their advantage trading. But Amia could shape spirit as well, force suggestions and change thoughts. He'd experienced firsthand how powerful such shapings could be.

"While shopping, I saw them."

Tan shook his head. "Saw who?"

Amia blinked and looked away from him. "My people. Aeta."

Tan laughed, cutting off when he realized Amia hadn't smiled. "But isn't that a good thing? After losing everyone you knew to the lisincend, aren't you happy to see others of your people?"

She sighed. "It's not that I'm not happy," she started. "It's just—"

"What?"

"It's complicated."

Tan could tell she didn't want to explain it any more than she had. While he didn't understand why she wouldn't want to see her people, he would let her decide when to explain to him the reason she struggled with it. In the meantime, he had a problem she might be able to help with.

"Roine thinks the draasin attacked."

Amia blinked and the troubled look on her face faded. "The draasin? It was draasin?"

Tan sighed. "I…I don't know. I've tried speaking to them but haven't been able to."

Her eyes lost focus and pressure built behind Tan's ears. A tingling sensation worked through him.

"What was that?"

Amia shook her head, the troubled look returning to her face. "I tried reaching through you to the draasin, but I can't tell either."

"Reaching through me? You can do that?"

She laughed softly. "I shouldn't be able to, but something happened when we escaped—"

"You mean when you shaped me."

She nodded. "The shaping was unintentional. I hadn't done that since I was young, but with the lisincend... it shouldn't have worked like that. Even when I shaped unintentionally, I never forged a connection like this."

"Do you feel the draasin in my head?" Tan wondered if she had shared in the pain when the connection had been stronger. Had she known the pain he'd been going through?

Had she been protecting him?

Amia leaned forward on her elbows, looking at the books. "I can feel *something*. I know it's there, but not what it is. I assumed it was the draasin."

"I can't feel it like I did before. Not since I spoke to it the other day."

"You connected to the draasin?"

"I didn't even mean to, but I was tired and my head had been hurting." Tan felt the need to explain, though Amia did nothing to make him feel that way. "Something I said upset it. Since then, I haven't felt the connection the same way."

Amia frowned and touched the back of her head. "Your head?"

Tan nodded. "Since we arrived in Ethea, my neck has been bothering me. It's been worse the last few days." And especially bad now, while sitting in the archives.

"Does it affect your vision?" she asked softly. "Does it keep you from seeing certain colors?"

93

Tan shook his head. "Nothing like that. Just the pain. A distant sort of ache. I knew it was the draasin, but I didn't know what I could do about it."

Amia sighed. She touched her head again. "I've been having pains as well," she admitted. "They've grown worse the last few days. I don't know what they mean."

Tan frowned. "Do you think you're feeling the draasin, too?"

Neither of them understood the shaped connection between them. Could she use the connection to speak to the draasin? Could she speak to the nymid?

"Not the draasin," she said. "This is different."

"What is it?"

She shook her head. "I don't know."

Tan watched her and frowned. "You have an idea."

She nodded. "I felt *something* while we searched for the artifact. I thought it had something to do with the lisincend, but it's only grown worse." She offered him a smile and tried to turn away. "Now that we're in the city and not running for our lives…" She shook her head. "The pain has gotten worse."

Tan grabbed her hand and turned her to face him. As he did, he realized what she feared. "You think you're feeling the shaping."

Amia didn't say anything at first, but then she nodded. "I think it's possible."

"How? What's causing the pain?"

"I don't know. I've never done a shaping like it before. I don't even know what it was I did in the first place. I've been testing different things to see if it will make a difference, but so far, nothing has helped."

That Amia tried various things to make the pain go away told Tan all he needed about how badly it bothered her. "Is that why you've been staying away?"

She didn't meet his eyes. "I've not been staying away, Tan."

"You have. I thought you were giving me space to understand the university, but that wasn't it, was it?"

She took a deep breath and looked up at him. Finally, she nodded. "At first, the pain got better when we were apart. Now, it doesn't seem to make a difference. In fact, lately, it surged worse, hot and terrible. I can't get rid of it now."

"Can you undo the shaping?"

Amia smiled. Sadness remained in her eyes. "I've tried. That was the first thing I did. But it didn't work. When you told me of the archives, I looked through the books here to try to find an answer, but there's nothing."

"The archivists wouldn't make books on spirit shaping available," Tan said. "There hasn't been a spirit shaper at the university in hundreds of years."

A hint of a playful expression teased at her eyes. "All it takes is asking to find what you need."

Tan frowned, thinking of the way the archivist looked at him, the way they treated his requests. Had he asked to access the restricted section, they would quickly have refused. He was just a senser, not even a shaper, and the restricted section was reserved for the archivists and Master shapers only.

But Amia *was* a shaper. And a spirit shaper at that. If she shaped her question, even the archivists couldn't refuse.

Tan laughed. Amia looked at him strangely.

The older archivist looming along the far wall shot him a look and then turned and hobbled away. The brief pressure behind his ears told him that Amia had shaped him in some way.

"I've been trying to find a way to get to the restricted archives to learn about the draasin," he explained. "But if you can walk in, you could help me find what I'm looking for."

95

She shook her head. "It doesn't work quite like that. There are thousands of works in what they call the restricted section. Some are kept locked so only certain archivists can access them."

"That's where you think the works you might need are hidden?"

She shrugged. "It is logical. If your university hasn't had a spirit shaper in as long as Roine says, it follows they would try to keep the knowledge protected."

"But maybe the work on the draasin isn't protected the same way. Maybe I can find out more about the draasin."

Amia smiled, but it was a sad expression. "I'll see what I can do."

The archivist led them into the depths of the restricted archives.

Amia had approached him directly. He stood near the far corner, looking for all intents as if he diligently worked at organizing a section of books. The man had short white hair shorn close to his scalp. Dark splotches were smeared across his face. He only looked up as they approached. Tan hadn't seen him in the archives before.

"May I be of assistance?" he asked. The man spoke with a thick accent Tan didn't recognize, though he doubted he'd recognize any accent in the city other than those from Galen. Like all the archivists Tan had seen, he wore a thick, gray robe that hung to thin ankles. He looked as ancient as the other archivists, but his eyes were bright and seemed to take everything in.

Amia glanced at Tan before turning back to him. "Your help would be much appreciated."

The man sniffed. "That is why I am here," he said.

Amia smiled. Tan felt a warmth radiate from her, a soothing sense she barely had to shape. The archivist did not seem to respond to it nearly as well as Tan.

"There are a few works I would like to find," she went on.

The man stood up and turned to her, waiting.

Amia glanced at Tan and nodded. When she turned back to the archivist, the surge of her shaping came as pressure in his ears.

"I would like to see your works on the draasin," Amia said.

The archivist blinked a moment as the shaping took hold, and then he turned and led them to the doorway near the back of the archives. Amia grabbed Tan's hand as they followed.

Tan was surprised by the sheer size of the archives. From where he'd been sitting, they archives weren't particularly large: a few wide dusty tables and rows of shelves. But behind the door, there was row after row of massive shelves. The archivist glanced at the shelves as he made his way through them, barely pausing when he reached an out-of-the-way corner.

Then he led them down a narrow stair.

Walls were darkened; only a few shapers lanterns hung on them. Amia shaped them and pale light bloomed.

The archivist nodded at her. "Thank you, Master."

Tan frowned, but Amia only shrugged.

They continued down the stairs. Light from the shapers lanterns guided them. Doors opened off the stairs, but the archivist continued down.

"Where are you taking us?" Tan asked.

The archivist paused and turned. "You requested to see the works on the draasin?"

Amia nodded. She sent another surge of shaping.

"Then we must continue to the lower archives." He continued down the stairs. "Few ask about the draasin anymore. They have been gone so long, few even know about them. Those who study such things expected saa and inferin to grow stronger in their absence, but that hasn't been the case." The archivist looked over his shoulder. "Might I ask where you learned of them?"

"How do people forget any of the great elementals?" Amia asked. "Inferin and saa do not serve quite the same as ara, golud, and udilm."

The archivist nodded. "Inferin and saa are lesser elementals only. Much like the nymid and thesn. But the draasin have been gone for nearly a thousand years, hunted and destroyed by the ancient warriors. One can only imagine what it must have been like when their wings filled the sky."

"Why did you say saa and inferin would grow stronger?" Tan asked.

The archivist looked back at him and frowned. They stopped at a lower landing and the archivist pulled a ring of keys out of his pocket. "It has been suggested that the greater elementals are essential to the world. Some think that in the absence of a greater, the strength of the lesser increases." He sniffed. "Alas, this has not proven true with saa or inferin in the absence of the draasin. Perhaps another elemental has appeared?"

Tan wondered if that were true. Could that be why the nymid had been so powerful?

The archivist sorted through his keys until he found what he sought and turned it in the lock on the door, pushing it open. Inside, a single bookcase stood in the middle of the room. The archivist nodded to it.

Amia lit the shapers lantern on the wall, giving a soft glow to the room as she and Tan made their way inside. As they did, the archivist pulled the door closed and left them alone.

"Is there anything here?" he asked.

Amia looked at the bookcase. Ancient texts filled the shelves. She pulled a few off the shelves and flipped them open, glancing at pages as she did. She frowned as she did.

"What's wrong?"

She shook her head, grabbing another book. This one had a leather cover embossed with symbols Tan did not recognize. "These have nothing to do with the draasin."

Tan looked over her shoulder, but the writing on the pages was made in a tight scrawl and done in the ancient language. "What are they about?"

Amia didn't answer. She pushed the book back onto the shelf and grabbed another, flipping through it.

Through the bond between them, the accidental shaping, Tan felt her growing more and more agitated. Whatever she saw bothered her.

He looked over at the door. Shaped as he was, the archivist shouldn't have left them here.

It was then he realized something was amiss.

The door seemed to have vanished, disappearing as if into the wall. "Amia?"

She shook her head as she grabbed another book off the shelves. She flipped through it quickly, the agitation becoming clearer. "These have nothing to do with the elementals at all."

He said her name again. "Amia—"

"What?"

She looked toward the door, toward where the archivist had left them in the darkness. Her face changed, the anxiety Tan felt through the shaping becoming fear. "He knew."

Tan frowned. "Amia… I don't know what you're talking about."

She moved past him and pushed on the wall, but it wouldn't open. Amia turned to him and shook her head. "The archivist. He knew I shaped him. And somehow, he resisted it."

"How could he know?" Tan asked. He touched the wall where the door should be but found nothing to grab hold of, no way to open the door.

The door was locked and they were trapped.

CHAPTER 10

Escape

AMIA STARED AT THE WALL, right where the door should have been. Tan pulled on her arm, spinning her so she faced him. "How could he have known?"

She shook her head. "I don't know. Only those of the Aeta have resisted my shapings, and then rarely. The only other time a shaping failed was when I tried shaping the lisincend."

Tan looked toward the shelves. Amia didn't say it, but the fact that the archivist had resisted her shaping made it more likely the draasin could resist as well. Tan had thought the lisincend able to ignore the shaping because they were twisted. The shaping they'd done upon themselves had made them impervious to Amia's spirit shaping. But what if that were wrong? What if Amia's spirit shaping could be ignored?

"We have to get out of here," she continued. She grabbed her head and rubbed at her temples, pain twisting her face. "If they know I can shape spirit…"

Tan understood. It was the secret her people had been trying to keep from the university for years. "How will we get out if we can't get past the door?"

Amia threw her shoulder against the wall. It didn't move.

Fear clouded her face when she turned to him. "Can you do anything?"

Tan shook his head. "Even if I'm a shaper like you think, I don't know how to control it. I can barely sense anything here in the university."

Amia sighed and worked to steady her breathing. She licked her lips and swallowed, turning back to the wall as she ran her fingers along the edge of where the door had been.

As she worked, Tan felt her anxiety building. She paused a moment and rubbed the back of her neck again, the motion the same as he did while trying to ignore the pain he felt buried there. But since the draasin spoke to him last, he hadn't felt the same pain.

Through the anxiety, another sense came, a pressure Tan had felt during their times in the mountains. It came like a voice in his head, a soft whisper that he could not ignore. A shaping, one that compelled him. *Protect me.*

He didn't think Amia had shaped him again. This was a remnant of the first shaping, the one that formed the bond between them, but he could not ignore the request.

His breathing quickened. The anxiety Amia felt bloomed in him. His heart fluttered.

Amia turned and met his eyes. Did she know the bond urged him now?

"Someone comes," she said.

"Can you tell who?"

Her eyes went shut for a moment as she sensed. When they reopened, renewed fear appeared there. "Not the archivist. It is another."

Another. Who would the archivist allow into the lower archives?

"Can you tell anything about him?"

Amia shook her head. "It's strange. He is...blocked...from me."

"You're not usually blocked?"

Tan didn't really know how Amia's sensing worked. With earth sensing, he had to intentionally try and reach out around him, to connect with everything around him. Was it the same for her?

"No."

The anxiety she felt surged again through the bond. *Protect me.*

It came louder this time: less of a whisper and with a sense of urgency.

He looked at Amia but couldn't tell if she knew what she was doing. Did she shape him intentionally or was this really the echo of the earlier shaping, now lingering within him?

Tan looked for another way out of the room. Walls of smooth stone surrounded them. The air held a dampness to it, a lingering scent describing their descent deep into the earth to reach the lower level of the archives. A sense of oppression came over him, as if the room itself squeezed down on them.

He looked to the heavy oak shelving. Faded stain looked as if it had once been dark. Some places were streaked as if moisture had damaged it. The books on the shelf drew his attention for a moment, but he looked away from them. There would be nothing in the books that would help him get Amia out of the archives.

As he turned, he wondered why the archivist would have led them here in the first place. If he knew Amia shaped him, did he bring her here to test whether she could shape, or was there another reason?

But what reason would he have for trapping her here?

He looked up at her again, worry streaking through his mind. "Is it a shaper?"

Amia frowned and tilted her head as her eyes briefly lost focus. "I think so." She looked over at him. "I can't tell so near the university."

Tan swallowed. Now the anxiety coursing through him was his own. "Can you tell what kind of shaper?"

She shrugged, fingers going to her temples and rubbing there for a moment as she shook her head.

Tan closed his eyes, straining to listen to everything around him, sensing as his father had long ago taught him to do. Amia might not be able to determine what kind of shaper came with the archivist, but could he?

Awareness of the earth filled him with the sensing. Tan had a sense of the age of the stone and the earth around him, a memory of what had once lived here. The bones of the archives were old, possibly older than the city. They felt everything differently than what Tan was accustomed to sensing in Galen. There was a sense of permanence, and anything that didn't fit with that permanence came as an abrasion.

He pushed beyond the walls of the room, stretching his sensing all around him. At first, he didn't think he would find anything, only more sense of the earth, the sense of him violating its space.

The person made their way down. Through his sensing, Tan couldn't tell how far away they were. Something reverberated deep in his mind, back where the sense of the draasin abided.

A fire shaper.

He blinked, releasing the sensing.

Amia looked at him. "What is it? What did you sense?"

Fire shapers existed elsewhere within the university, though they were rarer than other shapers. But with the recent explosion and what Tan had gone through with Amia already, he feared a different reason for his presence.

"A fire shaper," he said softly.

Amia nodded, already reaching the same conclusion Tan had come to.

Protect me.

The words rang in his head.

"We don't know where the artifact is anymore. Roine took it to the king," Amia said.

"Maybe they think you can find it again."

Amia shook her head. "I followed the shaping made by the key. Without that, I have no more connection to the artifact than you."

Tan had no intention of remaining where they were when the shaper reached them. Even without her urging, he would do whatever he could to get her to safety.

But where was safe? If the university was compromised, where else could she go and remain undetected?

Tan looked around, again trying to find a way out of the room. Other than the door—now hidden so he couldn't even see it—there was no other way out. He had nothing with him to protect them; he'd stopped wearing his hunting knife when he'd arrived at the university. His unstrung bow hung uselessly back in the room.

Could he shape a way from here?

He could sense the stone of the archives, could *feel* it. Was there any way to use what he sensed to draw on the stone?

But even if he could, where would they go?

Through the door led to the archivist and the shaper. Beyond the stone was only more dirt and earth, enough to practically bury them.

Tan looked toward the shelving again. If a shaping were to work, could he lead them *up*?

Protect me!

"They're nearly here," Amia whispered.

He had to try.

Tan hurried to the shelf and climbed to the top. Once there, he crouched, his head nearly brushing the ceiling. He touched the stone with the flat of his hand, letting his eyes close. As he did, he breathed slowly, steadily, simply sensing the stone.

Like the rest of the archives, the stone of the ceiling had been here for ages.

Tan breathed.

What did he do when he spoke to the nymid? To the draasin?

Tan thought about how he spoke to the ancient elementals, considered the way it felt when he spoke to them. It was different than speaking aloud and used a part of himself that felt deeper and more ancient.

Could he use that same sense?

Pressure built behind his ears.

Tan pushed out what he wanted, letting it press into the stone.

Fatigue washed over him as it did when speaking to the nymid and the draasin.

And then his hand sunk into the stone.

Amia gasped.

Tan blinked open his eyes.

Amia had climbed up the shelf and crouched next to him. "What did you do?" she whispered.

Tan looked up. His hand pressed into a hole in the stone where it seemed to have slid away, leaving nothing but darkness in its place. The hole was wide enough for one person to fit through.

"Go!" he urged, grabbing Amia and pushing her up and through the hole in the ceiling.

She reached up and touched the stone but jerked her hand back quickly. "It's hot."

Tan touched the stone. Not hot, but warm, as if warmed by bright sunlight. "We need to hurry."

As he spoke, he heard a soft *click*. The fire shaper reached the door.

Amia glanced back and then grabbed onto the stone, reaching through it. Then she pulled herself up, disappearing into blackness on the other side.

The door opened behind them.

Pressure started building behind his ears. If he lingered too long, a fire shaping might keep him from joining Amia.

Tan grabbed the sides of the stone and pulled through as the air in the room suddenly became much hotter.

Flames chased him through the hole in the stone, briefly licking at his boots. Once through, he rolled to the side. Light from the flames revealed a small, narrow room, much like the one below it. Another series of shelves lined the floor. Somehow, the hole he'd shaped managed to fit between the shelves.

Maybe the Great Mother watched over him after all.

Amia had already reached the door and pulled it open. She peered out and down, waving her hand toward Tan to follow.

He stood and wiped his hands on his pants. He started forward and stumbled, falling into the nearest shelf. The whole thing wobbled and books dropped around him. Tan caught one with a dark red leather cover. With surprise, he recognized the symbol on the cover and slipped it into his pocket. He could look at it later if they managed to escape.

A shout came from below.

"Tan?" She shot him a look and he nodded.

Amia raced into the hall outside the door and he followed her.

On the stairs, they paused long enough to see a woman with red eyes the color of flames staring at them. A dark smile peeled her lips back, reminding Tan all too much of Fur.

Amia cried out. *Protect me!*

The voice sounded loud in his mind.

She had tripped over one of the steps and jerked back, her hand blistered where she touched the stone.

Tan grabbed her, scooping her up into his arms as he ran up the stairs. "See if you can slow her," he said. His voice came out breathlessly.

Pressure built behind his ears as her shaping built.

When it was released, her shaping washed past him as it directed toward the fire shaper. Some of the intent carried through the shaped bond between them, as if he could hear it in his mind.

Stop.

Tan almost faltered.

The fire shaper did not slow.

Heat built in the air around them, dry and painful. His skin prickled and his mouth burned. Tan felt the same pain as when the Incendin hounds had treed him, back before he'd ever seen Amia.

Protect me.

He staggered up the steps, carrying Amia. The door into the main portion of the archives was too far away. They wouldn't make it in time. The fire shaper would catch them. After that, he had no idea what would happen.

Another step. The heat around him became unbearable. Sweat dripped down his brow, quickly evaporating as it did. The steps became hot, burning through his thin boots. Amia weighed heavily in his arms.

Tan had to do something. If only he could shape, but whatever he'd done to the stone left him feeling weakened. Even carrying Amia up the stairs was nearly more than he could manage.

Amia sensed his weakness and looked at him. "Leave me. Go find Roine and come back for me."

As she said it, different words echoed in his head. *Protect me!*

Tan could not ignore the demand.

Pressure built in his head, pounding through his skull. He staggered, nearly dropping Amia. And then a gust of wind whipped down the stairs. The wind seemed to split around him, parting so as not to blow him over. Behind him, the shaper screamed. The wind quickly silenced her.

Tan ran.

With Amia in his arms, the last few stairs seemed nearly impossible. Had he not been conditioned from years spent wandering the mountainous woods around Nor, he would have dropped her. As they reached the door, he found it closed and locked. With a scream, he slammed into the wood with his shoulder. It splintered open and they fell through.

Amia dropped from his arms. She grabbed his hand and pulled, dragging him through the archives. Tan followed, almost too fatigued to walk.

The younger archivist—the one who had been friendliest to him— looked over at them from behind a row of shelves. He started toward them, but Tan ignored him, concentrating on hurrying from the archives.

Somehow, they reached the outside. A fading sun dipped toward the horizon. The sky was swirls of orange and red where it disappeared, but otherwise no clouds drifted. The air felt cool and swirled around his pants.

Throngs of people moved through the street. Amia hurried toward them, quickly disappearing. Tan allowed himself a moment to feel relief, but persistent fear gnawed at the back of his mind. Where could she be safe?

CHAPTER 11

A Daughter's Duty

WHERE ARE YOU LEADING ME?" Tan asked. The farther they got from the archives, the more his strength returned. Fatigue still worked through him, but he didn't have the same sense of exhaustion as before.

She shook her head. "We need to get to safety."

"I thought we were safe in Ethea. That's why Roine brought us here."

She paused and met his eyes. "You might be safe in the city, but Mother made it clear I wasn't allowed to use my ability while we were here. I think the university Masters knew we were spirit sensers, but she didn't want to taunt them with shaping."

Tan remembered Roine's reaction when Amia confirmed her shaping ability. Scholars suspected the Aeta of having shapers but had never proven it. With Amia, they had proof. Now, not only Roine knew about her ability to shape, but the king did as well. It still didn't make any sense. Why would the archivist lock them in the archives? And why would he send a fire shaper after them?

And, perhaps more important, how had he resisted her shaping?

"That wasn't a university shaper," Tan said. "I recognized the shaping. I've felt it before. It was the same as when the hounds had me treed."

He took a deep breath and nodded toward a long stone bench along the side of the road. Amia walked him to it and he sat, resting with his head on his hands. With all the people moving around them, they were safe for now. How long would it be until the archivist found them again? How long until the Incendin shaper reached them?

And then what? Would they be able to hide from him in Ethea?

They needed to find Roine. He might be distracted with whatever the king had him doing, but he had to know what happened.

Tan looked around. With a throng of people filling the street, they wouldn't be able to reach the palace very quickly. And when they did, would he find Roine or had he disappeared on another mission for the king?

That left him feeling very alone. He had gone into the library searching for answers—to find something on the draasin that might help him understand the connection he shared with them. How had he spoken to them so easily when he could only speak to the nymid near the water?

Amia remained silent as they sat, leaving him lost in his thoughts. After a while, Tan pulled the book he had stuffed into his jacket and looked at the dark red leather cover.

"Where did you find that?" Amia asked, her eyes widening briefly.

"In the room we climbed to. After I—"

He hesitated. It seemed strange to admit that he'd shaped, but what other explanation was there? And had that been him with the wind blowing up the stairs? *That* had happened the last time he felt the same heat as well. Roine seemed convinced that Tan had shaped wind before and that his shaping had saved Amia from falling. Could he have done the same again?

Could he only shape when Amia was in danger?

Amia sat next to him, staring at her reddened hands. After a moment, she stopped and rubbed at her temples. "The book. It's about the draasin."

Tan recognized the symbol on the cover. Now all he needed was to understand the ancient language and he might be able to read it. "I grabbed it before we left. Maybe that will be of use."

Amia smiled and touched his hand. "The draasin have already proven their worth when they helped us escape Fur. Had it not been for them…"

Fur would have captured them. And then…well, he didn't know why they wanted Amia. Was it simply for the artifact or was there something more?

He watched her, but her face remained unreadable. The shaped bond between them didn't tell him anything more, but he *felt* as if she kept something from him.

"What now?" he asked.

She took his hand and met his eyes. "Now?" A hint of sadness that he didn't understand came across her face. She sighed. "Come. I'll show you."

They found the Aeta circling a small square to the east of the university. Without Amia guiding him, Tan wouldn't have found it. Ethea was a massive city, sprawling out from two separate foci. The university and the palace—separated by several miles, but visible across the entire city—each had a bubble of activity surrounding them. Roine had put them up in a part of the city partway between the university and the palace, easy distance to both.

As they walked, the city changed. The sun had fallen behind the horizon and lights flickered in most windows. Lanterns hung on posts along the street, casting bright light. A cool breeze billowed from the west, not nearly as powerful as home for Tan. The air stunk of the city, a mixture of sweat and ash and refuse piled near homes. More than anything, the stink of the city made him long for home.

Throngs of people filled the streets, all dressed so differently as to make it seem intentional. Most people moved in the same direction as Tan and Amia. Ethea drew from all over the kingdoms and beyond; traders came from Doma and Chenir, and some from as far as the Xsa Isles, a series of islands off the coast of Doma. Those from the Isles were easiest to recognize. Tan passed a couple from the Isles and couldn't help but stare as he did. The men wore their hair as long as the women and both kept it tightly braided. Tattoos marked the left side of the men's face and the right of the women's. Both had deeply tanned skin.

Amia offered him a smile when he turned away.

"Have you ever visited there?" he asked.

She shook her head. "The Aeta are wanderers, not sailors. But if you ever visit Doma, you'd see more than island folk."

"More?"

"Across the Natalin Sea. Par and Zulas and—"

"*Beyond* the sea?"

Amia laughed softly. The farther they got from the archives, the more they both relaxed. In spite of that, a certain tension tugged at him through the bond.

"The world is bigger than just the kingdoms, Tan."

He noticed a pair of men walking toward him, one with a large hoop in his ear and his head shaved, the other with bright orange hair and pale skin. Both wore brightly colored clothes styled differently than anything he'd ever seen. Neither seemed uncomfortable. No one else bothered to look at them; it was as if only Tan found them strange. He started to ask Amia about them, but didn't have the chance.

They turned another street and he saw the Aeta.

Before meeting Amia, Tan had only seen the Aeta a few times in his life. Each time they visited Nor, a celebration ensued. The Aeta brought their wagons into the heart of the Nor, circling the square. Music and dancers went along with nearly a week of trading. Most treated the visit as something akin to a festival. The Aeta welcomed it, often joining in the revelry, mixing their music with local sounds, unfazed by the delay in trading.

The last visit had been different. Lord Lind required the Aeta to camp on the outskirts of Nor, separating them from the village. Tan understood now they wouldn't have stayed long anyway, not with the hounds chasing them, but that hadn't changed his disappointment at the time.

The Aeta here generated much the same atmosphere as he remembered. Brightly colored wagons ringed a square. Lights from dozens of lanterns lit the street, casting everything in a warm glow. People from every direction made their way to the wagons, creating a crowd they struggled to push through. Music drifted from the square, the sounds of flutes and harps and other, stranger instruments floated about the voices of the people. A high voice sang, the sound little more than a melody from where they stood.

Tan smiled and looked over at Amia. The smile faded as he saw the look on her face. Concern mixed with the anxiety he felt through their bond. Tan took her hand, squeezing it, but she didn't squeeze back. "Aren't you happy to see your people?"

She kept her eyes fixed straight ahead. "I only learned of them earlier today. I hadn't thought I'd see them so soon. I hadn't thought about what I would do, not after what happened…"

"We don't have to come here," Tan said. "We can find Roine—"

Amia shook her head and stared ahead.

The crowd pushed them forward, driving them almost into the wagons. Tan didn't know how they would manage any trade at all with this many people here until he reached the edge. Then he understood.

The circle created a wall of sorts. Heavy metal railings were set in between the wagons, blocking off the square. Two openings allowed entry while two more let others out. A pair of heavily muscled men stood at each gate, carefully monitoring how many moved through. No one pushed too hard; those who did were sent away.

They reached the nearest gate. The wide man on the left wore a flaming red shirt tied around his waist with a thick cord of rope. Tattoos worked along exposed forearms. The tuft of hair on his chin was oiled into a point. Dark eyes looked at everyone carefully. The taller man next to him gripped the handle of a long knife he wore in his belt. A navy shirt unbuttoned to his mid-chest revealed tattoos much like the other man's. His hard eyes searched alongside the other man.

When the shorter, wide man saw Amia—really, the silver band around her neck marking her as Daughter—his face changed. He blinked and his eyes softened, his mouth opening for a moment before he nodded to her, dipping his head low. The other man frowned until he too saw Amia and then tilted his head low.

The first man looked back up. "Daughter. You are welcome within our circle."

Amia's mouth tightened and she took a deep breath. "May the Great Mother bless your trade."

The man nodded. The other man pulled aside a bar blocking access to the Aeta wagons and Amia started through.

When Tan tried to follow, the bar slipped back into place, preventing him.

"He may enter," Amia said.

The tall man stared at Tan for a long moment before turning and looking at Amia again. His eyes flickered to the band of silver on her neck. "Daughter?"

Amia nodded. "He provided safe passage as requested by the Mother."

The tall man's eyes narrowed. "Then his duty is discharged. He should have your thanks and nothing more."

Amia looked at Tan. "He has much more than my thanks," she said softly.

Echoes of the command shaped into him drifted into his mind, not nearly as loud or compulsive as what he'd felt within the archives. Still, the request seemed strange.

Protect me.

Tan wondered why he would hear it now.

The wider man grabbed the bar and lifted. The other resisted at first before letting it go. "The Daughter says he may enter."

"She is not *our* Daughter," the tall man objected.

"She is the Aeta's Daughter."

Both men turned.

Tan looked past them to see a slender woman with deep black hair. Her eyes were a soft shade of grayish green. A wide band of silver surrounded her neck. A loose yellow dress flowed to the ground. Streaks of color ran through it.

Both men tipped their heads, but it was the taller man who spoke. "Of course, Mother."

They waited, the wide man's hand on the bar, until Tan passed through the gate.

A few others behind him pushed forward but both men stood and slipped the bar back into place, blocking anyone else from entering the circle of Aeta wagons. A few quiet groans drifted toward him, but most people waited patiently. The two guards turned their backs on Tan and faced the throng of people pressing toward the Aeta.

Before turning, Tan caught sight of the archivist who had led them into the depths of the archives. The archivist frowned and turned away quickly.

Tan spun and looked to Amia, but she stood with her hands clasped in front of her, an uncertain look upon her face. She hadn't seen the archivist. Instead, she stared at the woman in front of her.

The Mother wore a serene expression and smiled at her. "Daughter. We felt your presence here." Her eyes tightened slightly and she gasped softly. "I sensed a great loss but didn't understand before now. What happened?"

Amia shook her head. "I would prefer not to speak of it here, Mother."

The Mother tilted her head, studying Amia for a moment. Then she turned to Tan.

He had the same sensation he had when speaking to the Mother of Amia's family. The Mother stared at him and seemed to look *through* him, as if reading his innermost thoughts. Like many of the Aeta, she would be a senser. From the way she made him feel, he suspected her skilled as well.

Could she know about the bond formed by Amia's shaping?

And if she did, would it matter?

A steady lantern burned inside the wagon, the bright light reflecting off stacks of metal pots and cases full of stones as Amia shared her story. Tan's eyes wandered, catching on the other collections in the narrow wagon. Rugs with fantastic patterns piled on a table. A few strange devices stacked in the corner. Clothing of all styles was neatly folded and set on shelves. Exposed walls were painted with the same bright colors as the outside of the wagons, each wall a different color, splashes of gold and red and orange surrounding him. Other items hung from pegs nailed into the orange wall. A large, dark bowl made of deep obsidian tucked into another corner.

Within this one wagon was incredible wealth.

The open window had been shut as soon as the Mother led them inside, another pair of guards standing watch. Noise from the trading filtered through, muffled somewhat. Tan still heard the music and burble of happy voices through it.

Tan had been surprised by how much larger this group of Aeta was than Amia's family. Nearly three-dozen wagons formed a wide circle around the square, filled with hundreds of people. Amia's tight expression stood in stark contrast to the laughter and music outside.

The Mother sat on sturdy wooden chair, her back stiff and straight as she looked at Tan and Amia. The serene expression on her face slipped as Amia spoke, telling about what happened with the lisincend and her people.

"How is it you escaped, Daughter?"

Amia took a deep breath and looked over at Tan. He still didn't feel the connection to her, as if the bond between them had severed as they passed through the gates into the circle of wagons, though he didn't understand why that should happen.

"Tan rescued us after we were captured."

The Mother looked at Tan. Eyes that shifted from green to gray studied him.

He met her gaze, refusing to look away.

"You risked the lisincend to save the Daughter?" she asked.

Tan shook his head. The Mother frowned, glancing to Amia. "I risked the lisincend to save the Aeta."

"And the others?"

Amia swallowed and tears glistened in her eyes. Tan wondered when she'd last let herself relive that awful night. He tried not to think about it. He didn't want to remember the casual way the lisincend burned the Aeta, turning each to ash before his eyes. He'd been unable to do anything, legs practically frozen in fear.

He deserved no credit for saving Amia. Had it not been for the storm that blew in, they would both have been dead.

Unless he'd somehow shaped the storm. He would have to ask Amia about that possibility later.

The Mother looked from Amia to Tan and then nodded. "I see. They did not survive."

Amia shook her head once and looked away.

"You did not seek the family," the Mother said.

Tan heard an accusation in her voice.

Amia didn't look over, as if unwilling. "I did not." She touched the back of her head, rubbing the spot Tan knew all too well. When the Mother glanced at her, she dropped her hand and looked away.

"You do not wish to help the People?"

Amia took a deep breath. She shifted, turning in her seat to face the Mother. "I did all I could to help my people. I failed."

The Mother frowned and leaned forward. "Many have failed when it comes to the lisincend. Why should you be any different?"

"I am one of the blessed."

The Mother nodded. "I sensed that when you arrived. It has been years since I felt the presence of one of the blessed. Had I known what happened to your family, I would have come sooner."

Amia shook her head. "I have not been in Ethea long."

The Mother sighed. "So few of our people are blessed. Not nearly as many as we once had. And to think we almost lost you to the lisincend." A mixture of emotions flashed across her eyes. "It is…unusual…that you traveled so deeply into Incendin that hounds chased you. Most understand not to venture so deeply. Even our caravan only passed along the outskirts of Incendin, and then only because…" She trailed off and shook her head, her brow flattening and eyes tightening. She reached her hand toward Amia. The other went to the band at her neck. "No matter now. The Great Mother brought you back to the family. This family is now yours."

Amia closed her eyes, rubbing at her temples.

As she did, Tan had a surge through the bond. The sense was distant and faint, but he felt it clearly and didn't understand. Sadness.

CHAPTER 12

Needs of the People

AMIA WALKED HIM TO A QUIET area within the ring of wagons. A cacophony of voices swirled around them, some shouting, others singing, still others humming or grunting. In spite of the noise, Tan remained focused on Amia.

The Mother left them, disappearing into the throng of shoppers to continue trading. When she left, she motioned to one of the nearby wagons and nodded, giving them privacy. Tan felt another surge of sadness from Amia.

"What is it?"

She swallowed and looked up, finally meeting his eyes. "The Aeta are my people."

He nodded. "Then why are you sad?"

"I've told you about the pain I've been feeling."

He nodded again. "You think it's from the shaping."

She bit her lip and glanced behind her. "I don't know if it is or not. Or maybe there is something else, another reason for me to have the pain." Troubled eyes scanned the circle, seeming to take everything in as she did. When she looked back to Tan, tears glistened in her eyes. "The Aeta are more than a people. They are a family. When we travel together, we do so for the benefit of the family." She took a deep breath, as if what she had to say next was hard for her. "When I lost my family, I knew I would have to find another. I am not the first to lose her family. Others have been lost, though never quite so brutally."

Tan frowned. "What are you saying?"

Amia forced a smile. "Seeing the Incendin shaper made it clear. I am not safe here. Not until we know what they were after and why the lisincend wanted me."

"The Masters can—"

"Can what?" she asked, interrupting him. "Can keep Incendin from sending their shapers after us? Can discover what I am and try to study me?" She shook her head. "The Aeta have survived centuries without the university learning of what we are. All they have is speculation."

"Roine knows."

Amia breathed out. "He knows. And if it hadn't been for the lisincend, he would not have known."

Tan turned and looked away from her, staring at the wagons. The bright colors that had seemed so vibrant and alive seemed cold and oppressive. Flames leaping from the large pit near the center of the circle reminded him more of the lisincend and Incendin. Nausea rolled through his stomach though he didn't really know why.

"Tan…" She squeezed his hand. "It's more than the family. You know that, don't you?"

He nodded.

"You…you could come with me. Outsiders don't often travel with the Aeta, but it's been known to happen."

He smiled sadly. His mother had traveled with the Aeta long before he'd been born. Another story he would never hear her tell.

He studied Amia and considered her offer. He *could* leave Ethea, travel with the Aeta, and perhaps help Amia learn what happened— why the shaping affected her as it did. But leaving meant he wouldn't learn about the draasin. After what he'd learned from Roine, he feared the king wanted them hunted and destroyed. Whatever else, Tan couldn't let that happen.

And then there was the issue of the fire shaper. He suspected she was from Incendin but had no way of proving it. Roine would take no action without proof.

Too much depended on him staying in Ethea.

He swallowed. He'd lost everything. His father, his home and mother, and his entire village. And now he would lose Amia.

This hurt more than anything else.

"You know I can't. Not until I know what's happening here. You could..." He trailed off, not knowing how to finish.

If she stayed, could he keep her safe? Would he learn enough about shaping to follow the one she placed upon him and protect her? Or would he fail as he had failed the other Aeta, as he had failed the Mother, and very nearly failed Amia? Had it not been for the draasin, he would not have protected her.

"You have to leave, don't you?"

She blinked slowly and then nodded. "I need to find answers. There are no others who can shape spirit other than the Aeta. And once I do..."

She didn't say she would return to him. He didn't need her to; he felt it through the shaped connection. But how long would that take? And how much would change before she returned?

But he couldn't refuse her the answers she needed. "Can they keep you safe?"

He looked her over. Her eyes carried much of the same sadness he felt. "We have managed to survive for centuries. We are the landless. We are the wanderers."

Something in her voice rang untrue, but he felt nothing different from the bond between them. The only thing Tan felt was pain. Amia would leave. "Where will you go?"

She shook her head, looking away, turning to face the fire. "The Mother leads. Were I to stay, in time, I would be Mother. As one blessed by the Great Mother, that has always been my responsibility."

Tan looked over toward the Mother. She met his eyes and nodded once. "You didn't answer."

Amia shook her head. "I don't know. Judging by some of the items the Mother had in her wagon, perhaps Doma."

Doma didn't have shapers like Ethea did, didn't have the capacity to push back Incendin if needed. And if Incendin had already shown the ability to push into the kingdoms, what would stop them from attacking in Doma?

"When will you leave?"

The sad smile that twisted her lips was answer enough. Soon.

She touched his arm and turned him toward the fire. "Come and celebrate with us before the wagons leave."

Tan wanted badly to stay, to be with Amia as long as he could, but memories of what had happened in the archives plagued him. Roine had to know about the Incendin shaper reaching Ethea. He had to know about Amia being unable to shape the archivist. As much as anything, he had a nagging concern about why. Only the lisincend had withstood her shaping.

And he needed to reach the draasin, to warn them of Roine and whatever the kingdom's shapers might do. "I need to find Roine…"

She nodded. "And I should meet the others of the family."

"How long?" He choked a little as he asked, but he needed to know.

Amia shook her head. "That's not how it works with the Aeta. And I don't know how long it will take to find another blessed by the Great Mother. Until I do—and until I can find out what happened when I shaped you, why it pains me as it does—I can't stay. You know there are none in Ethea who can help me with this."

Tan pulled her against him, hugging her tightly. "I don't want you to leave."

"I don't either. Had the archives been safer, I might be able to search them for answers. That had been my hope. But now…" She shook her head. "Now I will go with my people to find the answers I need."

She touched his arm. Pressure built behind his ears as she performed a shaping. A relaxing sense washed over him, but something else as well. A surge filled his mind, painful and sharp, before fading.

"What was that?" he asked, resisting the urge to pull away. He wanted Amia's touch to linger as long as possible.

"A gift. If it works, you will understand later."

"If it works?"

"I've never tried anything like it before."

"What will it do?"

She smiled again, this time sadder than the last. "Help you remember me."

CHAPTER 13

The Gift

TAN SAT ON THE LAWN NEAR a far wall of the university lawn, legs crossed on the grass, arms draped over his knees. The dark clouds in the gray sky matched his mood. The ache that had been with him the last few weeks was gone. With it, so was Amia.

He hadn't watched the Aeta wagons as they left town. Leaving Amia had been hard enough the first time; Tan wasn't sure he'd be able to do it again. Worse, he hadn't managed to find Roine. As far as he knew, the Incendin fire shaper was still in the city, searching for them.

Tan sighed. At least Amia had a chance to get some distance from Ethea. If nothing else, she might be safe a little while longer. Maybe she would find the answer to her pain.

The leather bound book lay next to him. Once he found Roine, he would return to the archive, find one of the books the archivist had shown him on how to read the ancient language, and do what he could to decipher this. Unless the archivist and the fire shaper found him first.

One hand fingered the cover of the book, running across the symbol. Shaped like a triangle with a branch leading off to each side, Tan recognized it as the mark for fire. More than that, he understood it to be the mark of the draasin. If only he could read the book.

Another reason he already missed Amia.

Tan pulled the book open and glanced at the page, scanning the words.

And understanding them.

He blinked. Could this have been written more recently than the others? Could this text not be as old as some? If that was the case, maybe it didn't have anything to do with the draasin. Other than the draasin frozen in the lake near the place of convergence, the great elementals had been gone from the world for nearly a thousand years.

Tan skimmed the next few pages. Each page described fire, detailing the elementals, describing conversations with saa and inferin. Another elemental was mentioned, but not by name.

And then Tan found a comment on the draasin.

"The most feared of the great elementals are the draasin. Massive creatures that once roamed freely, as the kingdoms spread, they recede from us, though only reluctantly ceding these lands. They are hunters, unmatched and fearsome in their power. Unlike the other great elementals, they have not been known to bond to our shapers. Few even possess the ability to speak to them, though who would risk such danger?"

Tan skipped a few pages, fascinated by the comments on the draasin. Whoever wrote this section must have seen draasin, or at least read of them. He found another passage and continued reading.

"While they are creatures of fire, they also live in the sky, and as such, have some power over the wind. Unlike saa and saldam, they do not fear the udilm. Only golud holds sway over the draasin, and they do so reluctantly."

Tan sat back, looking at the book. As he did, he made out the letters, the shape of the words, realizing that it *was* written in the ancient language.

Tan flipped through a few pages of the book. Letters from the ancient language covered every page. On each page, he read and understood the words as if he'd read them his entire life.

His head throbbed just thinking about it. How was it possible?

Tan closed the book and looked at the cover. Could the draasin have made this possible? Could the connection to the great elemental have granted him some of its knowledge? That didn't seem right. He'd been connected to the draasin since finding them in the place of convergence and he hadn't been able to read anything from the archives before now. What had changed?

As he sat there, he remembered what was different.

Amia.

She had shaped him before leaving. That shaping had pierced his mind, stabbing painfully through him. She said she gave him a gift, but how would she have managed something like this?

A lump formed in his throat as he thought about her. The bond between them still held—he could sense her distantly through it—but was nothing like it had been when she'd been in the city. Tan suspected that over time, the connection would fade. And maybe that was what Amia needed until she could reach another with the ability to shape spirit.

Pressure built in his ears and he looked up. Someone shaped nearby.

The courtyard remained empty. The chill in the air kept most of the university students inside and the gusting wind that blew through likely kept away anyone else. To Tan, the wind reminded him of home, a home he would never be able to return to.

Like the Aeta, he no longer had a home.

Thunder rumbled, followed by a loud *crack*, like the wind snapping.

Tan pushed to his feet, tucking the book back into his pocket to read later, and started toward the stone circle. There was only one person he knew who used it.

As he reached the stones, a small woman hurried away, moving quickly.

Not Roine.

Tan followed her. Could she be another warrior? There had once been dozens of warriors in the city, but as far as he knew, there hadn't been any in nearly two decades. Not since his mother had lived in the city.

The woman wore a deep blue hooded cloak. The hood settled about her shoulders, leaving auburn hair tangled in the hood's dormant folds. Other than her pale skin and lighter hair, she had much the same build as his mother.

She made her way from the university grounds. Tan kept after her. For all he knew, she was another shaper, but he'd never known any other shapers to arrive in Ethea this way.

The woman turned away from the palace, making her way up the broad street. Since the Aeta left, there weren't the same throngs of people on the streets. They were still crowded, just not quite like they had been even the night before.

Tan twisted, trying to keep her in sight, but she moved swiftly. Every so often, Tan caught glimpses of her dark cloak or her hair. And then he lost her altogether.

He stopped and looked around. He didn't recognize where he was. The buildings in this part of the city were built close together and made of wood rather than stone. Cobbles on the narrow streets were worn and some were loose, catching his feet as he walked. Faded signs advertised the shops, but most were too worn to make out completely.

The people here were dressed more simply than they were near the university or the palace. There were less of the bright colors of Doma. Fewer heavy drapes of Chenir. And he saw no sign of more exotic dress like those from the Isles. Only folk from the kingdoms. Most moved quickly, hurrying toward wherever they needed to reach.

Tan continued onward, looking for any sign of the small shaper, but he saw nothing.

As he waited, pressure built sharply behind his ears. Another shaping, this one more powerful than the last. The pressure faded with a burst.

Wherever the shaper had headed, he suspected she was gone now.

As he neared the university again, he saw Roine.

At first, he wasn't sure if he actually saw the old warrior. He was dressed in a formal jacket of forest green with deep black pants. Neatly combed hair had been brushed back from his head. It was the sword hanging from his waist that gave him away, the sword that marked him as one of the warriors.

Tan ran over to him. "Roine!"

Roine continued on as if he didn't hear.

Tan sprinted forward. A sudden gust of wind seemed to push him along. "Roine!" he shouted, this time louder.

Roine paused and turned. The frown on his face turned into a tight smile as he studied Tan running toward him. "You have learned to shape."

Tan nearly stumbled. Had Roine heard about what happened in the archives? Would he already know about the Incendin fire shaper?

"I—" Tan cut off, uncertain how to explain to Roine. "You heard what happened in the archives?"

"Archives?" Roine shook his head. "I merely meant the way you… wait—what happened in the archives?"

"There was a shaper." Roine frowned but didn't say anything. "Amia was with me. We asked the archivist to show us anything on the draasin—"

"Those are restricted, Tannen."

Tan nodded. "I know they're restricted, but I wanted to see them." He lowered his voice. "As I'm the only one who's spoken to one of the draasin in nearly a thousand years, I think it would be helpful to learn more about them."

Roine touched the hilt of his sword and blinked slowly. "You're right. There is much we need to learn about the draasin, especially since they've chosen to hunt so close to the city. That's where I was going, actually. I need to survey the damage and see if there's anything I can do to prevent another attack."

"That's just it," Tan began. "I don't think it *was* the draasin that attacked near the city."

Roine took a quick breath and shook his head. "I've seen the draasin, Tan. And I've read what I can of the restricted archives on the draasin. Most of it is written in the ancient language so I can't read everything, but there are translations from those who can." He shook his head again and ran his hand through his hair. "Most are warnings about the draasin, recommendations to avoid them when possible or kill them if necessary. And these from shapers—warriors—more powerful than me. No," he said, shaking his head. "The draasin are responsible for what happened near the city. I will do what I can to prevent them from attacking again."

"Then why was there an Incendin shaper in the archives?"

Roine looked and nodded toward the university entrance. They had almost reached the large curved archway into the courtyard. Roine rested a hand on Tan's arm and turned toward him. He lowered his voice and his eyes darted around as he spoke. "Why do you say that?"

"Because she nearly killed us."

"She?"

Tan nodded. "I think the archivist helped her. He brought us to the lower archives and locked the door. An Incendin shaper came for us."

"One of the archivists *brought* you to the lower archives?"

Tan nodded again.

Roine frowned, blinking again as if trying to clear his mind. "And you were with Amia?"

"Yes."

"Did she shape him?"

"It was the only way we were going to get access to those archives. If she hadn't shaped the archivist, he wouldn't have brought us there. At least, that's what we thought."

Roine frowned.

"The shaping didn't work," Tan explained. "He knew he was shaped and brought us into the archives anyway. He must have intended the fire shaper to find us. I haven't been able to figure out why Incendin would still want Amia now that the king has the artifact."

Roine let out a long breath and rubbed his hand through his hair again. His other hand drifted to the hilt of his sword, running across the symbols engraved there. As he did, the expression on his face changed, softening. "Her shaping should have worked on the archivist."

"That's what she said. She seemed surprised. The only time her shaping didn't work was when she tried shaping the lisincend, and then I think it almost worked."

"I was able to resist it to a certain extent," Roine reminded.

"I don't think she ever really tried shaping you."

Roine studied Tan. "No. Perhaps she did not."

"What would make a shaping fail?"

Roine shook his head. "I don't know anything about spirit shaping. No one does anymore. We haven't had a true spirit shaper in the kingdoms for hundreds of years. And then, we still had warriors with the ability to shape spirit."

Tan tried thinking about what little he knew of shaping. Since meeting Roine, he'd seen many shapings, but only once had a shaping failed. That had been when Fur tried sending a fire shaping at the draasin. He hadn't been surprised Fur failed in his shaping; sending fire at a fire elemental would not work, even as twisted as the lisincend were.

But did it work the same with shapers?

"What would happen if a fire shaper faced another fire shaper?" Tan asked.

Roine shook his head. "It depends on many things. Strength, skill, intent. Strength often trumps everything else, but not always. I've seen weak shapers deflect another's shaping, simply because they had more experience."

A thought began growing within Tan's mind. "What if the archivists were shapers?"

"Some *are* shapers. They are selective about who they choose to join the archivists, and will cull from the university when they find an appropriate candidate. Most are not."

"Maybe they're spirit shapers."

Roine shook his head. "Tan—most aren't even shapers. And if they were, we would have learned about it."

"Like you knew about the Aeta?"

Roine stiffened. "We suspected the Aeta for years."

"But you couldn't prove anything. And if they wanted, couldn't the Aeta shapers have shaped you to forget what they were capable of doing?"

His expression turned troubled. "It is possible," he admitted. "When I see him next, I will ask Jishun."

Tan shook his head. Roine couldn't wait to see the other Athan to learn whether he could shape spirit. And if he could, the archivist could shape Roine to deny it. Roine needed proof.

"And the archivists are the only ones who know the ancient language. Isn't that what you said?"

"They spend years studying the language. The newest archivists know very little of it. It's not until they've been an archivist for many years that they truly manage fluency."

Tan remembered the archivist telling him that it would take a lifetime of study. But Amia had learned it from a young age and the archivists managed to learn it. What if there was something more to how the archivists mastered the language? What if they were gifted it the same way Amia had gifted it to him?

"There's something I need to show you," Tan told Roine.

CHAPTER 14

The Archives

A MIA SOMEHOW SHAPED this knowledge into you?" Roine asked as Tan read to him in the ancient language.

Tan nodded, remembering the way it had felt as she performed the shaping. Pain and then warmth.

"But you had been studying it for—"

"Days only, Roine. Not enough to learn it. Not enough to read this," he said, tapping the cover of the book on the draasin.

Roine looked toward the university courtyard and closed his eyes. "If what you say is true…"

"It is."

Roine looked around, his hand still running along the hilt of his sword. "Then come. We need to return to the archives."

Tan watched Roine for a moment as he started toward the archives before racing after him. The archives were not far from the rest of the university, though they were set off in their own section, isolated from much of the city.

The squat building loomed into view. Roine didn't hesitate as he made his way to the archives and pulled the massive door open. Pressure built in his ears as Roine readied a shaping.

A single lantern glowed, giving a strange and darkened appearance to the entry hall. The air held none of the char scent he'd smelled the last time he was here, only the heavy musty odor from decades of moisture soaking into the stone. The smell reminded Tan of the abandoned mines in Galen he used to explore in the days before his father died. Most of the time, he had wandered them alone, but there had been a few times his father accompanied him. Each time he did, they made a game out of who could sense better than the other, trying to reach as deeply into the abandoned mines as they could while trying to detect signs of anything moving. His father always won.

Now it was his turn to win.

Tan pushed out with his senses, straining to feel for anything that would tell him if there were other shapers present, or even the archivist.

Roine looked over at him, brow arched. "Sometimes I forget how strong you are," he said softly. "You're already an incredibly gifted earth senser. With time, you have the potential to be just as strong a shaper."

Tan swallowed. Comments like that made him think of his parents, about what he'd lost and never known.

"I don't sense anything," he said.

Roine shook his head. "Nor do I. And that bothers me."

Tan frowned. "Why?"

"The archivists protect the archives. They are possessive about them, almost religiously so. That there would not be an archivist here…" He shook his head again. "It troubles me. Come."

They made their way to the back of the archives. Roine moved carefully, one hand hovering on the hilt of his sword. The muscles in his neck were tense and he stepped lightly across the stone. His head swiveled from side to side.

Tan crept alongside him, moving silently as he'd learned hunting in the woods around Nor. For the second time since coming to Ethea, he wished he had a weapon with him. Anything to keep him from feeling so helpless. Why hadn't he at least grabbed his knife before leaving?

"You were here?" Roine whispered.

Tan nodded. "He took us lower." He pointed toward the large iron door at the back of the room.

Roine looked around again, a shaping seeping from him. When satisfied, he reached the door and ran his hand along the outside edge. "It's sealed. Shaped closed."

Tan studied the door and saw what Roine meant. Where the iron met the surrounding stone, it had melted, seeping into the stone so the door couldn't be easily opened.

"Can you shape it?"

Roine's mouth was tight as he nodded. "Something like this took great skill. I may not be as skilled a fire shaper, but I should be able to…yes."

The pressure of Roine's shaping built and built until he released it in a flash. This time, Tan could almost make out what Roine did. The metal peeled away from the stone, curling out and rolling back toward the door. The stone itself shook, rumbling softly until it separated fully from the iron.

Roine pulled on the door and it opened with a soft squeal.

He let out a breath. "More skilled than I imagined. You must be right. I don't think one of our fire shapers would be able to manage such a shaping. Had I not shaped the stone at the same time…"

Roine started down the stairs. As he did, he lit the lanterns along the wall so they gave off a soft glow. "I've never been this deep into the archives. The archivists barely let me reach the back room, and that was when I was known as Theondar. As Roine…" He shook his head, peering into the depths far below. "Where were you taken?"

"Down."

Tan moved past Roine and led him deeper into the lower levels of the archives. Tan watched the landings, looking for the door the archivist led them into, finally finding it several levels down.

The door looked as it had before. Tan grasped the round handle with a lock in the center and twisted, pushing open the door. "This is where we were taken. The archivist locked us in from this side."

Roine frowned at the door. "Strange that it should be locked from the outside."

Inside, the room looked much as it had the last time Tan had been here. The single shelf stood in the middle of the room. Tan looked up, eyes taking in the dark hole in the stone of the ceiling, still surprised he had somehow managed to shape the opening. But if he hadn't, the fire shaper would have caught them. Who knows what would have happened next?

"What happened here?" Roine asked. "Why did the fire shaper burn through the ceiling?"

Tan shook his head, feeling a flush come over his cheeks. "That wasn't the fire shaper. That was me."

Roine jerked his head around. "You did that?"

Tan nodded.

"You *melted* stone?"

Tan frowned. "Melted? No, that was an earth shaping."

Roine laughed. The sound felt out of place in the somber archives, especially given as on edge as they had been. "That's a fire shaping, Tan. And a strong one. Didn't the stone feel hot as you climbed through it?"

It had felt warm to him—hot to Amia, he remembered—but he thought that had more to do with the stone moving than anything else. "Are you sure that's a fire shaping?"

Roine climbed onto the shelving and touched the ceiling. "Stone doesn't move like this, not when shaped. It will move, but slowly. More likely it would crumble away when shaped. This... this was heated." He looked down at Tan. "If I needed any more proof you could be a warrior, this is it. The strength you have... we haven't seen such shaping strength in many years. I think it's why you were able to speak to the draasin. It's why you were able to survive."

Tan swallowed. If only he could control it, but he had no idea what he'd done to make the shaping work. He'd focused on trying to push through the stone, but what else? What had he done then that he hadn't tried before?

He had tried pushing the same way he spoke to the draasin.

Was that what it took?

"This still doesn't explain where the archivists have gone. They wouldn't abandon the archives. This has been curated for over a thousand years, many before the rest of the university existed. Some of these works are so old, they crumble at the slightest touch. There should be at least one archivist." Roine jumped down, landing softly on a fluttering of air.

He made his way back out of the room and continued down the stairs, lighting the shapers lanterns as he went. After a few more flights, they reached a large circular level. A dozen doors ringed the room.

Roine whistled softly. "Never thought I'd see this."

"What is it?"

Roine made his way to the first door. Made of wide wooden slats with bands of iron holding them together, it had an ancient feel that fit the depths of the archive. The faint shapers lanterns reflected a dull light off the surface of the wood. Tan picked up a sense of age from the wood.

"A place the archivists claim lost, though few believe them." He turned, looking at the next door and running his hand over it as well. Roine looked back at Tan. "This building is the location of the very first archive. When the university was first founded, the archives were created as a way to store knowledge. The archivists claim to share their knowledge with any who seek it, but much is restricted, kept from even the Masters. Once, that was not the case."

Tan looked at the doors, wondering how they could be as old as the university. The wood should have deteriorated long before, but he couldn't deny what he sensed from it.

"What do they keep here?"

Roine shook his head. "None but the archivists know. Likely the earliest records, the first archives. Documents from when the artifact itself was created. Or maybe nothing. It's possible this is only their sleeping quarters." He looked over at Tan and smiled, then turned back toward the door. Roine ran his hand over the lock. Pressure from his shaping built and then faded. Roine shook his head, a frown deepening on his face. Another shaping formed, this time with more pressure, and then released. Nothing happened.

"Doesn't it work?"

Roine stared at the door. "The last shaping should have done *something*, but it is as if the door itself resists the shaping."

"We need a key."

Roine nodded. "The archivists must have them. And if none are here…"

Tan made his way around the ring of doors. Even the stone of this level felt different, as if heavier. Each of the doors looked to be made of the same dark wood banded together with metal. As he looked closely, he realized it wasn't iron, at least not any type of iron he'd ever seen before. The metal gleamed as dully as the wood and had a cool, smooth texture. His hand tingled where he touched it.

A shadow along the wall caught his attention. No shaper's lanterns lit the way here. The only light available drifted down the stairs but didn't quite reach this far back. Tan moved cautiously, sensing as well as he could, but felt nothing.

As he approached, he realized what he saw.

A body.

The back twisted grotesquely, as if thrown. The person's face looked upward, open eyes staring blankly. The hair looked singed. A stench came from it that he should have recognized sooner: the stink of a body rotting, but mixed with the scent of char and ash. In the forest around Nor, he'd come across carcasses, dead for days, that smelled much the same.

"Roine!"

Roine grunted.

Tan looked away, his stomach threatening to betray him. "I think I found an archivist."

CHAPTER 15

Another Voice

TAN STOOD OUTSIDE THE ARCHIVES, thankful to be back in the cool air. His lungs burned from a run to the university to find one of the Masters, which Roine had requested he do. The first one he came across had been Master Ferran. At first, Tan hadn't been certain he'd come with him, but when he mentioned Roine the Athan, his expression changed and he followed Tan to the archives.

Now Roine and Ferran searched the archives together, looking for signs of the other archivists while Tan stood outside, waiting.

The body they found was an archivist, but the younger one, the man who had been friendly to Tan. And now he was gone.

"Why are you standing here?"

Tan turned and saw Elle leaning against the building. Her arms were crossed over her chest, a stack of books clutched in them. Pale eyes gleamed as she looked at him. "Elle? What are you doing here?"

She frowned and stepped away from the wall. "Well, I came to find another book and the archivist wasn't there." She shrugged. "So I went back and found what I wanted."

"Did you see anything?"

"You mean, other than the rows of books I'll never get a chance to finish?" She shook her head. "I don't know why the archivist didn't stop me. That's never happened before. They always watch when I come into the archives."

Tan swallowed and looked away.

What would the archives have that would motivate an Incendin shaper to kill one of the guardians of the ancient books?

But leave the other archivist alive. Why would one of the archivists work with an Incendin shaper?

He sighed and shook his head. Roine wouldn't answer him. If Tan could face the lisincend and survive—and help recover the ancient artifact—why shouldn't he be included in whatever Roine planned?

Elle watched him, her frown deepening. "What happened in there? What happened to the archivist?"

He shook his head. "I don't know."

"You know something."

Tan shook his head slightly.

"Well?"

"What do you want me to say? That one of the archivists is dead? That we can't find any of the others? That Roine and Master Ferran are searching the archives but keep me out, afraid of what else they might find?"

Elle whistled softly. One hand rubbed behind her ear.

Before she had a chance to say anything more, Tan felt a massive buildup of pressure.

He looked around, wondering who might be shaping. Pain pulsed with the shaping in his head, pounding in his ears. He grabbed his head, biting down to push back against what he felt. Colors swam across his vision, leaving spots shimmering as if he'd stared at the sun for too long.

The pressure left, bursting away from him.

Tan sighed.

Thunder rumbled loudly, shaking the buildings around them. Faint trails of dust seeped from the archives' stones. The ground shook and for a moment, Tan thought it might split open beneath him. Elle gasped next to him.

And then it stopped.

Tan looked around, wondering what had just happened. The power behind the shaping was unlike anything he'd felt before, even more powerful than what he'd felt when they were running from the lisincend.

"What was that?" Elle whispered.

"I don't know. A shaping."

"I know it was a shaping," she said. She stood next to him, the top of her head coming only to his shoulder. The pale gray dress she wore looked huge on her. "But it was outside the city. For us to feel it…"

Tan looked down at Elle and blinked. She was right. The shaping *had* come from outside the city. He pressed out, trying to sense what might have come. At first, he thought he might not be able to discover anything, but then he felt something off. Near the outskirts of the city, where Tan knew were small farms and clusters of homes, the ground had been charred. Not destroyed, not like Nor. It came through the sensing as massive heat steaming from the ground.

The lisincend?

If it were the lisincend, it was a different kind of shaping than any he'd ever seen from them. But what else could make a shaping like that?

"You sense it, don't you?"

Tan turned to see Roine watching him. His dark eyes had an edge of anger in them. "I don't know what I sense."

Roine snorted and stepped away from the archives. Master Ferran came after. He had a few books in his arms, their titles obscured.

"I've warned you they were unsafe. That there was a reason the ancient warriors hunted them. And we've loosed them back on a world unprepared to face them," Roine said.

"That wasn't—"

Roine raised his hand to silence Tan. "You don't know what it was. But we both know what you sensed. And we both know the power required to work a shaping like we just felt."

"Roine—"

Roine shook his head. "No. The king was clear. If Ethea or the kingdoms were threatened, we would have to take action. I know you think the shaping holds, but that hasn't kept them from attacking. First near the borders and now near the city. How many died just now because of them? How many more will die before we can find them?"

Tan didn't know what to say. Roine was convinced the draasin had done this, that they had attacked Ethea, but Tan felt nothing of them. Wouldn't he have *felt* it if they attacked? Wouldn't he have *felt* it if they were so close?

Roine looked back at Master Ferran. "Summon as many as you can. What we must do has not been attempted in a thousand years."

Master Ferran frowned. "You demand the Masters appear? You may be Athan, Roine, and a skilled wind shaper, but you—"

Roine took a deep breath and let it out slowly. He looked over at Tan as he did. "Summon the Masters," he repeated, this time unsheathing his sword, the marker of a warrior. "Tell them Theondar calls."

A gust of wind lifted Roine, whisking him toward the palace. Master Ferran hurried off toward the university. He barely even glanced at Tan before leaving, though his deep frown told Tan everything about how he felt.

"What was he talking about? What does he think attacked?"

Tan sighed. Could the draasin really be responsible for the attack outside the city? Amia's shaping held, didn't it?

"I told you the lisincend destroyed my home."

Elle nodded.

"And Roine—Theondar—searched for something for the king. I helped him find it."

She looked over at him, her eyes wide. "What did he look for? What kind of power did he find?"

"We found something along the way, creatures long thought lost to the world, elementals of great power…" Tan swallowed. "When we searched for the king, we came across a massive frozen lake. Trapped beneath the ice were three of the draasin."

Elle gasped.

"You've heard of them?"

She nodded. "Only rumors. They are great fire elementals."

"Roine tells me the ancient warriors hunted them. They were considered too dangerous to live."

"And you?"

Tan shook his head. "They are elementals. They are a part of the world. Fearsome and powerful, but necessary. And…" He swallowed. "And they saved us from the lisincend. Had they not come when I summoned—"

"You *summoned* one of the great elementals?"

Tan nodded. "When they were frozen beneath the ice, one of them spoke to me."

If only it would speak to him now. If it did, he could ask what happened here, why it seemed the draasin attacked.

Tan closed his eyes and relaxed, breathing out slowly. *Draasin!*

He sent out the call with as much strength as he could. It left him feeling weakened.

"What was that?"

Tan blinked. "What was what?"

Elle had a troubled look. "I *felt* something. Almost like I could hear it if I tried."

Tan looked at her. How would Elle have felt him trying to communicate with the draasin?

No response came. *Draasin!*

This time, he pushed through the memory of the connection. He felt nothing there now, but it still had to be there. The connection couldn't have been severed, could it?

Or did the draasin choose to ignore him? Would they ignore him if they attacked the city?

After all the time spent wishing for the connection to change, now he *wanted* to speak to them and couldn't.

"You did it again."

The draasin hadn't answered, but Elle heard what he did. How was that possible?

"I'm trying to speak to the draasin."

Elle leaned toward him and shook her head slowly. "Why can I sense it?"

"I don't know. I don't think you should. When I did it before, the others with me couldn't tell when I did."

"Try it again."

"It doesn't matter. They don't answer. And if I can't get them to answer, then Roine is going to hunt them."

"You don't think they should be hunted?"

Tan thought of the way the draasin swooped through the sky, the way their powerful wings beat at the air. They were deadly hunters, but they did not deserve what Roine planned. Once the draasin were gone, the last of the great elementals would be gone.

"No."

Elle studied him for a moment. "Try it again," she said. "But this time, try doing whatever you do with me."

"It won't work with you," Tan said.

"Try it," Elle said.

Tan shook his head, but what would it hurt to try communicating with Elle? If it didn't work, he could tell her he tried. And he couldn't deny feeling curious whether it would work.

What had he done with the nymid and the draasin? How did he communicate with them?

Nothing particularly special. With the draasin, they maintained the connection, only releasing him when they chose. Speaking to the nymid had been different. But what about the connection could he reproduce?

He focused on Elle, trying to think about forcing a connection. And then he sent out a thought.

Elle!

He pushed it with as much energy as he had. Tan staggered forward under the effort.

Elle grabbed her head. "You *shaped* me!"

He shook his head. "I didn't shape anything."

"I felt what you did. It was a shaping."

Tan frowned. Could she be right? *Had* he shaped her? Was that how he spoke to the elementals? "Did you hear what I said?"

She frowned. "I think… yes. You said my name, didn't you?"

Tan laughed softly. How had Elle heard him? Even with the shaped connection between him and Amia, he hadn't been able to communicate with her the same way, but he hadn't really tried. Could he use their bond to speak? If so, he wouldn't have to feel quite so alone now that she'd left the city.

How can you hear this?

Elle laughed. "You asked how can I hear this."

Try speaking back to me.

Tan waited. Would Elle be able to talk to him the way he spoke to the elementals? The way he somehow managed to speak to her?

At first, he heard nothing.

Tan?

It came more like a whisper, but it was Elle's voice. She sounded nothing like she did when she spoke aloud and nothing like the draasin or even the nymid. It sounded wispy, barely there.

I hear you, but you're quiet.

It's hard to speak this way.

Tan nodded. The first time he tried speaking to the nymid out of the water, it had taken so much energy, he had barely managed to stay awake.

Have you ever been able to do this before?

Elle shook her head. *I can tell when there are shapings around me.*

I can as well. Did that make a difference?

Do you think I might be able to speak to the elementals?

If she could speak to him this way, there seemed no reason she couldn't speak to the elementals.

Tan started to tell her when the pressure of a shaping built behind his ears.

He grabbed his head. Elle did the same.

And then fire exploded in the night.

CHAPTER 16

The Draasin Answer

TAN RAN TOWARD THE FIRE. The shaping was familiar to him and nothing like the Incendin shapers. That meant draasin. But why?

The draasin wouldn't hunt near Ethea. There were too many shapers for that.

Flames leaped into the sky on the other side of the city, shooting in massive spurts like some sort of display. The air felt still and quiet and the heat of the flames already pushed away the chill. All around him, people ran.

Elle ran alongside him, struggling to keep up. At first, he heard her voice in his head, a distant whisper. Then she gave up trying to speak to him that way and shouted. "Tan!"

He started to slow. If the draasin attacked Ethea, he needed to know. He didn't know what he might be able to do. Speak to them, argue with them to leave the city. More than that?

Do you attack, draasin?

He sent the thought as loudly as he could.

It had been days since he spoke to the draasin, days since the connection had changed.

So it came as a surprise when they answered.

Little Warrior. You disturb the pairing.

Tan nearly stumbled.

He stopped at an intersection. People streamed around them, most running from the fire. One man stopped and glanced at Tan. Something about his face looked familiar. But then he disappeared, running through the street.

Tan stopped pushing against the flow of people and leaned against a stone building. A faded sign hanging out front showed a needle and thread. The lettering had long since disappeared.

Draasin?

A deep, annoyed rumble came through the connection. *You called the draasin, Little Warrior. Why do you bother?*

Do you attack? Have you come to my city?

Not his city—Nor was gone, destroyed by the lisincend—but Ethea was all he knew now.

There was a grunt and a sense of fire. *We hunt. It is the way it must be.*

Tan stared at the flames. Could the draasin be in Ethea?

Is that why he spoke to them so easily?

But if they were here, it meant Amia's shaping no longer held.

If only she were here—but at least she might be safe. Wherever the Aeta had gone, at least it was away from Ethea, away from the Incendin shaper who tried to attack. Away from the draasin. And maybe she would find the help she needed with the shaping.

Tan pressed a sensing through the connection to the draasin. It felt thready, nothing like the overpowering sense he'd felt of it when he first came across them at the lake. But there, distantly, he felt the distant sense of Amia's shaping.

It surrounded it, pressing against it like an invisible barrier, though remained solid.

The draasin did not hunt man.

Is that why you called, Little Warrior?

He formed an image of Ethea in his mind, sending with it the flames rising from the city.

This is not you?

Another grunt mixed with surprise.

And then a deep anger unlike anything Tan had ever felt.

The draasin fell silent and Tan wondered if they would answer. He focused his thoughts, trying to frame what he needed to send in a way the draasin would understand. *There are those who will hunt the draasin. They fear you are too dangerous.*

They may hunt. The draasin's tone had changed, growing angrier.

They are dangerous.

The draasin snorted with annoyance. A flash of an image came to Tan's mind. Was it flying?

Dangerous to draasin? There is little in this world we fear.

Would you fear warriors?

The draasin went silent for a moment. *We... are familiar with the warriors.*

Tan rubbed his head as he argued with the draasin. *The draasin haven't been seen in this world for a thousand years. There are other creatures of much power now. You have met Twisted Fire. They are the most feared creatures of this age.*

Tan couldn't ask the draasin to hunt the lisincend, but could he coax them into it?

Moments of silence passed. Tan sensed the something different from the draasin, almost like a conversation he could not quite hear. And then its attention turned back to him.

The draasin laughed bitterly. *You are clever, Little Warrior. But you are not wrong. Twisted Fire must be hunted, and for reasons you cannot fully grasp. You will come to us and we will hunt them together.*

How will I find you?

Before the draasin could answer, another explosion rocked the city.

Tan jerked around. This explosion was closer to him. And behind.

Something pulled at his sleeve. It was then Tan realized Elle still stood next to him, looking at him with a troubled expression. Her hair was pushed back behind her ears and her brow wrinkled. The expression made her look older.

"Tan!"

She was shouting.

"What?"

"Haven't you been paying attention? The city is under attack. We should get out of the streets until the Masters get it under control."

He blinked, noticing the noise and the chaos all around him. The throngs of people hurrying through the streets had turned, veering away from the university. Some shouted as they pressed forward, but most went silently.

Over it all, he heard a horrible cry.

Tan had never heard a sound like it before. The sound was pained and terrible and filled the air. Fire leaped above the street, shooting straight up like a fountain. Steam hissed with a continuous whistle.

Elle pulled on his sleeve again. Her face looked pale and sweat beaded on her skin. "We need to get somewhere safe. There's too much fire…"

"It can't be the draasin," Tan said. Whatever else, he believed the draasin would not do this. They were predators—hunters—but they wouldn't needlessly attack the city.

But they *were* the only remaining great elementals of fire. How could he presume to know what the draasin would do?

"Doesn't matter what it is," Elle said. "We shouldn't be here. Can't you sense it?"

He frowned.

As he started to ask what he should be sensing, he realized what it was.

Fire built around them and the temperature in the air rose. Tan had felt something like it before, but that had been when he rescued Amia from the cage of fire. This was the entire city.

Could it be the lisincend?

If so, how many lisincend were out there?

More than just the temperature was growing. A shaping was taking hold around him, making his head throb with its pressure.

What could make a shaping like that?

Unless… could the Masters be fighting back? If so, Tan had nothing to fear. They would drive back the Incendin shapers and the city would be safe.

But what if it wasn't? Tan might have the capacity to learn to shape, but he hadn't learned enough about it. He had no control. If he were caught near another shaper—caught like he and Amia were trapped in the archives—would he be able to do anything that might save them?

Probably not.

He was foolish to run toward the fires and the shaping. "Where can we go?"

Elle pulled him forward. "Come. There is a place I know."

She led him across the city, far from the palace and the university and into a section Tan had never visited. At one point, she paused, leaning against a faded wooden building as if she might faint. She swallowed hard and offered him a weak smile before continuing through the city.

The flames engulfing parts of the city seemed a distant and weakened thing from here. Fewer people were out on the streets and those who were moved quickly and with a purpose, much like Elle now did. Tan noticed their dress was simpler here; this must be where the locals lived.

They reached a series of steps leading down from a squat stone building.

She pointed. "Come."

Tan hesitated. "What is this?"

She spent a long second staring down the steps. After she had taken a deep breath, she looked over her shoulder. "Safety. Come on."

He shook his head. "Not until I know why you brought me here."

She shifted her weight. Her eyes mirrored the action, turning from the steps to the flames in the city and then to Tan. Hot air pushed on them as if practically burning the moisture from the air. Tan's skin felt dry and tight and his mouth felt like he'd finished running up the mountains in Galen.

Elle sagged slightly and leaned against the wall for support. "I had another reason for coming to the university, Tan."

"Another reason?"

"Most come here to learn shaping, and I wanted to learn that as well, but there was a different reason for me."

Tan frowned. "What other reason did you have?"

Thunder rumbled distantly. "Not here. Let's get down to safety first and I'll explain."

She turned back to the door. Tan heard a *click* and then a squeal as it opened. Faint light spilled out. Elle disappeared into it.

He stood for a moment, debating whether he should follow. What did he know about Elle? What did he know about anything in this city? So far, he'd come across Masters from the university who seemed more concerned about who he knew than about teaching. He'd met archivists who seemed to work with Incendin, and he'd followed a shaper into the city.

There was more going on than he understood—more than he was meant to know. He was meant to live in the mountains, to be surrounded by streams and trees and the gusting winds of Galen. Instead, all that had been taken from him. While Amia had been with him, he hadn't felt alone. Now that she was gone, he felt more isolated than ever.

Another explosion rumbled through the city, this one closer.

Fire flared against the sky. Again, Tan was reminded of the way flames had shot upward as they formed the fiery prison the lisincend had used to hold Amia. Flames continued fountaining upward, sending heat and bright light into the once-darkened night.

A shape swooped through the darkness.

Tan saw it as little more than a shadow, but he *felt* it moving in the night. Heat and fire radiated from it, but nothing more.

A terrible cry erupted from the darkness, a sound like nothing he'd ever heard.

Tan shivered and ducked down the stairs and after Elle.

She waited, brow furrowed and a worried look upon her face. Color had drained from her cheeks, leaving her pale. "What was that?"

Tan shook his head. It couldn't be. He would have known if it were, wouldn't he?

"Tan?" Elle repeated.

He swallowed and closed his eyes. His mind formed the image of the creature he'd just seen, a creature he'd last seen chasing the lisincend through the mountain passes. A creature he thought would not hunt near Ethea.

Tan took a deep breath. "It was the draasin," he said.

Behind him, someone gasped.

CHAPTER 17

A New Shaper

THE SMALL ROOM HAD BARELY ENOUGH SPACE for the tiny wooden chairs. Elle sat on one, her chair tipped onto only the back legs, and she balanced that way, staring blankly at the wall. Sweat dripped along her brow. Stone crumbled, spilling out from walls and through slatted boards overhead, layering dust with each additional explosion that rocked the city above.

Since he'd been in the room, Tan had heard at least two more explosions.

The painful cry of the draasin had not returned. Neither had any sense of the draasin, no matter how hard he tried to reach it.

Tan didn't bother Elle. Instead, he looked at the other person sitting in the room. He'd seen her before. In spite of a single lantern spitting pale, flickering light, he recognized the auburn hair trailing behind her head in a braid. Pale skin seemed even lighter than when Tan had chased her through the city. He had little doubt this was the same shaper he'd seen before. "I know you."

The woman stared back at him, watching him intently. The ends of her hair curled slightly, as if fluttered by an unseen breeze.

"You came through the university. You're a shaper."

The woman turned to look up at Elle. "You shouldn't have brought him here."

Elle turned and looked at her, her face pained. "I had to, Sarah."

Sarah frowned. "Had to? You had to do nothing but stay at the university and learn. Had you done that, you would eventually become strong enough to shape. And then—"

Elle leaned forward in her chair. "You know why I'm here. I'm still not certain why the elders sent you." She tipped her head toward Tan. "I found what we wanted. The reason I came to the university." Her voice lowered to a whisper.

"Where?" Sarah's tone changed, becoming interested. "In the archives? The archivists grant you access?"

Elle shook her head. "Not the archives. They hoard their books on the elementals."

Sarah sniffed and nodded. "As it has always been." She sighed. "Then what? What have you learned?"

Elle nodded toward Tan. "He hears them."

Sarah frowned. "What do you mean?"

Tan looked from Sarah to Elle. Sarah watched him, studying him with renewed interest. Elle looked as if she might vomit.

"When I first met you, I told you how I studied the elementals."

Tan nodded. "You thought studying them would help you learn to shape faster."

Elle inhaled deeply. "I told you about my grandfather… about how he was a water shaper."

Tan nodded. Roine had recognized the name of her grandfather.

"Your friend—the Athan—assumed I was from Vatten because I spent much time there as a child with my grandfather."

Tan frowned. "You're not from Vatten."

She glanced at Sarah before shaking her head. "I'm not. I only claimed Vatten as home to come here to study."

Tan started to stand. Could Elle be from Incendin? There was no reason Incendin wouldn't have shapers of water or air or earth. "Where are you really from?"

A mixture of emotions worked on Elle's face. "The kingdoms aren't the only place with shapers, just the only place where shapers can come to study."

"Elle?"

She shook her head. "Incendin is known for their fire shapers—"

"You're not from Incendin."

"The Masters screen for Incendin shapers. That's why they pay so close attention to where you come from. That's why Master Ferran spent the entire time in class harassing the rest of us to see where we're from. Until the Masters are convinced you're from the kingdoms, they won't teach you."

Tan thought about the experiences he had with the Masters and realized she was right. He hadn't wanted to say anything to Roine, but other Masters hadn't seemed particularly interested in working with him. Tan thought it had more to do with his age, but what if it didn't? What if it was as Elle said and they needed to convince themselves that he wasn't from Incendin?

"If not from the kingdoms and you're not from Incendin, then where are you from?"

Elle leaned back and answered. "My grandfather was a water shaper. I'm a water senser. Vatten doesn't claim the oceans for itself.

There are other places known for their mastery of the seas, places where the people have lived on the water for longer than the kingdoms have even existed." She sighed and her eyes closed.

Water? Ocean?

"Doma?" he asked.

Elle nodded.

Tan shook his head. "But… why? Why bother coming here? Why lie about where you're from?"

Sarah shifted in her chair and then stood, making her way to the door. She cracked it slightly and looked up the stairs into the darkness. Even with the door cracked as it was, the heat from the fire shaping pressed down the stairs and into the room. A low sound, like the beating of powerful wings, pulsed through the air.

Tan struggled, ignoring the desire to reach for the draasin. For answers.

Later. Once he understood what Elle was telling him.

Sarah shut the door and turned back to him. "Because the university will only train those from the kingdoms. Once, they would train any who chose to come. The only price requested was service." She sniffed softly. "You will learn."

Tan understood the price. His father had paid the price of service. His mother had gone to Galen to serve the king and pay for her education.

"What does this have to do with why Elle came to Ethea?" Tan asked.

"I came to learn shaping, but there was another reason. One that was as important for our elders."

Tan frowned. "The elementals? To learn to speak to them?"

Elle nodded. "Once, the elders in Doma knew the udilm well. They guided our ships and our shapers controlled the wind and waves, giving us power over the seas. For hundreds of years, our people enjoyed prosperity because of udilm."

"Not only udilm. But ara too," Sarah said. "They work together, often fighting, but with our shapers, we managed to coax the elementals to work together, to grant calm seas."

"And then something changed," Elle went on. She took a shaky breath. "Many years have passed since our last shaper appeared."

"Once, our people had dozens of water and wind shapers," Sarah continued. "Even some earth and fire shapers, though they were rare and they always were sent to the university to learn. Even some of our wind and water shapers came to Ethea, seeking to learn from the Masters here, hoping to discover if the kingdoms knew anything more of shaping than our shapers had learned from ara and udilm. Most who came stayed behind, built lives for themselves."

"That was how my grandfather came to live here," Elle said.

Tan didn't need for them to explain what happened. It was the same as had happened in the kingdoms. Over time, there had been fewer and fewer shapers. Even sensers became less frequent, leaving the kingdoms not only unprotected but disconnected from the elemental power that once defined the kingdoms.

"None of your people speak to the udilm anymore?" Could the udilm have disappeared? Maybe that really *was* why the nymid were so strong.

Elle shook her head. "It has been many years since any could claim the ability."

"And ara?" he asked Sarah.

She frowned at him, as if debating her answer. Then she shook her head. "Ara has not spoken to Doma in many years."

"So I was sent," Elle went on. "I have some ability to detect shapings. The ability is rare, but the elders thought it necessary for communication with elementals. They do not know for sure; none of them can speak to udilm. I was given everything we knew of the ancient language, taught to me from a young age like most from Doma, and told to see what I could find in the archives. Until you came, I hadn't found anything of use. Only old conversations, but nothing about how to find the elementals or how to start the conversation. Most of that is stored in the restricted archives."

Tan thought of the book on the draasin he'd found, how it had been much the same.

"And then I met you. You speak to not only one elemental, but two. And then you can speak to me." The last came out as a whisper.

Sarah turned sharply, studying Tan. "What do you mean he spoke to you?"

Elle swallowed. Sweat still beaded on her forehead and now she trembled slightly. "I don't know how to explain what he did. I hear his voice in my head. I can speak back. There is shaping involved, I think, but I don't understand it."

"If you find the udilm, what would you do?" Tan asked. Of all the questions he had, that one seemed the most important. More so after hearing Roine speak of what he feared from the draasin, how he intended to hunt them. The elementals were… a part of this world, something to be observed and learned from, appreciated for their beauty, not hunted and destroyed.

Elle laughed softly. "I hadn't expected to learn enough to speak to the udilm, let alone think I would have to answer that question."

What would you do?

Tan sent the thought with the same intensity he'd seen in Elle's eyes. After the way the elementals had helped him—the nymid saved both his and Amia's lives while the draasin hunted the lisincend, giving them a chance to survive—he felt somewhat possessive about the knowledge he'd gained. Learning how few could speak to the elementals only made him even more possessive.

I would ask to learn. My people need their help.

As he did through his connection to the draasin, he sensed more than her thoughts. Intent came through the connection. Tan sensed fear and uncertainty, but great need.

Why? What is it you need?

Elle didn't answer. But she didn't need to.

Through the connection, he caught the fleeting image of darkness and flames, shadows only. Had he not seen them before, he might not know what she feared. But Tan had spent too much time running from the lisincend not to recognize them, even obscured as they were.

There was something else he noticed, but it made little sense given what Elle had said.

"You didn't only come to Ethea to learn," he said aloud. "You came here to hide."

CHAPTER 18

The Demands of Fire

ELLE LOOKED AWAY and hid her face. As she did, Tan noted the redness staining her eyes. He tried pushing through the connection but couldn't. Either she blocked him or the emotion she felt prevented him from sensing anything more.

"What is it?"

Sarah watched Elle and then looked to Tan. "Growing up in the kingdoms, you can't know what it's like elsewhere in the world. The compromises made to exist."

Tan frowned.

"Doma has nothing like the kingdoms—no barrier and few shapers—so like most of Doma, she fears Incendin."

Tan took a step toward the wall and leaned against it. "The lisincend. They are horrible. They destroyed my home, everyone I ever knew and cared about."

Sarah nodded. "They have done the same in Doma. Especially when we don't send shapers to them."

Tan jerked around. "What? They want your shapers?"

Sarah looked at Elle. "Already we had few enough shapers, but with what Incendin requires, they have taken what few remain."

"What happens if you don't send shapers to Incendin?"

"What happens? Fire and devastation happen. Entire swaths of countryside are destroyed. Villages are decimated. Most choose to go willingly when demanded rather than subject the rest of Doma to the anger of the lisincend."

"I… I didn't know."

Did Roine? Did the king?

If they did, how could they do nothing about it?

She shook her head. Elle still hadn't looked up. "How could you?" Sarah began. "The barrier the kingdoms erected keeps the shapers of this land safe, but for how long? When it fails—and it *will* fail—you will understand what Incendin does."

"What happens to them? To the people who are taken?"

"No one knows. Those who are sent never return. The elders suspect Incendin uses them to build their own shaper army, but we haven't seen any signs of it."

The barrier. Tan felt sure of it. Using shapers taken from Doma, Incendin could attack and weaken the barrier—or even bypass it entirely.

He looked over at Elle. "You think the elementals might protect you?"

Sarah shrugged. "Some of the elders hope it might be so."

Elle looked up then and wiped her mouth. Vomit pooled near her feet. "Didn't you say the draasin chased the lisincend? If they fear fire elementals, surely they would fear water even more."

"Elle?" Tan asked.

She shook her head. "I'm fine."

Sarah hurried over to her and touched her on the head. A shaping built. Wind swirled softly, spiraling tightly around Elle's head with such control that Tan could only stare. When it settled, Elle leaned back.

"What is it?" Tan asked.

Sarah shook her head. "I don't know. I haven't seen anything like this before. Something works inside her…"

"Inside her?"

Sarah nodded. "A shaping, I think. One I'm not familiar with."

Tan thought of what Elle said about him shaping her. Had *he* caused her sudden illness by forcing her to speak to him?

If he had, could he stop it?

Elle blinked and looked up at Sarah weakly. "I'm fine."

Sarah watched her for a moment. Another shaping built, this time subtly and worked around her, pressing down and through her. Some of the color returned to Elle's cheeks. "That might hold it for now."

"What did you do?" Tan asked.

"I contained the shaping for now."

Elle looked at him and met his eyes. "What caused it?" Tan asked.

Sarah shook her head. "It's not clear. As I said, it's a type of shaping I've never seen."

Elle shook slightly, nothing like the steady trembling she'd been doing before, and pushed to stand. "Whatever you did helped. I'm feeling better."

"You shouldn't push yourself, Elle," Sarah warned.

"I said I'll be fine. Besides, I need to get back to my studies." She stared at Tan intently.

"I… I don't know what I can teach you," he admitted.

She smiled. With the color returning to her cheeks, so did the appearance of youth. "You can speak to the nymid. That might be a start."

Tan sighed. The nymid. If he could find them. "Maybe," he agreed, turning away from her. He didn't even know how *he* spoke to the nymid, let alone trying to teach someone else. Then there was the matter of finding the nymid.

And then there was the issue of what he'd learned. If what Elle and Sarah said was true—if Incendin demanded shapers from Doma—the threat from Incendin was even greater than they knew. Roine and the king needed to learn.

More than ever, he missed Amia, missed the connection they had, her ability to sense spirit and the connection it brought. Without her, he felt alone.

Could he speak to her as he did to Elle? She needed to know what had happened in Ethea since she left. She needed to know about the Incendin attack and about the possibility the draasin had attacked.

He sighed. How was that possible if the shaping still held? Unless there was a different explanation.

The draasin had wanted him to come to them, to hunt the lisincend with them. The bond wasn't clear enough *why* it wanted him to come, but what if there was something the draasin needed from him?

Tan stood and went to the door. Elle watched him but made no move to stop him, so he pulled the door open and glanced up the stairs. Hot air hit him, but nothing like before. The fires had died down. Distant shouts rang out through the city.

Nowhere did he hear the steady beating of wings. And nowhere did he hear the horrible cry of the draasin.

Instead, there seemed an eerie sort of silence, as if a pall had fallen upon the city.

Tan stepped up the stairs and into the street, ignoring Elle's protest. A few distant fires burned, casting a distant orange pall around the city that reflected off a hazy smoke shimmering in the air. He coughed as he inhaled it. A few other people emerged onto the street. Like him, they looked around cautiously, uncertain whether the attack had ended.

Elle came up behind him and touched his arm.

Tan turned, looking down at her.

"Was it like this when your home was destroyed?"

He shook his head. "That was worse. After the lisincend attacked, there was nothing left." The difference was striking. *Could* this be the draasin?

Elle turned to the north and stared at the steady glowing of the distant fire raging through a distant building. It stood taller than most in that part of the city, at least three stories, though he didn't recognize it. Since coming to Ethea, he hadn't explored much of the city. Most of his time had been spent at the university or the archives. And rarely Amia, though she claimed her distance more about the headaches plaguing her since they arrived in Ethea.

"This reminds me of Ushil," Elle said. Tears streamed down her face and her eyes were reddened. "When the shapers came. They took Aland, but he wasn't enough." She swallowed and turned to Tan. "So they sent their shapers. Fire shapers, mostly, but there was the other. The one we couldn't quite see." She shivered. "It took out most of the village before disappearing, destroying everything. We had shapers then, mostly wind shapers—none quite like Sarah—but at least Donal was there. If not for his shaping, more of the city would have burned."

Sarah stepped up behind her and touched her lightly on the shoulder. Wind gusted softly, clearing some of the smoke and haze, and Sarah took a deep breath. Her back seemed straighter and she stood taller. "I will do what I can for Doma," Sarah said.

Elle blinked.

"Continue your studies. What you learn might be important." Sarah looked at Tan, meeting his eyes. She blinked and touched her hair, smoothing it. "Perhaps more than the elders ever knew."

Elle touched her head. "What if…" She trailed off, looking at Tan.

Sarah smiled sadly. "I will be here a little longer if you need me. But then I will need to return. If the lisincend truly move freely, then I will be needed. For now," she continued, looking out at the city and the fires still burning there, "there is much for me to do."

With that, she took off on a soft shaping of wind, moving quickly toward the glowing flames.

CHAPTER 19

Master's Plan

MUCH OF THE CITY had not been affected by the fires. As Tan made his way through the city, he saw patches of destruction, where charred and burned buildings toppled over, some falling on neighboring buildings and setting them alight while others spilled into the street, leaving piles of smoking wreckage. But interspersed were rows of buildings untouched by flame and fire. In these areas, Tan could almost imagine nothing had happened.

Elle trailed him silently. Though her color had returned, something still seemed off with her and she followed a step behind until they reached the area near the university.

Unlike other parts of the city, few people stood in the street here, almost as if afraid. Tan expected to find shapers, both Masters and students, but saw none. Elle gasped softly. Tan wasn't certain if she did so aloud or if he heard it through a shaping; the constant pressure behind his ears made it difficult to tell.

The destruction was heavier here. The great arch leading to the courtyard had fallen, crushed to the ground in a heap of stone and ash. Powdered residue from its collapse hung in the air, filling it even more than the smoke from still-smoldering fires around the courtyard. Tan pulled his shirt up over his mouth to keep from breathing it in, but still coughed, the sound echoed by Elle.

He made his way past the pile of stone that once had been the archway and stepped into the courtyard. Where trees and grass had once grown green and vibrant, now there were only black, charred remains. The stone around the courtyard crumbled but stood otherwise stout. Black ash hung on the stone where flames had licked at the walls. In a few areas, stone had vanished, leaving a gaping hole revealing private quarters or lecture halls. Tan could not see to the top of the university but wondered if the roof had sustained much damage.

The air hung heavy and still, almost unnaturally so. It took Tan a moment to realize the air was likely shaped into stillness. Any wind would allow lingering flames to jump to nearby buildings, spreading the fire throughout the city.

"Where are all the shapers?" Elle asked.

Tan glanced at her, looking for lingering signs of her illness, but saw none. Then he shook his head. They should be here. The university should have been protected. Where would they have gone?

He couldn't tell if the university was harder hit than other places in Ethea, but he hadn't seen stone destroyed quite so thoroughly elsewhere. What type of force must have struck here?

Tan turned and started out of the courtyard. The university had never been his home. Possibly he would have come to see it that way in time, but he'd only been in Ethea a short while. Not nearly long enough to feel connected to it, not the way his mother spoke of it before she'd passed. But seeing it destroyed like this made him regret the opportunity he would never have.

And what of the archives?

He hurried away from the university. From what he'd seen, the archives were even more valuable than the university, and the ancient tomes were much more susceptible to fire.

When he reached the archives, he let out a breath. It still stood.

Like at the university, stone crumbled and flames had crawled along the walls, but something pushed back against it, almost as if the stone itself had resisted. The great doors to the archives were twisted and bent, but still stood.

Tan pushed them open. All looked untouched, as if the chaos out in the street hadn't managed to reach inside. Nothing moved. Had the archivists not returned?

When he turned back to the door, Roine stood watching him. Soot covered his face, leaving his silvery hair streaked with black. His eyes looked drawn and tired. Parts of his shirt were singed, but it was otherwise intact. He had his sword in hand. In spite of the early morning light, the blade had a sheen, as if it glowed.

"Are you harmed?" he asked.

Tan shook his head.

Roine took a quick breath and nodded. "I thought you might have been at the university," he said. "After what I saw there..."

"I saw it too."

Roine nodded.

"How are the archives intact?" Tan asked.

"The stone that makes up the walls of the archives," Roine said as if that explained everything.

Tan frowned. "I don't understand."

Elle had turned from him and touched the wall. She gasped softly. "They're cool."

Tan looked at the walls. The air still felt hot, practically burning his lungs with each breath. The ground outside was hot, like stones baking in a blazing sun all day. "After everything that happened? How can the stone still be cool?"

Elle cocked her head as she ran her hand along the stone. "I can…" She trailed off, her eyes going distant. "There is something about it," she continued. "I don't think I'm meant to know it, though."

Roine sniffed. "Not as a water shaper, you're not."

Elle turned and frowned at him. "Not a shaper. Not yet, at least. And what do you mean?"

Roine shook his head. "The archive is one of the oldest buildings in the city and certainly older than the university. Those who built it infused shapings into its creation."

Elle stared at the stone. "There is more than only shapings here."

Tan touched the stone. His hand tingled. Something reverberated in his head with the sensation, like a memory. Almost, he could hear a distant, low rumbling voice in his mind.

"Golud helped with this," he said softly.

Roine furrowed his brow in a frown briefly as he nodded. "Golud did. Not many know." The comment carried a hint of a question.

"How did this happen?" Tan asked him.

"Ethea was attacked. And we were unprepared."

"Incendin? Was it the lisincend?"

"Not lisincend. You've seen the devastation they bring firsthand. What happened here was different."

Tan sighed. He couldn't deny what he saw last night, the shape circling overhead, but he hadn't felt anything from the draasin. "It doesn't make sense," he said softly.

Roine snorted. "Doesn't it? You think this the work of Incendin and it might be, but the draasin were involved as well. I *saw* one in the sky. And maybe they work together."

"The draasin wouldn't—"

Roine cut him off with a wave of his hand. "They both serve fire."

Tan shook his head. "I've told you the draasin despise the lisincend. The draasin were the reason Amia and I escaped in the first place! They wouldn't cooperate with the draasin."

"You saw it, didn't you?"

"They wouldn't help Incendin. Not Twisted Fire."

Roine laid a hand on his arm. It was a gesture meant to be soothing, but to Tan it felt harsh and unwelcome. "We don't know how they think, Tannen." He raised a hand when Tan opened his mouth to argue. "You know what they want you to know. They are elementals, born of the deepest power this world knows. How can we know what drives them, what motivates them?" He shook his head. "They serve fire. As do the lisincend. They are a natural pairing."

"No. They're not. There's nothing natural about the lisincend. That's why the nymid and draasin despise them."

Roine shook his head and let out a slow breath. "I can't argue with you about this. The decision was made already. What happened tonight only confirmed it. I came to find you, to see if you were alright. Now that I see you are, I want you to go to the palace—tell the guards I sent you—and you will be safe there while I'm gone."

"Roine—"

He shook his head. "No. I am leading a dozen shapers after the draasin. We can't afford another attack like this one, not if we want to be able to push Incendin back. Tonight alone, we lost two shapers. We have so few already... another attack like this and we won't have enough shapers to hold the barrier. And then when

Incendin attacks." Roine shook his head. "I'm sorry, Tan. This is what must happen."

They made their way back to the street and Roine studied him, as if waiting to see what he would say. When Tan said nothing more—there really wasn't anything for him to say—he turned and made his way toward the university.

Elle watched Tan rather than Roine. Her eyes were wide and her mouth pressed into a thin line. "What will you do?" she asked.

Tan shook his head. Nothing made sense. The draasin wouldn't attack the city. They were predators—hunters—but hunted for food, not sport. But what had he seen? Was it possible the draasin worked with Incendin?

Could he find out? Did he dare chase the draasin himself?

Could he dare not?

"You wanted to speak to the elementals," he began. If he focused, he could just begin to sense the draasin at the edge of his mind. Even when they didn't speak to him, they were there, hovering at the edge of his awareness. If he closed his eyes, he could almost see them, could almost *feel* what the draasin felt. He would use the connection to find them.

And then what?

Then he would have to find proof, somehow, the draasin had not attacked Ethea, proof enough even Roine would believe.

Tan had no idea what that might be.

CHAPTER 20

Search for Healing

A SENSE OF QUIET HUNG OVER THE CITY, something heavy and palpable. Smoke drifted leisurely, in some places creating a dense fog in the air that obscured what should be a rising sun. Fires still burned throughout the city, though with less urgency, leaving a fading orange glow that reflected off the smoke and fog. Few people wandered the streets. Those who did made a point of not looking at him.

He had nowhere to go. He'd tried returning to his room, but fire had destroyed the building. Much of the floor he lived on had burned. Had he any possessions, they would have been lost. It was the second time fire had claimed the place he called home.

Tan stood on the street overlooking the palace, debating.

Roine wanted him to go to the palace and wait for his return. Waiting meant until after Roine hunted the draasin, after the last of the great elementals were destroyed.

Could the draasin really be responsible for the attack on the city? Shouldn't he have some warning if that were the case, some sign from the draasin through the connection they shared?

But the draasin had not answered again. And Tan couldn't deny what he saw circling in the sky.

Besides, what could he do? He could shape—he no longer doubted his ability there—but had no control, certainly not enough to chase after the draasin. Even were he to find them, what could he say?

Tan took a seat on a stone bench and stared at the palace. Within its walls was the king, the one person who might be able to persuade Roine to refrain from attacking the draasin, to go with him and search for more information. But the king would not, not with the threat of Incendin still hanging over the kingdoms. The worst part was that he understood. The threat of Incendin was that significant.

What he needed were answers, but no one alive understood the draasin.

Tan reached into his pocket for the leather bound book on the draasin. He traced the symbol on the cover, working his finger around the embossing before finally flipping the book open. He still marveled at the fact that he could read the ancient language—that Amia's shaping allowed him to read.

And missed her.

He skimmed over the sections recounting conversations with the draasin. Names were mentioned without reference, likely those who had spoken to the great elementals, shapers—warriors—from a different and more powerful time. A time when speaking to the elementals was less rare. A time when shapers were more common.

A section caught his eye and he slowed to read it carefully. It was different than the earlier section and written in a different hand, this a tight script.

There are scholars who feel the draasin should be hunted to extinction. Their explanation takes less of a philosophical explanation than a practical one. We have seen the progression of elementals over time; their power is not static.

Master Phelan predicts similar changes for fire. Who can argue with his logic? He references geologic changes to make his point, reminding the Scholars how the oceans have receded over time, shaped and changed to draw this land from their depths. As they do, so too does the udilm influence. Such change is not without another. Inland waterways have grown more common, lakes and rivers rushing through where only salt water flowed before. The nymid have flourished and grown more powerful, seemingly at udilm's expense.

Could not the same, it is suggested, happen with Fire? Would the lesser be more compliant than the greater?

Tan hesitated. The archivist had made a similar comment as he led them into the archives. Had he known?

Could Roine? Would they actually *want* the draasin destroyed so another elemental could replace them? Was that why the draasin wanted him to come?

"What is that?"

Tan looked up. Elle stood, watching him, arms crossed and pulling the baggy dress tight over her chest. Her eyes flicked from the book to him and she bit her lower lip.

"It's a book I borrowed from the archives."

Elle grunted. "Borrowed. Wish I could have borrowed a few books from the lower archives, but the Athan wouldn't let me back in, not after the archivist was found dead."

Tan slipped the book into his pocket and stood. "The archives weren't safe. You don't understand what happened there—"

"You said an Incendin shaper chased you."

178

He nodded.

"But you haven't seen her again."

"No, but that doesn't mean—"

"Doesn't matter. The archivists have reclaimed the archives. None of the old archivists. I think they sent the younger archivists to clean up the mess after the city was attacked by the draasin."

Tan started to argue but closed his mouth. Arguing wouldn't change what happened and he couldn't deny the draasin weren't involved. Only he wanted to know why. Did the draasin know the elemental powers could be replaced? Would the lesser elementals gain power if they were hunted to extinction? He knew little about the other elementals—saa and inferin—but they were nothing like the draasin.

"Where are the older archivists?" Tan asked. He thought of the younger archivist, now twisted and dead at the bottom of the stairs. Of the archivists, he had been the friendliest, nothing like Master Yulan or the man who locked them into the archives.

Elle shrugged. "I don't know. They're a secretive group."

Tan waited for her to say more. When she didn't, he laughed. "Secretive? Like you have any room to comment?"

"I'm not…" She trailed off, her face going pale. Her eyes flicked up and she swooned in place.

Tan reached for her, but she steadied herself before needing any help. "We should find Sarah," he said.

Elle took a deep breath and drew herself up. She studied him with an annoyed expression, biting her lower lip as she pushed her hair up over her ears. She still trembled, though it was less than before. "Why do you want to find Sarah?"

"I don't know what she did before, but she helped when you were sick. She can help again."

How much of it was his fault? How much had trying to force the connection between them caused her illness? If Sarah could do anything to help, he needed to find her.

He pulled Elle through the street. They weren't far from the basement, and he could think of no place else to find her. That Elle didn't resist told him how unwell she was.

When they reached the steps leading to the basement, he found the door open.

Tan led them down, stretching forward with sensing. A soft breeze fluttered behind them and into the room, swirling cool air around. Shaped—the pressure behind Tan's ears told him shapings took place around him nearly constantly, and certainly more than he'd ever felt before while in Ethea—the breeze provided welcome relief from the heat.

Did Elle feel the same shaping? Was that how he managed to communicate with her? Or was there another reason? Had he actually shaped her as she thought?

"I'll be fine," Elle said.

A soft snort came from behind them. Sarah stepped forward and with a quick shaping, pressed down on Elle's forehead. She was dressed differently than before. A long green cloak hung from her shoulders with the hood thrown back. A long satchel hung over her shoulder. Her eyes flashed a pale blue as she looked from Tan to Elle. "It's worse than before."

Elle shook her head. "Not worse."

"You nearly collapsed," Tan reminded her.

She shrugged. "The heat. I needed water."

Sarah shook her head. "It's more than that. If we had a water shaper…" She looked toward the open door. "Many of the Masters leave Ethea. They search for something, but I can't tell what. Only a few remain, and none I would trust."

Tan frowned. "Trust? For what?"

Sarah looked at him blankly. "To remove the shaping."

Elle stood. Her long dress hung around her, draped over the floor. "Really. I'm fine. Can we get back to—"

She didn't finish and slumped to the ground.

Sarah grabbed her, scooping her up. She pressed her hand against Elle's head again, letting it linger longer this time. Pressure built with her shaping and then she looked up at Tan. "She grows weaker. It's as if her mind fights the shaping. Do you know what happened to her?"

He swallowed and forced himself to meet Sarah's eyes. "Only me."

"Can you fix it? Remove whatever happened?"

"I don't know what happened. I wouldn't know how to begin."

Sarah sighed and leaned Elle back to the ground. "Great Mother bind us," she whispered harshly.

Tan had only ever heard his mother say something like that.

Sarah stood and faced Tan. Her eyes flashed brightly. "Were there water shapers remaining in Ethea I trusted, I would take her to them, but I've been away too long…" She said the last to herself. "You spoke to the nymid?" she asked Tan.

He nodded. "I can't reach them from Ethea."

"Can you find them?"

"There's a place… but I don't know where it is. I'm not sure I could find it."

Sarah grunted and turned toward the door, annoyance sweeping through her. "Time is not on our side. The girl needs help." She spun and met Tan's eyes. "Will you help her, Tannen?"

He looked down at Elle. What he needed was to understand why the draasin had attacked. Find a way to slow Roine. But Elle was his friend. He had so few in Ethea. "I will."

"Good. Then you will go to the nymid. Though not as powerful as udilm, they should suffice for healing. As she is a water senser, they will bond to her easily."

Tan didn't bother correcting her about the nymid's strength. "I only know of one place to reach the nymid, and it's far from here."

Sarah looked up at him. "I will see you reach them."

Tan looked over, thinking of only one way she could manage to get him to the place of convergence. He'd traveled on a wind shaping before and nearly died. What Sarah suggested would require even greater distance.

"Are you…" He hesitated, not sure how to ask. "Are you strong enough for what you're suggesting?"

Sarah sniffed. "Strength and control are not the same things."

Tan stared at her for a moment. "Do you have the necessary *control* for what you're suggesting?"

How could he even be considering this? A shaping like what she suggested would be difficult for a shaper as powerful as Roine. How could a wind shaper claim the ability to send him as she suggested?

Elle shook again.

Sarah's mouth tightened into a thin line. She pressed another shaping against her friend.

If Tan had caused this illness by unintentionally shaping Elle, how could he not?

"You will need to hold a focus in your mind. I can lash the shaping to it." Sarah looked up at him. "I won't be able to summon you back. You will be on your own to return."

Watching Elle, the color again drained from her face, he knew what he had to do.

"When do we go?"

Sarah lifted Elle from the floor and nodded toward the door. "Now."

They stood in the courtyard of the university. Elle supported herself but leaned against one of the damaged walls, eyes looking around blankly. As before, no one else was around. Sunlight strained to push through the haze still hanging over the city, but especially here, where the destruction seemed the worst.

A single tree still stood in the courtyard though its branches were blackened and all the leaves had scorched off it. Either Sarah or another shaper kept a steady breeze blowing, cooling them; otherwise, the heat still burning within the stone would be overwhelming.

"We need to hurry," Sarah said, watching Elle. "When you're gone..."

Tan looked over the Elle. "What happens when we're gone?"

Sarah shook her head. "My shaping might not hold. So you will move quickly."

Tan turned and looked at Sarah. She watched him, eyes intense.

"You will hold the nymid in your mind. Focus on them. They will help heal her."

Tan took a deep breath and nodded. If he could find the nymid. There was no guarantee he could find the place of convergence. The last time had been an accident, the nymid drawing him to them.

Sarah nodded curtly. "You must hold onto her."

Tan turned and grabbed onto Elle. He remembered the terror he felt traveling this way the only other time he had, and that had been with Amia.

Elle grabbed his arm. Her hand felt so small, but she squeezed tightly. Even ill, she nodded.

Pressure burst behind his ears.

A sudden gust of air swirled around and then lifted them.

"Hold the nymid in your mind!" Sarah called.

A tingling chill settled upon him, washing over his head.

As it did, Tan focused on how he'd called to the nymid, trying to visualize the place of convergence in his mind. He didn't know how Sarah's shaping worked, but he would do what she asked to help Elle.

At first, they went slowly, but the wind built steadily, rising like a cloud beneath them. Sarah nodded and the pressure burst, like a dam breaking, and they went soaring out of Ethea.

The view was like nothing Tan had ever experienced. Roine's shaping had carried them urgently, done out of necessity or else the lisincend would have attacked them. The control to this shaping amazed him.

There came a sensation of speed and movement as wind whipped past. Strangely, he felt safe, nothing like what he'd experienced before, almost as if the wind itself knew where it was taking him, blowing him like it would a leaf on a breeze.

Elle clung to him, gripping his arm in panic. With the wind swirling around him, he couldn't see her clearly, almost as if the wind funneled up and around him to prevent him from seeing her. Occasionally, she would grunt and grip his arm more tightly.

Tan listened for the connection to the nymid.

Nymid!

He quested for them, holding the image of the lake where he last saw them in his mind, but he couldn't reach them.

Instead, another image crept in, tints of orange and red, mixed with a throbbing in the back of his head.

He pushed the sense of the draasin away.

Elle shook in his arms, the tremor lasting painfully long moments.

Tan reached for the nymid again. He felt something in his mind and held onto it, latching tightly.

They whipped through the air, reaching a peak before starting back down.

Now they moved more quickly, picking up terrifying speed. Tan tensed, uncertain if Sarah's shaping had enough control to slow their landing or if they would crash into the ground. Had it not been for the nymid, the last time he'd traveled this way, he would have crashed.

As they dropped, a brief tingling washed over him and then was gone.

Tan didn't have time to wonder what it was, only enough for the brief worry over whether something went awry with Sarah's shaping, when smears of brown appeared below him, growing rapidly closer.

Elle roused and must have seen the same. She tensed, holding onto him tightly.

"Tan!" The wind swallowed her shout.

The ground loomed closer and closer. They did not slow.

Now they were close enough for Tan to see huge boulders and rocks rising up to meet them.

They were moving too fast to slow.

The ground became distinct.

If he did nothing, they would crash. Was this what Sarah had intended? And where was the lake, the valley, *anything* from the place of convergence?

Could he even do anything? Were he to summon some sort of shaping, they still might crash.

A panicked thought raced through his mind—what had he done in the archives?

He strained to remember the sensation, forcing it the way he would force the conversation with the draasin. But that had been using fire. Tan didn't know what he needed, but a fire shaping wouldn't save them.

He shifted his focus, thinking of how he'd called the nymid. Water would cushion their fall, though might not keep them from shattering bones throughout their bodies.

In his mind, he envisioned the stone shifting, dissolving into liquid that would catch them but not leave them maimed. Pressure built softly behind his ears. Tan didn't know if it was what he did or the residual effect of Sarah's shaping.

Another gust of air came at them, whistling up from below.

Tan kicked his feet, trying to keep from hitting the ground too fast.

When his feet struck, they sunk into the stone.

He slipped into a sense of warmth up to his chest. Then he took a breath and let it out. The sense of warmth pressed against him, making it difficult to take another.

Elle was shouting.

She still held his arm, gripping it tightly. Dust settled from the wind and he saw only the top of her head. Her shouting became muffled before dying off.

He pulled on her, but she didn't move. Whatever they sunk into was thick, like mud.

And, he realized, it probably *was* mud if his shaping worked.

He continued to sink, slowly dropping lower into the ground, as if being swallowed.

Let us OUT!

Tan sent it no differently than he would speak to the draasin.

Pressure burst in his ears.

And then he was squeezed.

It came as if the earth itself squeezed him, pushing him up and out of the muck.

When his arm came free, he pulled on Elle, trying to draw her up and out. She came slowly, drifting from the mud, but she came.

His chest freed and he leaned toward Elle and grabbed her, lifting her as much as he could. Her eyes were closed and her chest didn't move.

Tan jerked his legs free at the same time the ground pushed him all the way free. He fell to the side.

He lowered Elle to the ground and checked her for obvious injuries. There were none. Then he tipped her head to the side. Some of the thick mud had gotten into her mouth and started to harden. Tan pulled it free. It came out as a long, thick string.

She sucked in a deep breath.

He put an arm beneath her neck, cradling her to him. Elle shook for a moment, each breath becoming easier before she finally opened her eyes.

She blinked. Redness rimmed the whites of her eyes. A weak cough came from her chest. "I thought you didn't know how to shape," she said.

He laughed nervously. "Apparently I don't."

"Maybe you don't shape the stone into mud the next time?"

Tan laughed again. "I hope there isn't a next time. I don't think I want to travel like that again. The last time I did, I nearly drowned. If not for the nymid, I might have. And this time, I thought to help by trying to shape water. Instead, I think I shaped earth."

Elle pushed herself up and spit more of the mud from her mouth, her lips making a sour expression as she did. "Roine—Theondar—was right about you, wasn't he? You *are* able to shape all elements. You can be a warrior."

"I don't know what I am," he admitted.

"At least you're honest." She leaned forward, looking around. "Now, where are we?"

They weren't in Galen as intended. The were nowhere near the place of convergence and the nymid. And now… would Elle's illness overwhelm her before they could find help?

Tan stood and looked around. The bleak landscape was familiar. It took a moment for him to realize that it was because he'd seen something like it through his connection to the draasin. The air had a heavy sort of haze to it, much like the smoke they'd seen in Ethea, though this felt different. Heat radiated up from all around. The bright sun burned overhead, making them sweat in their thick jackets. It dripped from his forehead to run into his eyes, burning them.

There could be no doubt where they were. Now he only had to figure out where to go.

"This is Incendin."

Elle looked over at him and nodded. "I've been to the border a few times. Most from Doma do though it's not quite this bleak. At least along the border we see some life, even stunted as it might be. This… this is barren."

A sense of oppression radiated from the landscape. They could die here and no one would know. What happened? How had the shaping gone wrong?

"Is this where Sarah wanted you to bring me?" Elle asked.

Tan shook his head. "I was supposed to bring you to the nymid. She placed a shaping on me that would draw us to them."

Elle blinked. Already the color faded from her cheeks. How much longer before Sarah's shaping failed and the convulsions returned?

"Looks like you drew us to the draasin instead."

Tan blinked.

The draasin.

Had the draasin *drawn* him here the same way the nymid once pulled him to the place of convergence? But why? Did it want him to remove the shaping Amia placed on them, or could there be another reason? The last time Tan spoke to it, the fire elemental wanted Tan to find it.

And now he had.

But they were stranded in dangerous Incendin. Anything could be deadly here—and likely was.

He took a step away from Elle. The movement triggered something in a nearby plant and sharp barbs spat away from it. Tan jumped away before they struck his leg.

Apparently even the plants were deadly here.

Tan stretched out with earth sensing. They would need water. Perhaps he could find the nymid even here. And then he would find the draasin.

As far as he reached, he found no water nearby.

That meant no nymid. No healing for Elle.

He sensed something else looming large not too far from them. It resonated off the deep connection in his mind. The draasin was out there, somewhere. And it waited for him.

CHAPTER 21

An Offer of Help

THEY STARTED ACROSS THE BARREN ROCK, slowly weaving their way down the slope. A wide, open valley spread before them, a flat bottom near the center making it look like a river had once run through here. Elle moved slowly, wincing each time she touched the rock, and needed to stop often. So far, the tremors had not returned.

Tan didn't seem as affected by the heat as her. He didn't feel cool but wasn't as painfully uncomfortable as Elle appeared.

They avoided the plant life growing around them. Thorny bushes seemed to spring from the rocks themselves. A few stunted brush trees grew in the shade of larger rocks. Nothing else. After their first experience with the plant trying to kill them, Tan sensed each one, trying to gauge what the plants would do as they passed. Some, like the twisty, stick-like plant rising up between a pile of huge boulders, seemed benign. Others, like a low, brown clump of grass gave off a dark sense and Tan knew to avoid.

The sense of the draasin moved ever closer to them.

The sun rose steadily overhead. In Galen, Tan had known several phases of sunrise. There was the initial lightening, when the sun first crested the horizon. The air still carried with it a crispness and bite, regardless of the time of year. Then, when the sun peeked overtop the trees, it would stream down toward the forest floor. In Nor, that sunlight would slowly warm the town, burning off any fog that might have rolled in off the nearby streams. The sun wouldn't last for long before falling again behind the towering trees throughout the forest.

In Ethea, the sunlight had been different. Always warmer, Ethea was farther south and much flatter than most of Galen. Once the sun pierced the horizon, it began warming everything. Only the city buildings blocked the early morning light, and they did so poorly.

Here, the sun shone hot and bright. Somehow, it also seemed closer than in the kingdoms. As they made their way along the rocks, it continued climbing, rising both higher and closer at the same time.

Elle slowed. "I need to rest." Her voice came out in a harsh whisper and her cheeks were nearly white.

Tan nodded, and they took shelter behind a tall finger of rock. Everything around them looked much the same, but as they came down from the rocks, more and more of the stunted scrub plants grew. Tan sensed danger from most of them and didn't risk going too near.

"I think we're getting close," he said.

Elle nodded. She hadn't asked where he led them. She stared at the ground, her lids growing heavy as she did, and rocked slowly in place.

The walk drained her. And when she fell, beaten by the sun and heat and whatever shaping he had accidentally placed on her, he would have to carry her.

Would he have the strength he needed?

They seemed to be moving west. If that were right, they would eventually reach the kingdoms. There they would have to pass through the barrier, though they would have passed across it on their way to Incendin.

Tan leaned against the rock. The heat had finally caught up with him too, leaving him drained and tired. He could lay here, wait for the sun to fall into darkness…

A low howl erupted.

Tan tensed and looked around. He recognized the sound. Hounds.

When they got his scent, they would track him until they caught him.

What could he do? He was too tired to shape, too tired to go on, but if he didn't, they would both die here.

What other choice did he have?

He reached toward the sense at the back of his mind and listened for the draasin.

Draasin!

He sent the call with as much strength as he could generate, but after climbing along the rocks all morning, it wasn't much.

When there was no answer, he sent another call.

Draasin!

He hesitated before sending the next message. Showing weakness to the draasin was dangerous, but if he did nothing, they would either succumb to the heat or the hounds would find them.

Tan needs your help.

At first, there was nothing but silence.

And then, softly, like a great stretching of wings and claws, came the sense of the draasin. It crawled toward the front of his mind, the sense of claws digging painfully into his mind. Much like the first time he'd spoken to the draasin, he felt them painfully, nothing like the harsh, quiet presence he felt while in Ethea.

The draasin was close.

Little Warrior.

The thought came like a terrible burst of thunder and ripped through his mind.

Tan grabbed the sides of his head, squeezing, pushing with his palms as if to press the sounds of the draasin back and away. The voice echoed through his mind before fading.

You have come as required.

Tan shook his head, squeezing his eyes closed against the pain of the draasin's voice. If he couldn't push it back—if he couldn't get some control of the power behind the sending—he might not remain sane.

What had he done the last time he had been this close to the draasin?

Nothing. Amia had helped him then. It had been her shaping that kept the draasin from attacking them. But had her shaping protected his mind?

He pushed against the sense of the draasin, forcing it toward the back of his mind.

It slid away slowly, reluctantly, and with so much pain, it felt as if the creature's talons dug into his mind as it did. Tan continued to push, creating a separation in his mind until the draasin no longer threatened to overwhelm him.

Only then could he turn his attention to the creature.

You came to Incendin. He didn't want it to come out as an accusation, mostly wanting to get a sense of whether the draasin understood where they were. Such things didn't really matter to the draasin. But there was more to it for Tan.

After what Roine suspected, he needed to know if the draasin worked *with* Incendin.

We spent many years beneath the cold and ice. We sought the warmth and the sun.

193

This is the land of Twisted Fire.

The draasin seemed to grunt. As it did, it threatened to push a greater presence on him, pressing toward the front of his mind. *This is the land of the Mother. Twisted Fire cannot claim it.*

Tan glanced at Elle. She stood in place, rocking slowly.

Why did you summon me? He no longer doubted the draasin had summoned him, pulling him away from Sarah's shaping. Did they fear being hunted by Roine?

The draasin snorted. *You will hunt with me. It has been many years since a warrior joined the hunt.*

Tan blinked. *Others hunted with you?*

The draasin laughed again. *You think yourself the first to speak with us? Draasin have existed before nearly everything else and will exist long after everything is gone. Such is fire.*

Tan had a fleeting sense of time, almost like a flickering flame that rose brightly in his mind, starting as a tiny spark, quickly spreading and growing, consuming everything around it.

In response, he pushed an image of water and wind mixed with the hard earth he stood upon.

The draasin laughed. *Nearly everything. The others as well. Such is the will of the Mother.*

Tan thought of how the nymid worked to hold the draasin in the lake, freezing them in place. The shaping had been augmented by the other elementals, golud and ara serving alongside the nymid to restrain the draasin. How must it feel, spending nearly a thousand years in captivity, a thousand years spent freezing at the bottom of the lake in the place of convergence, held there by the nymid, golud, and ara?

Are you angry for what they did?

The draasin seemed to pause and consider before answering. Tan sensed a simmering rage coming from the draasin.

We… accepted the necessity. The others went willingly, but they remained for the same millennia.

You don't… Tan didn't quite know how to ask what he wanted. … *want revenge for what happened?*

Would revenge serve the Mother?

Tan suspected there was more to the answer, but couldn't tell what.

Elle crumpled to the ground.

The motion startled him and he reached for her, lifting her motionless form. Her eyes rolled back in her head. Dried sweat smeared across her face, mixing with dirt and remnants of the mud they'd landed in. At least she still breathed.

Tan looked toward the south, toward where he felt the draasin. He couldn't tell where they were any more directly than that.

I did not come to hunt.

Why come then, Little Warrior, if not to hunt?

Before he asked for help, he needed to know if the draasin were responsible for what happened in Ethea. He flashed an image of the attack in his mind. He showed fire burning through the city, the destruction taking place, and then, last of all, the fleeting image of what appeared to be one of the draasin soaring overhead.

Was this you?

The draasin was silent. It tried to claw its way to the front of Tan's mind, but he pushed back, holding it there, keeping it in place deep in his mind.

Was this you?

Tan repeated the question with more force.

The draasin seemed to stretch, attempting to pull away from him. Tan held on, refusing to let it disappear.

Answer this question!

There came a low rumble.

Not only in his head.

Tan looked up. A heavy-throated roar echoed around him. Massive wings beat at the sky, blotting out the sun. The draasin's long, sinewy body slipped through the air. Spikes rose from it like thorns. It twisted its head and golden eyes stared at Tan.

He stared back.

Feeling the draasin in his mind did not capture the enormity of the creature. He should feel afraid. Flying over him was a hunter unlike the world had seen in a thousand years. A predator capable of destroying him in a single snap of its enormous jaws. The last time he'd seen the draasin—really seen them, not like the shadowed image he had of it flying over the city—they had chased the lisincend, easily catching and swallowing one of the powerful creatures. Before that, he'd seen them crawl out of the ice after being trapped there for a thousand years.

In spite of that, Tan could not feel fear.

The draasin might destroy him, but flying as it did seemed more like posturing than any real threat. And then there was the shaping placed on it by Amia so long ago.

Tan reached across the connection. The shaping held.

The draasin laughed.

We may not hunt man. But if we are threatened…

Tan almost smiled at its clever solution.

I am no threat to the draasin.

Another burst of laughter, this time in sync with the beating of its massive wings. Hot, dry wind swirled each time it did, pounding at the air. *You confine the draasin. You seek to use the draasin. How is that no threat?*

Tan shook his head. *I seek only to understand.*

He stood, waiting for the draasin to decide. Either it would attack him or it would not. Nothing Tan could do would allow him to survive an attack. His survival was up to the Great Mother now.

And then the draasin settled to the ground.

Massive wings tilted slightly, letting it glide slowly down. As it landed, huge claws pinched the rock, piercing the stone. Steam rose from its nostrils as it snorted.

Why have you come?

The tone of the draasin had changed.

Was it you?

He had to know. If Roine was right—if the draasin attacked Ethea—nothing else mattered. Not him or Elle's illness.

The draasin's head tipped back and it looked down at Tan with its bright golden eyes. *That is draasin.*

Tan's heart sunk. Roine had been right. The draasin had attacked Ethea.

But that meant Amia's shaping no longer held. Why did it seem to him it did?

Why? Why attack the city? Why fight against the shaping?

The draasin lowered its head until it could look at Tan, meeting his eyes. *When you released us from the ice, there were but three draasin who remained. The youngest had lived only a few cycles.*

The youngest?

Tan thought of the smallest draasin that had pulled itself from the ice. The creature had still been massive.

Why would the youngest attack Ethea?

The draasin tipped its massive head. *The youngest would not. She had barely learned the art of the hunt. But Twisted Fire...* The draasin trailed off and snorted softly. *Twisted Fire captured the youngest. I do not know what happened.*

The lisincend captured one of the draasin—it might explain the attack—but how had they twisted her into following them?

There was much pain from the draasin, anguish over what happened with the youngest. If the lisincend—Twisted Fire—captured one of the great elementals, what would it do to it?

Could she be coerced into attacking?

Another snort that seemed so much like a sigh. *I would not have believed it possible for draasin to be controlled by another but the Daughter...*

A shaping of spirit, but how would Incendin have learned? How would they have a shaper capable of shaping the draasin?

Where is she now? Will she attack again?

She is elsewhere.

Tan had the distinct sense the draasin didn't share something with him.

Elle moaned softly and started to shake.

Tan lifted her and pulled her against his shoulder. She trembled violently. After a moment, the trembling eased.

She will not last long.

Tan looked up. The draasin had stepped nearer to him, moving silently across the stone. The creature's hot breath steamed toward him and he blinked.

You know what's wrong with her?

The draasin dipped its head. *A darkness burns in her.*

What had he done to her? What had his shaping done?

If the draasin could sense the darkness, could it undo it?

What is it?

I... do not know.

She said I shaped her. Can you undo it?

This is not your shaping, Little Warrior, and I can do nothing to save her.

Tan swallowed. Then Elle would die. He couldn't get her to safety quickly enough and had no way of healing her without the nymid.

This land is not appropriate for one such as her. She requires water.

An image of massive waves crashed through his mind. Within the waves was a face, driving the waves forward.

Tan nodded. *We came searching for the nymid.*

She is not of the nymid.

Tan frowned. *The udilm? I don't know where to find them.*

Tan wasn't even certain whether the udilm still existed.

The draasin snorted. A flash of fire burst from its nostrils.

Tan raised a hand to his face to shield himself, but the fire didn't burn him.

You speak to the nymid but you have not sought the udilm? The draasin seemed amused by the possibility.

Tan only nodded.

Then come. I will bring you to udilm.

You will bring me?

An image of him climbing atop the draasin flashed into his mind.

Tan took a slow breath. Speaking to one of the massive elementals was terrifying enough, now it wanted him to *ride* it?

What will you do? Why are you helping?

The draasin shook its head. *Not what I do. It is what Little Warrior must do.*

And what is that?

You must help save the youngest.

The draasin waited for Tan. It lowered its head, bringing its massive jaw close to the ground. Enormous teeth filled its mouth, and its golden eyes were nearly as large as Tan's head.

The decision should be easy. Go with the draasin and get help for Elle. But what would the draasin require of him if he went? How could he help find the youngest?

And if Tan were right, doing so meant rescuing the draasin from Incendin. He wasn't a shaper—not yet at least, and certainly not with any level of control; there was nothing he could do to save the youngest draasin.

Elle shook against him again, this time more violently.

The tremor lasted longer than the last time. As she shook, he held her, holding onto her head and neck so she didn't injure herself. When the shaking stopped, he pulled her back. Blood trickled down her mouth. Tan pried open her lips and saw she'd bitten her tongue. A deep gouge worked through it, oozing blood.

Another tremor started.

He held her close again. He had to do something to help her. If he did nothing—if he refused the draasin's offer—she would die.

You can find udilm quickly?

The draasin snorted. *Quickly enough, Little Warrior. Come.*

With a sigh, Tan stood and carried Elle toward the draasin. Heat rose from its spines. Tan held Elle away from the draasin, trying to protect her from its heat.

And then, grabbing onto one of the thick spines on its back, he climbed atop.

CHAPTER 22

Flight

THE DRAASIN'S HUGE WINGS beat against the air with rhythmic precision. Each flap of the thick wings sent the creature higher and launched it faster. Tan leaned against one of the thick, heated spines on its back, surprised the spine didn't burn him.

He clung to Elle. She slumped across his lap, cradled and protected from the wind by the spines and the arch of the draasin's neck. Tan worried most about the heat. Sitting atop the draasin felt like a furnace. Even taking a breath was difficult, his lungs practically screaming with the effort. What must it be like for Elle?

The draasin flew high into the sky. Streaks of brown streamed past below them. In a flash, they passed out of the desolate browns of Incendin and over lush green fields.

The speed was terrifying and intoxicating. Wind whistled and rushed past his ears. Pressure pushed against his head continually, like a steady shaping. He wondered if the draasin shaped as he did or if their power came from something else.

A dark shadow swooped in the distance before turning away. The other draasin.

Tan could not speak to the other draasin. Somehow, he had bonded only to this one. But could he? To save the youngest from Incendin, he might need to speak to the other draasin.

Why do I only speak to you?

The draasin arched its neck and one golden eye glanced back at him. Steam snorted from its nostrils. *You have not tried speaking to the others.*

Could I speak to them?

The draasin's eyes shifted, almost as if arching its brows. *It is possible.*

How am I to help if I can't speak to the youngest?

The draasin snorted in answer.

You don't know, do you?

The draasin swung its head around and glanced at Tan. Then it turned to face forward again. *We have been unable to save her.*

Tan felt the frustration the great elemental felt at admitting its failure.

Where does the other go?

She cannot help in this. She will wait.

There was more, but the draasin shielded it from Tan.

They flew onward. The wind turned cooler, though it still gusted off the heated back of the draasin, leaving a misting spray in the air. The cool mist settled on Elle. She twitched, but the tremors had eased since leaving Incendin. She did not awaken and her breathing came slowly.

What would happen if the draasin were gone?

The draasin seemed annoyed by the suggestion. *Draasin have been here since the first.*

If you disappeared, would another take your place?

For a moment, Tan wasn't sure the draasin would answer.

Fire is different than the others. The others battle for supremacy, but none can replace the draasin while we live.

Tan sensed he would get nothing more from him. *What's your name?*

The draasin snorted again but did not look back.

Tan repeated the question. *I would like to know what to call you.*

The draasin's massive tail swished behind it, sending them sliding toward the north. *Names are meaningless to the draasin.*

This time, Tan snorted. *You call me 'Little Warrior'. Names are not completely meaningless.*

The draasin are True Fire. We do not have need of names.

Yet you use them. What is yours?

The draasin snorted again, this time in annoyance. *I am called Asboel.*

The name resonated in Tan, triggering a memory. Somewhere, he had heard that name before.

Massive wings pulsed against the wind, driving them higher and higher into the sky. As they did, Tan realized why he recognized the name and had Amia to thank for it. It was a word derived from the ancient language, a word meaning ancient and fire and power and strength all mixed together. If not for the ancient language, he would have no word for this draasin's name.

But he had also seen the name *Asboel* before.

In the book about the draasin, it was one of the words that stood out, a word he hadn't recognized even after receiving Amia's gift that allowed him to understand the ancient language. Something had been written in that book about this draasin, if only he could remember what it was.

I am Tannen.

The draasin snorted again. Tan sensed it trying to use his name and failing.

You are Maelen.

Tan frowned, struggling to decipher the word, saying it a few times before making the translation.

The draasin helped, sending an image of a tiny barbed creature battling against the draasin. The barbed creature didn't back down before the draasin and used its barbs to pierce the soft places around the draasin's nose.

Tan laughed. *You may call me Maelen. How much longer, Asboel?*

Fire erupted from the draasin's nose. A spray of steam washed over him, somehow failing to burn the flesh from his face.

Tan looked down. Far beneath him was a vast expanse of blue. He didn't know when they had left the grassy plains to soar above the ocean, for there was little doubt in Tan's mind they flew above the ocean. From where they were, he saw no sign of land. *How will you find udilm?*

The draasin laughed softly. *Maelen must call udilm.*

Tan blinked. He would have to call the udilm. Only—he didn't know how.

Asboel stretched his wings wide and tipped them, letting them glide. They slowly started to descend, swirling in a steady circle as the draasin took them closer and closer to the water.

Tan had no idea how he would call the udilm. He'd never spoken to them—had only really spoken to the nymid and the draasin—but Asboel seemed convinced he should be able to do so.

I don't know how—

Elle started shaking, more violently than before.

Tan grabbed her, pulling her against his chest. The tremor wracking her this time shook her nearly so hard as to throw her off the back of the draasin. Tan held her head, hoping to keep her from biting her tongue as she convulsed.

Her flame grows weak, Little Warrior. You must summon udilm.

Tan looked at the draasin, wishing he could explain himself better. How to explain ignorance to a creature that seemed to know everything? How to explain feeling weak and helpless? In time, Tan might have the capacity to become a shaper, but he did not have the knowledge or experience necessary, especially not now that Elle needed him.

I have never spoken to udilm. I do not know how.

The draasin chuckled. This time, the sound did not come in Tan's head, but as a deep rumbling from the back of the draasin's throat. He felt it through the thick spines of the draasin's back as the sound slowly rolled through its body.

You must learn to embrace your strength, Maelen. There is much fire within you or else I would never have heard you.

What does that mean?

The other warriors were not quite so ignorant.

I am not a warrior.

The draasin chuckled again. *Perhaps not by your standards. You fear the unknown but should not. The Mother has a purpose.*

Tan tried to think of what he knew of speaking to water. How had he connected to the nymid, and was there anything he could do that would let him talk to udilm?

He knew of only one way.

Elle might not survive. *He* might not survive.

But she would certainly die if he did nothing.

Do not go far, he instructed Asboel.

The draasin snorted. *You do not command the draasin.*

Tan listened for what else might come through the connection. When he was convinced the draasin was not angry, he turned and dove from its back.

Wind swirled around him as he fell, holding Elle in his arms. He imagined tiny, translucent faces appearing in the wind, almost grinning at him as he dropped from the draasin toward the shimmering water below.

The fall took only seconds, but in that time, the temperature dropped significantly.

And then they plunged into icy water.

The sudden cold sucked all the air out of his lungs. Tan kicked, trying to stay near the surface, but huge rolling waves kept threatening to pull him back under.

Another wave crested over his head.

Tan glanced up. Asboel circled, bright golden eyes staring down at him. Steam rose from his nostrils, and his long, barbed tail swished behind him, swinging in time with the slow beating of his wings keeping him hovering in place.

The wave hit, blocking everything else from view.

Elle slipped from his grip.

Tan kicked, trying to grab her but missing.

The wave tossed him. He had a moment where his head was above water and he sucked in a deep breath of air and then the wave crashed down on him once more. The weight of the water forced him down, deeper and deeper into the cold.

With nothing but blackness all around him, he couldn't find Elle.

What had he been thinking to jump into the water? Even in the lake at the place of convergence, the water had nearly drowned him.

What made him think he would survive in the ocean? And with Elle?

Tan felt something near his leg and reached for it, praying to the Great Mother it was Elle. When his hand reached where he thought he felt something, whatever he'd felt was gone.

With lungs burning, he tried kicking back to the surface but couldn't. The water resisted him, pulling him deeper.

Panic washed through him.

He kicked, flailing against the water.

Draasin! Silence answered his call. *Asboel!*

The connection felt faint, weaker than it had ever felt while in Ethea.

Could the water obstruct him from connecting to the draasin? Even were he able to communicate with the draasin, what could he do? Could he plunge into the water and save him?

Was there anything *he* could do?

Water swirled around him, streams of black and blue and shimmery. The pain in his chest became unbearable, but if he took a breath, he would suck in nothing but water.

Survival overwhelmed any attempt to shape.

And then he couldn't kick any longer.

The pressure in his chest—the burning pain—overwhelmed him.

Breath whispered from him, sucked away by the swirling current.

And then he saw light.

CHAPTER 23

Restored

HE HAD NO WORDS for the flickering lights around him. Translucent blues and greens and pinks blended together, sparkling in their intensity. Shimmery shapes moved around him in swirls, looping like cresting waves. Tan had the sense of immense power.

The udilm.

With the realization, he reached out.

Help me.

He sent the request with the same intensity he'd used when speaking to the nymid. There, the pale green movement had swum through the water, slipping and sliding like something small and alive. What he sensed here was massive, larger even than the draasin.

Tan's vision began to fade. The colors drifted away.

Udilm!

He sent the request with more urgency, tinged with the same edge he used with the draasin. But there was a difference this time, and he sent the request like a surging wave.

Who disturbs?

The thought came slow and steady, pressing into his mind until it crested to the front.

Tannen Minden. He used his full name, though did not know if it mattered to the elementals. *A friend of mine suffers and needs your help.*

The water parted slowly and Elle drifted closer to him.

Arms splayed apart, hanging off to her sides, her head lolled back on her neck. Her mouth hung open and her eyes stared blindly.

Elle was gone.

But the water elemental could save her as the nymid had saved him.

Please. She is a child of water.

The water swirled, sliding over her slowly, deliberately, before withdrawing. Tan had the sensation of a wave rolling against the shore.

Darkness has touched her.

Twisted Fire. A shaping Asboel did not recognize.

The water surged more urgently at the mention of his name. *You speak to the draasin?*

Yes.

The wave receded, pulling away from him and leaving him floating.

He didn't open his mouth or attempt to breathe. Like the last time he'd been beneath the water—when rescued by the nymid—he'd not had the need to breathe underwater. Whatever shaping they did kept him alive in spite of that.

Could they—and would they—do the same for Elle?

Water rushed back toward him, slamming around him. Tan did not fight. Nothing he could do would matter anyway, not against the onslaught from the udilm.

You did not fear coming.

Like the others, the thought built slowly until filling his head.

I knew fear.

But still you came.

I know the power of water. I have spoken to the nymid.

Water receded again, this time for much longer than before.

He was left staring at Elle, watching her pale face with the water streaming around, her hair hanging limply around her head and her long dress swirling around her. Tan touched her hand and it felt cold. Could even the udilm do anything to save her now?

Then water crashed against him.

Tan held tightly to Elle's hand.

He Who is Tan.

Tan smiled. As the draasin had a name for him, so did the nymid.

You speak to the nymid?

A low rumbling of water swirled around him. *All is connected, He Who is Tan.*

Can you help her?

The udilm washed over Elle, separating him from her. Colors swirled around her, infusing her with the same translucent light he saw elsewhere around him. *You speak truly, He Who is Tan. She is a child of water. She will be restored.*

And with that, Elle's eyes flickered.

Steam rose from her body, pressing out through her mouth and ears, as if the udilm pressed out a shaping that burned through her. Arms and legs twitched, but differently than before, finally moving slowly through the water, swimming in place.

A smile crossed her face.

Elle?

You found them.

Her voice echoed loudly in his head, more loudly than ever before.
Not me. The draasin.

He shaped a vision in his mind of them atop Asboel, rising high above the clouds.

I rode a draasin?

Tan laughed and nodded.

The smile spread across her face and she looked upward, as if to see through the water into the sky. *Thank you.*

He heard the thanks radiate all around, directed not only at him, but at the udilm as well.

Water swelled over them, swirling around her.

What now? Tan asked.

She may stay, the udilm answered. *She has questions. We will see her returned in time.*

And me?

You committed to the Eldest.

With the comment, water surged, sending Tan up in a rush.

The change in pressure built around him and water slid from him. He streaked up through the water, cresting from the peak of a wave and flying higher.

His lungs burned. This time, he remembered to take a breath.

And then heated mist pressed upon him.

He looked up to see Asboel swooping from the sky, diving beneath him and twisting until Tan landed on his back, nestled between a pair of thick, hot spikes.

The draasin pulled up from the dive, streaking back into the sky, powerful wings beating the air. Tan leaned back against the draasin's spikes and tried sending a message to Elle but felt nothing in return. The water obscured the connection.

She lives.

Tan looked up to see Asboel watching him, his head tipped in such a way so that one enormous eye could see him. He blinked and then turned back to watch where he flew.

She lives. Udilm healed her.

The draasin snorted. *You sound surprised, Maelen.*

How is it I can speak to both draasin and udilm?

Asboel snorted. *You ask the wrong question.*

Tan shook his head. Speaking this way tired him. He had gotten much more practice than when he first learned to do it, but it still tired him. Amia suspected it a form of shaping, though Tan could not understand how that could be. He had no control over shaping, not like he did with speaking to the elementals, though he had no idea *how* he managed to speak to them.

What is the right question? Can I speak to golud and ara?

I cannot say.

The udilm called you the Eldest.

Asboel snorted, seeming amused. *Perhaps now I am.*

You were not always?

You have much to learn, Maelen.

Asboel fell silent and Tan closed his eyes, letting the wind blow past him. His heart fluttered from the terrifying speed, but there was an exhilarating sense of freedom found soaring through the air that he'd never experienced.

He didn't know where the draasin carried him, though now that Elle was better, he wasn't sure it mattered. They had a task for him, but he still had no idea how to accomplish what was asked. How could he reach the youngest? And if he did, how would he be able to help?

How would Twisted Fire coerce her?

He asked the question without really meaning to do so, but as he did, he thought he knew.

Had Amia not shaped the draasin? Had she not coerced them?

The shaping of the Daughter, Tan began, feeling along the connection he had to Asboel, *does it hurt?*

The draasin snorted a burst of fire. Steam rose around his face, blowing over Tan but not burning.

It is... restrictive.

Would you hunt man if it were not in place?

Tan couldn't tell. From his conversation with the draasin, it seemed too intelligent to risk attacking shapers, but Roine spoke of warriors hunting the draasin out of fear. Would the draasin retaliate?

The draasin did not fully answer. *We hunt to eat.*

Tan sighed. If Amia could shape the draasin to prevent them from attacking man, could another spirit shaper do the same? Could that be what happened to the youngest of the draasin?

Who, other than the Aeta, could shape spirit?

He could come up with only one answer. The archivists.

But if she had been shaped, what could Tan do? Even were he able to communicate to the young draasin—and nothing he'd seen told him that would be possible, especially as he hadn't spoken to any other draasin but Asboel—would there be anything he could do to remove a shaping?

No, but there was someone who could.

If only he could find her.

CHAPTER 24

Finding the Aeta

ASBOEL CIRCLED HIGH OVERHEAD, spiraling above the kingdoms.

Tan's skin tingled when they crossed back over the barrier. He recognized it this time as they did, the sense like plunging into a cold bath, not nearly as uncomfortable as diving into the ocean had been. Mountains rose around him and he recognized them as well, leaving him feeling a hint of longing for his home as they passed over Galen. If only he could return home, trail through the mountains as he once had done, carefree except for whatever chores his mother asked from him.

But he had no home, not any longer. Even if he did, hadn't he seen too much to return to such a simple lifestyle? Could he really even go back to that time, knowing what he did? He thought of what he had been through—learning of the nymid and the draasin, of meeting Amia and learning of the artifact—and realized he could not. Nor may have been his home, but even were it still around, he had outgrown it.

And with that realization, he understood why his parents had returned to Nor in the first place. They were shapers who served the kingdoms. If they served as a part of the barrier—if they kept the kingdoms safe in any way—wouldn't he have done the same? And his father… he'd answered the king's call, gone to protect the kingdoms from Incendin. As an earth shaper, he would have known better than most what he risked were he not to go.

Tan felt foolish for the anger he'd felt for so long. Anger at the king for sending his father off to war with Incendin. Anger with his mother for trying to coax him into going to Ethea to study at the university. And anger at Incendin for destroying his home and everyone he'd known. Strange how it took Incendin attacking to set him free to learn what he might be capable of.

He sighed, sensing for Amia as they flew.

The connection to her was there, but faint. At this distance, he couldn't speak to her, regardless of how hard he tried. It felt much like when he tried speaking to the draasin while in the water or when he tried speaking to Elle once he was back atop Asboel.

Finding Amia was the only way he knew to try and help the draasin.

Asboel continued to circle. They moved out of Galen and across the center of the kingdoms. Somewhere down below would be Ethea. Asboel could tell his difficulty and circled back to the north, moving away from Ethea.

She was still somewhere in the kingdoms, that much he felt to be true.

Tan drifted as they flew. The effort of trying to find Amia drained him nearly as much as speaking to the udilm. And once he found Amia, the real work would begin. They would have to find the youngest of the draasin, learn what Incendin wanted with the elemental, and then try to undo whatever shaping they had worked upon her.

But it all depended on finding Amia.

As he drifted, the connection grew.

It started quietly and then built, slowly rising in his mind, flowing like the sense of the udilm. Tan's eyes flicked open and he looked down. Where would the Aeta have traveled?

Beneath them, the landscape had changed from lush grass back to mountainous peaks and thick forest. Asboel took him back to Galen.

We have passed this way once.

The great elemental snorted and continued onward.

As he did, Tan realized the draasin used the connection within his mind to track Amia, somehow pulling along it to search for her. He dropped, tipping his wings toward the ground so they angled downward, diving toward the treetops. Galen, but no part of Galen he knew.

Asboel must have sensed something through Tan telling him where to find Amia, but why would the Aeta come to Galen... and why would Amia have returned here? After what she'd been through, Tan wouldn't expect her to willingly venture so close to Incendin.

It seemed unlikely, but he couldn't deny the strengthening connection.

He sat upright, one hand gripping a heated spike, the other pressed behind him as he leaned down and over to peer beneath Asboel. He saw no sign of an Aeta caravan, though he might not through the trees of the forest.

Amia!

Tan pressed out with as much strength as he could muster.

Asboel snorted.

Had he heard?

After struggling to connect to the udilm, he had realized that speaking to the draasin was different than speaking to the nymid. And speaking to nymid was different than to udilm, though they were both elementals of water. He didn't know how he spoke to Amia, though he thought the shaped connection made it possible. But how had he spoken to Elle?

Amia!

He repeated her name, pushing a sense of him and the draasin through the connection. It faltered at the back of his mind, a flickering presence he could almost reach.

The sense grew stronger.

Tan grabbed onto it, pushing himself into it as he called for Amia.

And then, faintly, he heard a reply.

Tan?

He sensed concern and, strangely, relief.

Where are you?

Overhead.

There was confusion and then a sense of agitation. *You shouldn't come for me. Tell Roine to return you to Ethea. The Aeta... it's not safe here.*

Not safe?

I'm not with Roine.

Then how... NO!

Tan sat upright on Asboel. The word had come through like a command, a snap of a shaping. It burst in his ears, piercing through his mind before washing over him and fading, disappearing into nothing.

Amia had tried to shape him. And failed.

Tan shifted, looking to Asboel. *Can you find them?*

The draasin swung his head. *I see movement. Many small carriages.*

Tan saw as if through Asboel's eyes. The image looked twisted and blurred, tinged with reds and oranges his eyes would never see, but the wagons were Aeta wagons. They were stopped, spread out in a circle

217

around an open area visible through the trees. Asboel saw the wagons with incredible detail, enough so that Tan could make out the Aeta standing alongside the wagons, but not enough for him to see Amia.

But why had she tried shaping him? Why hadn't she wanted him to come?

Something is wrong.

Asboel snorted. *You finally sense that, do you, Little Warrior?*

What is it?

There was another spurt of flame from Asboel's nostrils and a sound much like a frustrated sigh. *It is like Twisted Fire but different.*

The lisincend are here?

More than simply Twisted Fire.

What else?

Feel for yourself, Maelen. There is fire nearby. I feel it burning, powerful and bright. But it is dark. Twisted. I have only sensed its like one other time.

He could not sense the lisincend, but he did not have the same sensitivity to fire as Asboel. But if the lisincend were here, and if what Asboel suspected was true, they would find the youngest of the draasin.

Which meant Amia and the Aeta were in danger.

The lisincend are near!

Tan sent the message to Amia with urgency and fear. If she didn't know about the lisincend, then she needed to know. And if she did and thought to protect him, he would let her know that he did not fear them.

You should not have come.

The voice that came was not Amia.

It sounded harsh and dark and rough with violent anger.

Asboel must have heard it too. He banked, turning to the side, flapping his massive wings in the wind.

As he did, Tan realized why.

Flames lanced toward Asboel, striking him in the stomach and disappearing.

Fire did not hurt the draasin, but a deep rumbling roar erupted from its mouth.

Another finger of flame struck at him and then another. Each pierced his stomach and faded, none reaching Tan.

Asboel twisted, rolling in the air, flicking his massive tail.

As he did, Tan saw what attacked.

A line of shapers stood atop a nearby peak. One faced Asboel with hands outstretched. Fire arced from his hands toward the draasin.

Next to the fire shaper were two others. They were smaller, thin, and reminded Tan of his—

They are wind shapers!

Asboel grunted. With a flick of his tail, he shot up into the sky, wings beating quickly as he searched for altitude.

Gusts of wind swirled, throwing them from side to side. Tan clung to the spike rising from Asboel's back, holding tightly as the draasin spun in the sky, wings and tail struggling to regain control in the wind.

Flames shot from his mouth.

For a moment, they steadied.

The sky darkened suddenly. Thunder rumbled across the sky. Rain sleeted down, piercing his flesh.

Asboel roared.

There were too many shapers.

With a dawning horror, he realized it might not be Incendin attacking the draasin. This might be the kingdom's shapers. Which meant Roine was here. That was why Amia had wanted Roine to take him away, but why? What would she have feared?

Asboel?

The draasin flipped, straining against the wind and rain. His tail snapped behind him, attempting to keep them steady, but the overwhelming power of the wind and rain was too much.

Asboel began to lose altitude.

If they reached the ground, Tan suspected the earth shapers would be next. After what he'd seen of how the archives withstood the flames in Ethea, he didn't want to risk earth shapers reaching Asboel.

But what could he do?

He sensed Asboel's frustration. Mixed with it was a deeper emotion. Panic.

Asboel did not want to be captured again. The time spent trapped within the ice made him all too aware of what might happen were he recaptured.

Tan closed his eyes and let out a steady breath. If he could only control the wind… shape it as Roine thought he'd shaped it once before…

Pressure built behind his ears, rising steadily. As it did, Tan pushed out a request, a thought shaped much like how he spoke to the draasin and udilm, asking for the wind to calm.

The pressure eased.

The wind died suddenly, as if the air held its breath.

Asboel roared furiously. In the moment the wind stopped, he pounded at the air, driving them into the sky, pushing against the thunder and rain.

Tan tried another shaping, this time asking for the skies to clear.

The familiar pressure built in his head, popping as it released. The rain slowed to a trickle. Dark clouds split to the side, giving a brief glimpse of the sun.

In that moment, Tan thought they might succeed, that whatever weak skill he might have at shaping might be enough. And for that moment, he felt pleased.

And then something struck with terrible force and they fell from the sky.

CHAPTER 25

A Fall and a Surprise

ASBOEL CLAWED AS THEY SPIRALED toward the ground. His massive head dipped and twisted, rotating so the thick spines on his back pointed toward whatever attacked. The clouds thickened again, turning the sky black. Rain pelted them with thousands of tiny needles. Tan cowered between the spines on Asboel's back but still felt exposed.

The great elemental turned, twisting his head. As he did, Tan caught sight of what attacked them.

The youngest.

She was larger than he remembered. Her eyes glittered a hazy green. Teeth snapped at Asboel's head. Claws raked his sides, severing a few of his spines, barely missing Tan as they did. Spines like those on Asboel's back steamed where the rain struck, creating mist around her.

In spite of the ferocity of her attack, Asboel did not fight back.

Why don't you fight?

Tan pressed the thought at Asboel as they spiraled toward the ground. Trees reached for them, massive trunks stabbing at the sky like spikes visible through a growing layer of fog.

Asboel responded by pressing an image into Tan's mind.

He saw rocks not unlike those they had found in Incendin. He had a sense of the hot sun beating down. A trio of eggs nestled atop the stones. A draasin curled around them, long tail lashed protectively. One of the eggs cracked and a long snout pressed out.

The youngest. *His* youngest.

Asboel could not harm his child.

What of the others?

Asboel snorted and fire leaped from his mouth. *The Mother took the others. She is all that remains.*

And Tan understood why Asboel would not attack.

This was the reason Asboel had brought him here, the reason the draasin worked with him, expecting that Tan could do something to save the youngest, but without Amia, there wasn't anything he could do.

Was there?

Hadn't he heard another voice in his head? Had the youngest spoken to him?

Tan focused on the sense of the draasin. He felt the vague sense of something else, dark and angry. How to know if it was the youngest?

He reached for her, pulling through the connection as he had with Asboel. *Please...*

The attack intensified. Had she heard him?

Claws raked toward his face, nearly striking him and throwing him from Asboel's back.

Tan pushed harder, straining through the connection she had created.

Stop!

He sent the command with all the energy he could summon. Pain and pressure snapped behind his ears, splitting through his head. His vision blurred for a moment before clearing.

The youngest dropped away.

And then Asboel grunted and plunged toward the ground.

Tan gripped the spines on Asboel's back. His legs flew off the draasin, floating in the air as they fell. The treetops raced toward them. Another moment and Asboel would crash into the trees, carrying Tan with him.

The draasin might survive, but Tan had no expectation of surviving a fall like that.

Asboel!

The draasin grunted.

What is it? Tan asked.

I cannot move.

Fly! Tan demanded. Pain exploded in his head.

Asboel roared. Flames shot from his mouth, streaking toward the trees. Wings beat at the sky. His long, barbed tail snapped from side to side.

And then they climbed back into the sky.

Tan settled back into place atop the draasin. *What happened?*

Asboel turned and looked back at Tan. His golden eyes blinked slowly. *You happened, Maelen.*

Tan frowned. *I don't understand.*

You commanded stop and I could no longer fly.

Tan blinked slowly. *I didn't command anything. I tried to get the youngest to stop attacking you. I couldn't think of anything else to do.*

You placed, the draasin paused and Tan had the sense of him searching *through* Tan for the right word, *a shaping.*

224

What kind of shaping would command the draasin to fall from the sky? Tan could think of only one.

A spirit shaping might work, but only from a powerful spirit shaper. He couldn't perform a spirit shaping, but he knew someone with strength enough to shape the draasin.

But how would Amia have shaped them?

Where is the youngest now?

She has fallen.

Tan's breath caught. *Fallen?*

The draasin snorted, the sound rumbling through it. *She lives but does not move.*

Whatever else happened, at least the youngest had not been hurt, at least not badly. Tan would take solace in the knowledge.

What now?

Asboel snorted. *Now you free her.*

Tan shook his head. Without Amia, what Asboel wanted was beyond his ability. *I must find the Daughter.*

Asboel snorted again. *She has found us.*

With that, he dove toward the ground, this time with more control. His wings folded enough to settle them between a pair of massive pine trees rising atop a crest. As they landed, Tan jumped from Asboel's back, happy to be on the ground again.

Tan stood among the trees and inhaled deeply, smelling the crisp scent of the forest all around him. A steady breeze blew through the trees, playing at his hair and swirling around his shirt. Strange that he should return to Galen in such a way.

He looked around. Below him, a broad valley stretched in the distance. A long lake settled in the middle, blue water tinged with a hint of green. On the distant mountains, the peaks were covered with snow.

225

Tan had been here before.

This was the place of convergence.

Did you know we returned?

Asboel turned and looked at him. *This is a place of the Mother. There are but a few like it. How would I not know?*

What did it mean that they returned here? Had Amia led the Aeta to this place or had they come accidentally? When he found her, he would have so many questions.

But first, they needed to find the youngest.

Shapers attacked you.

Asboel sniffed. *They tried.*

Tan suppressed a laugh. Asboel was too proud to admit to the fear he felt during the attack. Tan recognized the terror at the possibility of recapture, the way he'd fought against it with everything in his being. Had Tan not been there, had he not somehow managed his shapings, Asboel might have fallen.

They will search for her as well.

Not only the shapers, but Incendin. Twisted Fire.

Tan had nearly died that last time he'd been here with the lisincend. Had it not been for the nymid and the draasin, he would have. And the artifact would have fallen into the hands of Lacertin. Tan didn't know what Lacertin intended to do with the artifact, or how he would use it against the kingdoms.

They needed to find the draasin first. And Tan needed Amia's help.

He crouched, looking through the trees toward the lake as he waited for a response. Asboel squatted on his haunches, wings folded around him. Somehow, he reminded Tan of the lisincend and Fur in particular, especially the way his head and eyes flickered all around, his wide nostrils flaring as he scented the air. Steam rose from his nose as he breathed.

Amia still had not answered.

Tan felt her, though, and knew she was near.

He waited.

He felt movement from the connection to Amia, but her silence told him something must be wrong. When they found her, he would learn what it was.

Your people will soon come for us.

Tan looked over at Asboel. His golden eyes blinked slowly and his tail twisted around one of the trees. *My people would not attack you.*

He sent the thought with more irritation than intended, but how could he feel anything else? Roine knew how the draasin had saved them from the lisincend, yet it seemed he still chose to attack. And without he draasin, the king wouldn't have the artifact that so many had been lost trying to reach. Whatever else, they were *not* his people.

Asboel snorted. *And the Daughter?*

Tan shook his head. He didn't know what would happen when he found Amia.

He didn't have to wait long.

The soft sound of tinkling bells made their way through the forest.

Tan looked down toward the narrow path running through the trees. Only the topmost part of the wagons was visible. They were brightly painted, some in yellows and others in reds. Flashes of other colors were visible through the forest: fleeting glimpses of the wagon drivers or other Aeta. He heard no voices or laughter, nothing like he expected to hear from a joyful people like the Aeta.

Still, there came the sense of Amia, but he heard nothing to tell him she knew he was here.

Careful, Maelen.

Tan turned and looked at Asboel. *What is it?*

He sniffed at the air softly. *Do you not sense it?*

Tan shook his head.

Fire. Powerful.

The youngest?

If she had awoken after her fall, they risked another attack. Tan didn't know what he had done the last time but didn't think he would be able to replicate it, not enough to save both of them again.

And if she attacked, the Aeta were in danger. The youngest would probably not even realize if she destroyed a wagon full of Aeta. Amia had already lived through that once before. Tan would do what he could to protect her from it again.

Not the youngest.

Tan stared toward the Aeta wagons. *Twisted Fire?*

But he didn't think it likely. A buildup of heat marked the lisincend presence. When they had come to Galen before, the forest had become unseasonably hot and dry, nothing like the cool breeze blowing through now.

But if not the lisincend, then what did Asboel sense?

Tan crouched behind a tree as the wagons wound below them. *Watch over me,* he sent to Asboel.

You think to command me again?

Tan shook his head. *Not command, but we work together.*

Asboel snorted. A sense of amusement came through the connection. *I will watch.*

Tan nodded and turned back toward the Aeta wagons. Time spent in the forests around Nor gave him skill moving stealthily through the trees. Earth sensing ability allowed him to recognize when he disturbed the sense of calm through the forest. Tan used both as he made his way down the slope, working carefully so as not to disturb loose soil. He stepped lightly, avoiding obvious branches and letting his feet settle before moving onward. Each step carried him closer to the Aeta. And with each step, a sense of dread grew within him.

At first, he couldn't place what he felt.

His skin prickled as if dry and tight. His ears popped, though he didn't know whether that came from a change in altitude or a shaping. A nagging, raw sense irritated him at the back of his mind. And the wind gusted strongly.

As he reached a slight overhang where rock jutted out, he crawled atop it, clinging to the surface as he stared toward the wagons. What bothered him about the Aeta here? Why did Amia's lack of communication worry him so much?

A small shape emerged from one of the wagons and looked around the forest. Tan recognized the shape and almost gasped.

He had seen her before, though the last time had been deep within the archives. He had only caught a glimpse of her then, but it had been enough, burning a memory of her into his mind. And he understood the fire Asboel sensed. She had nearly captured him once before.

An Incendin fire shaper traveled with the Aeta.

CHAPTER 26

Shaping and a Friend

T AN BACKED OFF THE ROCK AND CROUCHED among the trees, thinking about what he knew.

The Aeta traveled toward the place of convergence with Amia. He could not reach Amia, but sensed something was wrong. An Incendin fire shaper rode openly with the Aeta. And the draasin twisted by either a spirit shaper or Incendin lay somewhere in the forest.

And then there was Roine and the other shapers. They were here as well. Had they chased the draasin here or had they come for another reason?

It couldn't all be a coincidence.

But why?

What would bring both Roine and Incendin back to this place?

He could think of only one thing that would.

Tan needed to find the youngest and do what he could to break whatever had happened to her. To do that, he needed Amia, but if she was here with Incendin, he feared her trapped or injured. Anything he did would draw the attention of the Incendin shaper. And then Roine and his shapers would move in, determined to attack the draasin.

There were too many parts for what they needed to be successful.

He made his way back up the slope toward Asboel. As he neared the draasin, there was a heavy pulsing in his ears. A shaping built, and it was close.

Tan moved quickly, running up the slope as quietly as he could.

Shapers are near!

He sent the warning as quietly as he could, directing it with as much skill as he had.

Tan reached the pines where Asboel had been.

The clearing was empty.

He felt a pulse in his mind—nothing more—and looked up. Asboel rested in the upper branches of the pine tree, clinging to it with his massive claws, his wings still folded around his body. Enormous nostrils flared wide, spreading out and diffusing the steam that billowed out.

The pressure of the shaping built behind his ears. The shapers were near.

Were they kingdom shapers or Incendin?

Tan focused, holding his breath as he did. *Hold on.* He sent a request to the wind as he let out a breath.

The pressure eased with a pop.

Wind suddenly gusted, tearing through the trees.

Someone nearby shouted. Pressure built again. Thunder rumbled. The ground shifted beneath his feet. Tan pushed out a request for it to flatten. He steadied himself before asking the ground to push out in a rolling wave, building it within his mind similarly to how he spoke to the udilm. At the same time, he shifted his focus, asking the trees and the earth to obscure Asboel.

The ground rolled out and away, fading into the forest with a rumble.

"Lacertin!"

The shouted name pierced the wind, which then settled, dying slowly down as if it had never been whipping around him.

The shapings he had attempted failed.

Tan stood in the middle of loose needles and branches. He tried pushing on the wind again, but it didn't answer, not as it had before. And the ground, now solid, would not respond.

How could he think to go against fully trained shapers? He barely knew what he was doing. His only skill was the ability to speak to the elementals. That didn't translate to strength or skill in shaping.

"Not Lacertin!" Tan shouted.

Thunder cracked again and Tan's ears snapped with it, bursting with a sudden explosion. A streak of lightning shot from the sky, blinding him. When his vision cleared, Roine stood before him. He held his sword in hand, runes catching the light of the forest and casting strange shadows.

Roine waved his hand and the wind died completely. The air fell still and silent. He looked at Tan with a hard glare, anger clear in his eyes.

"Tannen. Why have you come here?"

Tan flicked his gaze around the small clearing. How many shapers had Roine brought with him? Enough to capture or kill Asboel? Given how difficult a time the draasin had staying in the air with the shapers focusing on him, it might be enough.

But only if Asboel was allowed to attack; doing so would confirm everything Roine feared from the draasin.

"I won't let you destroy them, Theondar." Calling him Roine when he stood in the place of convergence, determined to destroy the draasin, felt wrong.

His eyes narrowed. "We have been through this. You saw what they did in Ethea. The world is dangerous enough without the draasin free."

"It was not the draasin in Ethea," Tan said.

Roine snorted. "Not the draasin? I saw the creature with my eyes, Tannen! I chased it from the city. Do not think I can't tell the draasin."

Tan shook his head. Movement to either side told him there were shapers there, but the change was subtle and masked somehow. He felt a void in his ability to sense the forest and suspected the earth shaper responsible for that. Could Roine have brought Master Ferran?

But it was the Cloud Warrior standing before him he should fear. If Roine decided to attack Asboel, there was nothing Tan could do to stop the draasin from fighting back. And that would only weaken the kingdoms more than they already were.

"How many draasin did we free?"

Roine blinked and frowned at him. "What? You know how many we freed."

Tan nodded. "Tell me, then. How many?"

Roine looked around the clearing. Tan felt pressure build in his ears: Roine sensed for Asboel. Probably the earth senser did as well. Could the shaping Tan worked around the tree hold them off long enough to convince him?

"There were three."

Tan nodded. "Three. And how many did you follow here?"

Roine fixed him with a glare. "What are you getting at?"

"Only that you have followed one of the draasin—the youngest at that. Do you know where the other two draasin can be found?"

Roine's eyes narrowed. "Do you?"

Tan nodded.

Roine took a step toward him. That small step carried with it the subtle hint of a threat.

This was about more than the draasin, but what else? What had he missed?

Tan raised his hand and took a slow breath, letting it out with a request to the ground. The earth rumbled softly in response. "Don't."

The shaping served a dual purpose, not the least of which was drawing the attention of the earth shapers. They turned and quickly settled the rumbling.

Roine shook his head slightly. "You have learned to shape."

"I have learned to ask," he answered. "Which is why I know Incendin is responsible for the attack on Ethea. The tool may have been the draasin, but not the intent."

"Tannen…"

Tan shook his head. "No. The draasin were trapped for too long. And now they are free. I must live with the repercussions, but you need to know the draasin did not attack Ethea."

"And I know I'm as much at fault in releasing the draasin," Roine said. He paused, letting his words sink in fully. "Incendin would not be able to reach Ethea, Tan. You know the barrier—"

"I know the barrier could not hold the lisincend. All of Nor learned that lesson."

"Tan—"

"No, Theondar. You don't believe the—" he lowered his voice so it didn't carry to the other shapers "—shaping will hold the draasin, but I *feel* it."

"And I have seen what the draasin can do. I saw the way the draasin attacked Ethea. I know what the archives tell us the draasin were like before they disappeared."

"From archivists who work with Incendin?"

Could the archivists have an ulterior motive? He still didn't know why the archivist had let the Incendin shaper into the archives. And what of the archivist Athan? Was he corrupted as well?

Could they *want* the draasin gone?

But why? What purpose would that serve anyone?

"Why have you come here?" Roine asked him.

Tan took a deep breath, thinking about how to answer. What would Roine believe?

"I came to help the draasin," he answered. "I believe Incendin has twisted the youngest, forced her to go against her nature. And I'm here to do what I can to help."

Roine watched Tan for a moment and then shook his head. "I'm sorry, Tan. The king made his decision, and it's one I agree with." He took another step forward. "And I'm afraid I can't let you do that."

Tan sensed Asboel's concern for him and he sent a nearly silent plea for patience. *Follow me quietly.*

Roine frowned slightly. "Where is it? Where is the draasin?"

"You should know there is an Incendin shaper looking for her as well."

"Incendin?" He blinked and his face seemed to change for a moment before hardening again. "How do you know?"

"I saw her. She's the same one who attacked us in the archives. She's with the Aeta."

"The Aeta? Why would an Incendin shaper travel with the Aeta?"

"I don't know. Why don't we go and find out, Theondar?"

Tan felt the earth shaping disappear with a soft pop. Now gone, the other shapers waiting near Roine were suddenly visible. Tan counted at least five but knew there must be more. Three fire shapers alone had attacked Asboel while they flew toward this place.

The two small wind shapers watched Tan carefully. One of the men, a bald man named Alan he remembered meeting near the palace, watched him warily. The other seemed more interested in looking around the forest. Ferran turned out to be the earth shaper hiding them. Tan tried carefully sensing to learn who else might be waiting in the forest, but something obstructed him. Ferran watched him with a hard expression.

Roine took him by the arm and led him away from the clearing and the watching shapers. "When the king learns of this—" he started and then lowered his voice as they reached the edge of the towering pines. "I saw the attack," Roine whispered.

Tan frowned. "What attack?"

Roine turned, his mouth tilting into a tight smile. "The draasin fighting. I saw what happened."

Tan's heart raced. "If you saw it, then you know I'm telling the truth about them. Why else would the draasin attack each other?"

They made their way down the slope. Tan's ears popped slightly. Roine shaped.

"Something is off here, Tan, but I'm not certain I know what it is."

"Wait—" he started, and then realized how loud his voice must be. "You *believe* me?"

Roine took a sharp breath. "I thought the draasin attacked Ethea. I saw one of the creatures shooting fire upon the city. But when we chased it here…" He shook his head. "Why would the draasin return to this place?"

Tan waited.

"I believe you speak to the draasin, but I hadn't believed they could be trusted, even with what you claim Amia shaped."

"Roine—"

He smiled. "Not Theondar now?"

Tan snorted. "Roine is my friend. Theondar—"

A smile tugged at his mouth. "It's as useful a distinction as any."

"What changed your mind?"

"I saw you riding the draasin."

"And?"

"I have never heard of anyone riding one of the draasin. I have rarely heard of anyone even *speaking* to the draasin. When I saw that, I realized there was much I didn't fully understand. And if I didn't understand, I couldn't hunt them, not without knowing for certain."

Tan stopped. He stood on the outcropping of the rock, looking down at the narrow road the Aeta had traveled through, listening for Amia—or something that would tell him she was at least alright. He felt her as a quiet softness at the back of his mind but dared not reach out to her, not while knowing the fire shaper was among the Aeta. And if the Aeta welcomed the fire shaper, might they know, too, about Amia's ability and think to use it somehow?

He sighed. Once, the Aeta had given him joy, but since meeting Amia, he had known nothing but sorrow around them. And now the soft tinkling of their bells had long since faded. He sensed their presence within the forest not far from here. They neared the water but were moving quickly—far faster than he would expect. From there, they would continue toward the rocky mountains. And once there...

"I know what they want," he suddenly realized.

Roine frowned. "What who wants?"

Tan let out a shaky breath. *Why would Twisted Fire want to reach the Mother?*

Tan sent the question with needle sharp focus to Asboel.

The draasin stirred within his mind, speaking as softly as he'd ever heard. *Twisted Fire cannot reach the Mother.*

But if they did?

Tan sensed alarm from Asboel. For the great elemental to feel alarm was answer enough.

Move, but silently.

He hoped his shaping obscuring the draasin held.

"We need to hurry," Tan said, speaking aloud to Roine.

"What is it, Tan? Why do we need to hurry?"

Tan looked at Roine, meeting his eyes. The attack on Ethea made sense now. They had not only attacked the city, they had created a diversion, drawing the kingdom's shapers away and after the draasin.

But that hadn't been the entire purpose of the attack. Tan felt it with certainty.

"Did they take the artifact?"

Roine frowned. "What? How would you know they were after the artifact in the attack?"

"Did Incendin reach the artifact?"

Roine shook his head. "No. The artifact remains secure. The king gave it to Jishun, one of the Athan…"

The archivists were compromised, regardless of what Roine believed. "Then we must assume Incendin has the artifact."

"But why? What do they hope to do with it?"

Tan shook his head. "I don't know, but they have the Aeta and they're heading toward the mountain where we once found a pool of liquid spirit. Whatever Incendin plans, that must be the reason they came to this place."

He still didn't know why. What would Incendin gain by returning here? Why risk so much?

Roine looked up the slope. "I need to stop them. We may not have managed to learn the key to using the artifact, but I don't know if Lacertin managed to learn. And with the archivists involved…"

Tan nodded. "Go. I will meet you."

Roine set a hand on his arm and shook his head. "It's not safe, and you're not fully trained. Your mother would have killed me if I let you go."

Tan smiled sadly. "But she is no longer here to stop me. And I don't think you could, either."

"Tan—I'm a fully trained warrior, able to shape the elements. I would have little trouble stopping you."

Tan smiled and turned, finally letting his shaping disappear with a pop. As he did, Asboel appeared where a massive boulder had once stood. "And I have one of the draasin to help."

CHAPTER 27

Spirit Shapings

ROINE STARED AT ASBOEL, unable to take his eyes off the massive fire elemental. He stood as if frozen in place. Then, slowly, he turned to meet Tan's eyes. "How did you obscure him from me?"

Tan shook his head. "I didn't obscure him."

Roine frowned. "There was a shaping. And for me not to notice... for Ferran not to notice—" He shook his head, rubbing his hand through his graying hair. "You will be dangerous one day, Tan."

Tan looked over at Asboel. The draasin's bright golden eyes watched them, an unreadable expression on his leathery face. *Twisted Fire seeks the Mother. That is why they came here.*

They brought the Daughter.

Tan nodded. *Why is that important?*

Asboel sniffed softly. His annoyance came through the connection. *I am uncertain.*

We can't let them reach the Mother.

No.

I will do what I can to help the youngest, but this must be done first.

Asboel blinked, staring at him intently. *Yes.*

Tan sent out a quick sensing, listening to the forest. Deep within the forest, hidden by trees near the edge of the lake, the youngest draasin still lay unmoving. How much longer would she remain like that?

If he were closer to the water, he would ask the nymid for assistance, even if only to hold her there until he could reach her. Once he had Amia with him, he might be able to find a way to remove whatever effect Incendin had worked on her. Until then, he didn't want her attacking again, especially not if Asboel would not fight back.

"We need to reach the mountains before the Incendin shaper," Tan told Roine.

"What do you think they will do?"

"They have Amia. I can't reach her, not like I should be able to."

Tan could feel her presence and knew she still lived, but didn't dare reach through the connection in case another spirit shaper was with her. What would happen to Amia if they knew he was here, if they knew the draasin had come?

Roine frowned and waited for Tan to explain.

"When I saved her from the lisincend near Velminth, she shaped me." Roine's eyes widened slightly. "I don't think it was intentional. But since then, we've been connected. At first, I felt only the effect of her shaping urging me on. Over time, it has deepened, becoming a connection to her. If I focus, I can speak to her."

"Like you speak to the draasin?" Roine eyed Asboel carefully.

Tan nodded. "Like that, but different. It is different with her than with the nymid or udilm too."

Roine looked over. "You spoke to the udilm as well?"

Tan nodded again. "They weren't easy, nothing like speaking to the nymid. And I nearly died trying to reach them." He *had* died—if only for a while—speaking to the nymid the first time, though Roine didn't need to know about that. "Had I not found them, I think Elle might have died. She had been shaped…" Not by him, not according to the draasin and udilm. Had it been a *spirit* shaping that made her ill?

But if that was the case, had the same happened to Amia?

Roine glanced at Asboel and nodded. "We have much to speak about when this is over."

Tan only nodded.

"What do you have in mind?" Roine asked.

Tan walked over to Asboel. The draasin watched him, his long tail flicking to each side, and then he lowered his head, allowing Tan to climb on his back. The warmth of the spines along his back felt nice after the chill of the air. "We need to reach the Aeta. I need to rescue Amia."

Roine looked from Tan to Asboel and nodded. "I can't protect you from the others. I may be Athan, but they heard the king's request directly. They know he wants the draasin gone. No offense," he said, nodding to Asboel. "So if they attack, there's not much I can do."

Tan took a deep breath and nodded. "I'm not as worried about the kingdom's shapers. It's Incendin we need to fear."

"I will do what I can."

Let's go, he told Asboel.

The great elemental peeled his massive wings from his body and took off with a jump.

As they cleared the trees, his wings struck the wind, pushing them higher and higher. A shaped gust of wind threatened to catch them, but Asboel roared through it. Lightning streaked toward the ground and thunder followed.

Roine—Theondar the warrior—took to the skies on a shaping of wind and fire.

Tan sensed Amia already moving around the lake. The last time they'd been here, it had taken days to make their way around it. In their wagons, the Aeta moved with a speed Tan wouldn't have expected.

If they traveled much longer, they would reach the northern mountain. And then it was a short climb to the top of the rocks to reach the cave. Whatever Incendin planned would happen there.

We need to reach the cave first.

Asboel's reluctance was evident, pushing through the connection. Tan understood. After a thousand years trapped beneath this lake, the draasin would not want to return.

The Mother...

You do not need to remind me of the Mother.

Asboel banked and they soared high above the lake, moving through wisps of clouds. Tan couldn't make out anything below them other than the dense, deep green of the forest ending abruptly at the sharp edge of the water. The lake splayed out across the valley before ending in the rocky mountains to the north.

Can you see anything?

Asboel grunted. An image of the ground beneath them came into his mind with nearly as much detail as if he were walking along it. Tan was amazed at the level of detail. If this was how the draasin saw all the time, it was no wonder they were feared hunters.

Asboel grunted again, this time more amused than anything.

Tan used the image from Asboel to track along the lake's edge. As he did, he pressed out with a sensing, straining from the distance to listen. He sensed them nearing the wide river at the end of the lake. Once they passed it, they would move easily into the mountains.

He felt something. Asboel felt it, too.

243

The draasin twitched, suddenly diving toward the ground.

What is it?

You felt it.

Yes.

Good. Fire burns below.

Twisted Fire?

Perhaps. I cannot tell.

Tan recognized frustration from Asboel. *The youngest?*

No. She still slumbers.

Tan saw her in his mind, lying flat against the ground near the lake. A tree cast shade over her, blocking her from the sun. She did not move.

Then what?

Even as he asked, he knew. He *felt* the shaping, hot and powerful.

And with it, he felt another sense, like a voice in his mind. This was soft and distant, but he'd heard it before.

The nymid.

And they were hurting.

They try to burn their way across the river.

Yes.

But the nymid…

The nymid suffer with what they do.

Tan sensed a strange satisfaction from Asboel. Whatever he claimed, the centuries of suffering left him with some anger.

This is where we must make our stand.

Tan couldn't let the nymid be injured. They had protected him, saved him when the lisincend attacked. Now it was his turn to help.

This would be where he would try to stop the Incendin shaper. This is where he would rescue Amia. And then he would attempt to free the youngest.

Asboel dived and Tan hung to him tightly.

Wind whistled around his face, streaming translucently around him. As they descended, Tan thought he saw tiny faces, flitting about before disappearing altogether. Tan's ears popped with the speed of the descent.

And then Asboel pulled up.

The change happened rapidly. Tan's stomach felt like it dropped with the quick change. He was thrown against Asboel's back.

Amia!

There was no use hiding their presence anymore. Once the fire shaper saw Asboel, she would know they came for her.

His sense of Amia stirred deep in his mind.

Amia!

He repeated her name, this time shaping a snap to her name.

Answer please!

Asboel roared. The shaper had attacked him, striking him on the stomach.

Twisted Fire hadn't hurt Asboel, and this shaping didn't either. But Tan felt something else, like a subtle calling in his mind that writhed toward Asboel. Without his connection to the great elemental, he might not have recognized what happened.

A spirit shaping.

They try to shape you, Tan warned. But who? Not Amia, but that meant another spirit shaper. One of the Aeta?

Then you must protect me, Little Warrior.

How?

You ask Fire how to use spirit?

I can't use spirit.

Asboel laughed darkly. *If you can't use spirit, why does the youngest lie at the edge of the water?*

245

Unlike with the other elements, nothing he had done made him think he could shape spirit. But Amia could, and through her shaping of him and their shared connection, was it possible that it seemed like he shaped spirit?

He would ask questions later. For now, he would do what he needed to protect the draasin.

Tan focused on Asboel's mind, focused on everything he could sense from the great elemental. He felt the enormity of his mind, the age and wisdom gained from centuries of life. The sheer vastness nearly overwhelmed him.

Over everything, Amia's shaping lingered, creating a barrier. Mixed with it was the sense of another sliding across the draasin's mind, trying to influence Asboel.

Tan pressed *through* his connection to Asboel and wrapped himself around the draasin's mind. He held that sense, tying it off to isolate the draasin. As he did, he wondered if he separated Asboel from Amia's shaping, as well.

The other shaping slid over him, a foul sense, and then snapped away.

Asboel grunted and roared.

They dove toward the ground.

The draasin landed with his claws splayed, his mouth dripping flames, heat and steam blooming from his nostrils.

The Aeta wagons were near. Tan sensed Amia within.

Go. Find the Daughter, but hold what you do. I will watch for others.

Tan had no idea how to hold what he did; he had no idea *what* he did, but he nodded and sent a quiet affirmative as he jumped from Asboel's back onto the ground.

Asboel took to the air in a flap of wings and another roar of flames, leaving Tan on the ground.

Where was Roine? Moving as only a warrior could, he should have been here by now. Instead, Tan saw no evidence Roine ever reached the Aeta. Could he have been spirit shaped?

Without Roine, saving Amia had become much more difficult.

The lake was on his left, lapping softly at the shore. The wide river that had once slowed the lisincend was in front of him, draining with a swirling rush into the lake. The Aeta wagons had slowed, too, stopped at that point, and the fire shaper stood at the river's head. Another shaper—another fire shaper, Tan suspected—stood next to her. He was tall and broad-shouldered. His clean-shaven face sneered.

Tan did not look at either of them.

Instead, he stared at another man, older and stooped of back, but still with a sharp, surprised expression. Tan recognized the man, though the last time he saw him had been back in Ethea. The archivist.

Tan suddenly understood the spirit shaping that had attacked Asboel. She had thought him a spirit senser somehow able to ignore her shaping, but with new realization, he recognized he was more. He was a spirit shaper. That was how he had ignored her shaping.

Steam rising from the river from the fire shaping started to blur his vision.

The energy came as sharp pressure behind his ears. More than that, he felt the strange dry tingling of his skin. Now Asboel's comment made sense: Tan sensed shaping itself.

The river suffered, more than when the lisincend had attacked. Then, even with Fur, the water had slowed the shapers. The nymid had helped, surging the river wider than the lisincend could handle, but something here was different than what the lisincend had done.

Soon, the river would burn away. The power funneled into the river boiled the water, drying it up and damaging the nymid.

The shapers watched him through the fog of the steam rising over the river but didn't move.

The archivist pressed on him.

Tan felt his presence, thick like oil sliming over his mind, but soft and gentle with attempted subtlety. He clawed at it, uncertain what the archivist would do if he managed some shaping of him. As he did, he felt the shaping sinking into his mind, clinging to it. There was nothing he could do to fight; he was not a spirit shaper.

But Amia was.

He reached for the distant connection to her, feeling along it. *Amia!*

A faint stirring answered, barely enough for him to know if she was there.

He tried again, this time with an image, using what the draasin had shown him of how to send images. He pushed through an image of the archivist, sending it to her. If she were injured or unconscious, she might not be able to respond.

The thought only made him more anxious.

The stirring increased, drawing toward him.

Tan didn't know if it was even Amia responding. If the archivist was a shaper, would it be possible *he* recognized what Tan tried to do?

He strained, reaching for the draasin but unable to hear him, as if straining against water. And he was too far from the nymid or udilm… unless he could reach the water.

Tan ran toward the lake.

When his feet touched the cold water, sudden tingling washed over him.

Nymid!

He stood in the water, waiting for the nymid to respond, needing the nymid to respond. The sense of the archivist crawled across his mind. With each passing moment, he felt his presence sink deeper. Another moment or two and Tan might not be able to make his own choice.

The nymid didn't answer.

Tan couldn't do this on his own. He needed help, but if not the nymid...

Draasin!

He feared using Asboel's name, knowing from the draasin there was something important in naming, but there came no response.

Nothing happened.

Had Asboel been influenced by the archivist?

Panic set Tan's heart racing. He plunged deeper into the cold water of the lake, letting it reach his waist. *Nymid!*

He sent the thought like a rolling wave, trying to remember how he'd spoken to the udilm. Maybe speaking to the nymid as the udilm would speak to them would trigger a faster answer.

Silence.

The crawling sensation in his mind stopped.

Tan felt suddenly afraid. He'd done nothing to stop the archivist, nothing that would keep him out of his mind.

It left only one answer.

The shaping had taken hold.

CHAPTER 28

Return to Water

THE URGE—THE *DESIRE*—TO RETURN to shore was nearly overwhelming. Every part of him wanted to climb back onto shore. The sense almost overwhelmed him.

Instead, Tan dove into the water.

Cold sucked the breath from his lungs. He didn't fight, letting himself sink, drifting to the bottom of the lake.

The lakebed was deep here where the river ran in, and he slowly drifted downward. Pressure to return to the shore continued to build within him, but he recognized this was not his own. The water began to warm, the turbulent current around him slowing. The fire shapers nearly succeeded.

Tan would die here.

He couldn't reach the nymid, the sense of the draasin had cut off from him, and Amia wouldn't answer. He was alone.

And Roine still hadn't arrived. He wouldn't, if the archivist had shaped him.

Had the kingdom shapers tried attacking him? It seemed they had. If not for his weak shaping, whatever they attempted in the forest might have prevented him from finding Amia.

Had the kingdom's shapers already been influenced by the archivists?

If Jishun were involved, it meant the king himself might have been shaped. If so, then the entirety of the kingdoms was at risk.

Unless someone did something to stop them.

But he wasn't a shaper—not yet—with barely any control over the weak ability he had. His greatest strength was speaking to the elementals, and if they wouldn't answer, he had no strength.

Amia needed his help, though. Even if he didn't feel the gentle urging of her shaping for him to protect her, he would want to do what he could, whatever it was.

He would have to figure out something on his own.

How could he stop a spirit shaping?

He'd done something to help Asboel. Could he do the same for himself?

Tan focused on what he'd done, thinking of how he'd encased Asboel's mind. This time, rather than pushing out through the connection to the draasin, he focused it internally, wrapping himself around his own mind. As he did, he realized what it was he did, practically *saw* the shaping of water and air he used to create a sort of shield. He had done something like this before, only without knowing what he'd done.

His ears popped.

And the oily shaping from the archivist separated from him with a *snap*.

Tan gasped.

Asboel was there, shouting in his mind.

MAELEN!

Tan pushed back, pushing the sense of the draasin away from him.

I am here.

Relief flooded through the connection. *You disappeared.*

Tan snorted. *Not by choice.*

Fire. It is nearly complete.

Is there anything you can do?

Asboel sent an image through the connection. Kingdom shapers attacked him from all sides: wind and fire and water. As long as Asboel remained in the sky, the earth shapers couldn't reach him. He fought, but grew tired.

Go. Save yourself. I will finish this and help the youngest.

Asboel roared through the connection. *You will not fight alone, Maelen.*

Can you stay above the attack for now?

Asboel seemed annoyed he had to ask. *Yes. What will you do?*

Tan could think of only one thing he *could* do. There was only one way he would be able to remove the archivist's influence off the youngest and the shapers. And that required Amia.

I will fight.

Asboel roared approval.

Tan saw as if through his eyes as the draasin soared high into the sky, piercing through the dark clouds threatening rain and thunder, streaking through the lightning and fire, ignoring the wind. He reached a place of quiet and calm and turned, looking down at the lake.

Tan turned to the water. The nymid were nearby. They must be, or else he would have needed air long ago.

The Daughter needs your help again.

Soft murmuring, almost voices. And then, *He Who is Tan.*

Tan smiled tightly. *Can you help?*

A green shape, like an elongated face, came into view. Since seeing the udilm, Tan had begun to wonder if the nymid truly shared the same strength as the ocean elemental. Seeing the nymid now, he recognized something he hadn't seen when floundering in the ocean with Elle. They were much the same.

The Daughter suffers.

Tan nodded. It was his fear.

Fire will boil the source.

Tan nodded again. *The water they take can be returned.*

They destroy.

They are like Twisted Fire.

The soft murmuring increased. *Twisted Fire cannot return.*

Tan frowned. *They are not twisted fire, but work with them.*

Twisted Fire cannot return, the nymid repeated.

I will do what I can to stop—

In their agitation, the nymid interrupted him. *Do not let Dark Fire reach the source.*

I will do what I can, but I will need your help.

The face of the nymid twisted, looking out toward the shore. *You command water. You command fire.*

I don't know how. I have no control.

The nymid seemed amused by the statement. The face turned back toward him. *We will help, He Who is Tan.*

With the words, the shimmering green shape of the nymid swirled around him, coating him as they had once before, creating a type of armor. The armor would shield him from the fire shapers, but he would have to protect himself from the spirit shaper. As long as his shaping of water and wind held.

Prepare.

Tan frowned.

Water swelled around him, swirling and rolling. A strong wave pushed from behind, pressing Tan up from the sandy bottom of the lake. He rode atop the wave, moving up and up as the water surged.

And then the wave crested.

He took a deep breath.

The river was nothing but a heavy cloud of steam. Tan couldn't tell if any water ran through it anymore, but it likely didn't matter. The river had narrowed enough that the shapers could cross.

Aeta wagons rolled, moving steadily over the land the river had occupied. Tan saw the wagons as flashes of muted color through the fog. Wood creaked as it rolled. A few voices shouted.

The wave coursed down, slamming into the wagons.

Tan landed with a splash. Water swirled around his ankles, tugging at his legs as it flowed into the lake. Hot air tried to burn him, but the nymid armor pushed against it.

The sudden wave had sent the wagons into disarray. Some pressed forward, horses frantically attempting to pull the wagons free. Tan focused on the ground and sent out a request with a breath, shaped like he had when he had landed in Incendin.

Mud formed beneath them, slowing the horses.

Tan prayed it would slow the shapers as well.

He reached the nearest wagon. He sensed someone moving inside and listened for Amia. It wasn't her. Moving on, he stopped at the next. Again, he sensed but found no sign of her.

Going wagon to wagon would be too slow.

He closed his eyes, ignoring the sounds of shouting and the creaking of wagons around him. He ignored the splashing waves slamming at them again and again as the nymid did what they could to help. He ignored the growing heat in the air as the fire shapers tried to undo what the nymid had done.

Through it, he focused on his connection to Amia.

The sense was weak. Whatever the archivist did to her—and Tan had no doubt the archivist was responsible—it kept her from reaching him. But he could still sense her, deep within his mind. And she had nearly responded to him before.

He followed what he sensed of Amia.

She was near. He felt certain of that.

Tan moved away from the wagons. This time, he reached through his connection to Asboel. *Show me where she is.*

The draasin turned and an image tinted with the strange draasin orange and red sight came into his mind.

He knew where to find her.

Tan ran toward her wagon.

It appeared out of the steam as bright blue and green. He had seen the wagon before when they were in Ethea, before she felt the need to leave. Had the pain she'd been feeling had anything to do with the archivist, or had it truly been from her shaping of him?

They would learn together. Once he rescued her, he wouldn't leave her alone again, regardless of what she said.

The door to the wagon slammed open. The tall, wide fire shaper stepped out.

He saw Tan and smiled.

Tan ran at him, ramming his shoulder into the shaper, knocking him back.

A blast of fire lanced toward him. Tan didn't have time to move. The fire struck him square in his chest.

And then disappeared.

Tan looked down to make sure he hadn't been harmed, but saw no sign of fire. He'd not even felt any heat. Whatever the nymid had done protected him even better than the armor he had worn the last time.

The fire shaper lunged.

Tan stepped to the side. He had no weapon to slow the fire shaper, nothing to stop him. The man was solid, built like a blacksmith, but moved with a dangerous grace.

Another burst of fire, this time spreading out in a wide shower.

It passed over him, disappearing as it did. Somewhere behind him, someone screamed. The fire shaper cocked his head to the side.

In that moment, he ran at him again. Tan needed to get past the shaper to reach Amia.

This time, he slammed his shoulder into the man's stomach. The fire shaper doubled over with a grunt. Tan brought his knee up, trying to kick him. The fire shaper recovered enough to grab him and began bending him forward.

The fire shaper was stronger than Tan and crumpled him.

His vision started to cloud. Heat pressed on his neck, slowly but steadily, rising in intensity. Tan suspected that with enough time, the shaping would overwhelm even the nymid armor.

He had to do something.

He pressed out with the same request he'd used before, asking the earth to soften. His ears popped as the shaping washed away from him. For a moment, he thought it might work, that the ground might soften enough for him to trap the fire shaper. Then the shaper directed his shaping downward, heating the ground. Somehow, this stabilized him.

He laughed. "An earth shaper? I will need to learn what trick you use to stop the fire."

"Not… only… earth," Tan grunted.

He might not be a strong shaper, but he could speak to the elementals, especially in this place—the place of convergence where all the elementals existed. And he needed their help.

With that, he begged the wind for aid.

He sent out the request on a light breath.

At first, nothing happened. Then wind began swirling around. Translucent faces appeared in the wind. Were they ara? And if they were, could they help?

Tan, son of Zephra, needs your assistance.

His voice disappeared from him with a flutter of wind.

Zephra.

The name came through softly, barely a disturbance in the air.

Tan nodded.

Please. Help.

Wind swirled, raging around the fire shaper. Tearing at him with tiny fingers.

The man grunted and released him.

Tan kicked him and then pushed past, barreling into the wagon, not waiting to see if he would follow.

Inside, the wagon was more sparsely decorated than the last time he'd seen it. Long, leathery skins lined the walls, most painted with strange symbols with a dark ink. Or blood, he decided. The obsidian bowl he had seen before rested near the center of the wagon. Fire danced within it.

A few other implements lined the floor. Hooks and wire with thick barbs ran along the ground. Something wet and sticky clung to them.

Blood.

Tan turned away, looking for Amia.

He found her chained to the far wall. A clamp held her mouth closed. The chains swirled around her arms, biting into her skin. Blood trickled down and onto the floor. More symbols were written on the floor, the trail of blood leading to Amia.

Tan shivered.

"Amia?"

She shuddered slightly but didn't try to speak.

Tan ran to her, kicking the barbed wire out of the way. He nearly stumbled on the hook lying across the ground, but caught himself and threw it to the side.

Two long screws held the clamp over her mouth. Tan twisted them until the clamp fell free, dropping to the floor. Amia gasped.

Finally, she looked up. "Tan?" she whispered.

He nodded.

"What happened? How are you here?"

He smiled tightly. "It's a long story. I need to hurry to get you free."

"The chains—"

"I know. I'll get them free."

"No—"

She didn't get the chance to finish.

The door to the wagon slammed open and the bald fire shaper stepped inside.

When he saw Tan, he smiled.

"A warrior," he said appreciatively. "Untrained, but still strong. Too bad you will not live long enough to learn how to use your abilities."

He didn't move, but Tan had the sense of movement.

The fire in the obsidian bowl surged, rising into a pillar. Tan had seen something similar from the lisincend before, but this shaper was not one of the lisincend.

With a dark smile on his face, he pressed the fire toward Tan.

Tan didn't have time to react.

The armor might protect him, but it would not protect Amia, not from this fire.

Without thinking, he pulled through his connection to Asboel, pulled from the great elemental, and drew fire into himself.

The flames extinguished with a hot gust of air.

The obsidian bowl cracked.

The fire shaper looked from Tan to the bowl, shaking his head as he did. "What did you…"

Tan didn't wait. He grabbed the hook he'd tossed to the side and swung it up and around, surging with a building pressure behind his ears. The hook connected with the fire shaper's head. He fell with a loud *thunk*.

Amia stared at him.

Tan took the hook and worked it in the back of the chain, leveraging it back and forth. When it was lodged as far as he could get it, he pressed down with an assisted surge. The chains cracked and fell to the ground around Amia, who shook softly in a way that reminded Tan of Elle.

He grabbed her, scooping her in his arms.

She continued shaking. "How are you here?"

"The draasin."

"But the shapers… the archivist… he's one of the Aeta."

Tan blinked slowly. Aeta. Of course he would be. "I saw him."

She looked up and met his eyes. "Has he…" She hesitated, and a soft touch brushed his mind. "Has he shaped you?"

"He tried."

Amia blinked. "You knew?"

"I felt what he attempted."

"How did you…"

Tan shook his head. "I don't really know. I had to protect Asboel," he answered, saying the draasin's name before realizing what he did. Amia would likely learn it from him anyway.

Amia smiled. "Asboel. Fitting, I think. You learned what they did to the little one?"

Tan nodded. "It's why she attacked. It's the reason he summoned me." Tan paused near the obsidian bowl, looking down into it. More of the strange symbols had been carved into the stone itself. Tan reached for the bowl to touch them, but Amia slapped his hand away.

"Don't!"

He turned. "What is it?"

She shook her head. "I don't know. It increases their power, draws from a different source, I think. They were using it in a shaping."

"What kind of shaping?" As he asked, he looked around the room again and thought he understood. Whatever it was involved Amia. "What did they need you for?"

"I'm not sure. I *should* know, but the archivist... he does something that keeps me from understanding."

"I think he shaped the kingdom's shapers as well."

Amia's eyes widened slightly. "And Roine?"

He still hadn't seen Roine since they had separated. Where had he gone? What did that mean?

Had Tan said anything to Roine that might have helped the archivist with whatever he had planned? He didn't think so. Roine already knew everything he'd said.

But where was he?

And where was the archivist?

CHAPTER 29

Escape from the Aeta

T HEY STEPPED OUT OF THE AETA WAGON. Steam still rose around them in a blanket of fog, but voices escaped, shouting. Tan set Amia down, letting her walk. "Can you get us through here safely?"

She looked up at him. "I…"

She didn't have the chance to finish; she shuddered violently. Tan caught her and held her close to him, waiting for it to pass.

It was the same illness that had overcome Elle. Not his shaping, as he'd feared, but something the archivists had done. With Elle, it had progressed quickly until she could no longer function. How much time did Amia have?

When it stopped, she looked at him. "I can't shape. When I try…"

He nodded. The convulsions. Whatever they had done prevented her from safely shaping. There had been only one way to heal Elle, and that had involved getting her to the udilm. Tan didn't think the water elementals would help this time. For Amia, she needed spirit.

Reaching spirit would be dangerous. Especially if the archivist and the Incendin shaper headed there as well. But for Amia, he had to try.

Someone emerged from the fog. A tall Aeta, bright clothing marking him as one of the traders, stood and looked at them. When he saw Tan and Amia, he yelled.

How could one of her people allow this to happen to her? How could the Aeta turn on their own?

These were questions he would have answered later, he told himself as the Aeta trader pulled a long knife from a belt sheath and started toward them.

Tan sent an angry request on the wind.

It responded with a soft breath of an answer, blowing through the wagon, lifting the fog. More than that, it sent the Aeta staggering. He tripped, stumbling into the thick mud.

The archivist stood before them, suddenly revealed from within the fog. Yulan. He studied Tan with his bright eyes and his shaping built, pressing on Tan's mind. As he did, Tan understood what the archivist did and he pushed against it, sealing his mind from the outside influence.

The archivist shifted his attention to Amia.

If Tan did nothing, he could harm her. "Why?" he demanded. "They are your people!"

The archivist glanced at him, for a moment taking his attention off Amia. "Isn't that reason enough? Must the People wander forever?" He shook his head. "Banished out of ignorance. Now… now it is our time."

Amia shook violently. Whatever the archivist was doing harmed her.

Tan roared, startling the archivist. With it, fire burst from his hand and struck the other man in the chest, knocking him back with the heat of the attack. The archivist twitched and didn't rise.

Had Tan just used a shaping to kill?

He shook off the thought. Not to kill—to protect. Had he done nothing, Amia would have suffered.

"There is another," she whispered weakly.

Tan glanced at her and nodded.

When he neared the water's edge, he felt heat rising, so he turned and saw what he expected: the other Incendin fire shaper.

Her touch was subtler than the other shaper's had been. She swirled heat and smoke and fire from the ground itself, sending it in a torrent around them, pressing against the nymid armor.

"Why are you here?" he demanded.

The shaper smiled darkly. "Because Fur was too weak to do what was needed. He sacrificed too much, but I've learned how to have fire serve me."

Her voice was hoarse and reminded him of the lisincend. She held a wide band of silver—the Mother's—in her hand. Blood stained it.

The heat threatened to swallow him, powerful and intense and painfully hot. Tan swallowed as he took a step back but her shaping kept him from the water. Amia shrank against him. Were he a more powerful shaper, he might be able to push back the fire. But he wasn't that skilled shaper. Not yet. He did, however, have another ability, one this fire shaper didn't.

Asboel!

Tan sent the thought like a needle toward the circling draasin. Reaching Tan would be dangerous for Asboel. He would have to come through whatever the kingdom's shapers had planned. But Asboel was one of the great elementals, a creature of fire itself.

He streaked toward the earth like a bolt from the heavens.

Tan felt him roar in his mind.

The fire shaper felt something as well. She turned her attention away from Tan as Asboel plunged from the sky.

With a wave of her hand, she sent heat and smoke whistling around her.

Asboel responded with a snarl. Flames leaped from his mouth and nose, ripping through her shaping. He roared again, this time aloud. The sound echoed across the valley and he landed with a snap of his tail. It caught the shaper and sent her tumbling away. Tan grabbed onto his spines and swung atop, pulling Amia along with him.

You bring another.

The Daughter. We need to reach the Mother or she will die.

Asboel sent his frustration.

Without her, I can't help the youngest. I do not know how.

Asboel snorted. *Very well.*

They launched into the air.

Shapers attack. Hold tightly.

As Asboel sent the command, a blast of wind struck them, funneling around Asboel's wings. He spun, flicking his tail to regain momentum, but couldn't.

Tan focused on the wind shaping, feeling the current of air. With a soft request to ara, he begged the wind to release Asboel.

The wind died and they shot upward, propelled by ara.

You grow quickly, Maelen.

I did not shape that.

Asboel snorted amusement. *No shaping. You speak with ara. She is difficult. Fickle.*

I am the son of Zephra. I think that is why ara responds.

You continue to underestimate yourself.

A vision of the ground came through his connection to Asboel. Beneath them, fire raged, burning everything to ash. Dark flames licked the ground, twisting and writhing, building to horrible size. Aeta wagons disappeared in a flash. Through Asboel's eyes, Tan saw the Aeta die, turned to ash and char. It was the second time he'd seen Incendin destroy the Aeta.

He pushed away the image. He would shield Amia from it as long as he could.

They reached the clouds. Again, rain tried tearing through them. This time, Asboel sent a snarl of fire around them and the rain turned to steam, filling the sky with a heavy cloud like the fire shapers had attempted on land.

He banked, turning rapidly, spinning toward the mountain. As he did, Amia shook again. The convulsion lasted longer, and Tan held her until it passed.

Thunder rolled behind them, distant at first. It came again, closer this time. Was that Roine? If the archivist had shaped him, Tan didn't want to come across him until Amia had been healed.

Hurry, Tan urged.

Asboel surged forward.

They reached the peak of the massive mountain. Below them, a gaping hole in the stone dropped down deep into the mountain. The last time he'd been here, he had come through the mouth of the cave. This time, he would come as Lacertin had come.

They dropped through the mountain. Asboel would be vulnerable here. He wouldn't be able to stretch his wings. The draasin could use his fire, but any other attack would be limited.

They touched down on hard stone, Asboel sinking massive claws into the rock.

Tan looked around before climbing off Asboel's back. A lush forest grew within the mountain, shaped by the ancient warrior shapers. Grasses and trees grew where they should not. A soft glow radiated from the tunnel.

The shapers were here.

He looked where the pillars had once been, now fallen. The pillar formed by the draasin had fallen first, released when Roine helped free the draasin from the lake. Ara and golud had followed quickly after. Only the nymid lingered. Even now, there was a sense of the nymid within the mountain, more than his armor would account for.

Amia shook again. The tremor lasted longer than the last.

When it finally subsided, he took her and carried her carefully from Asboel's back. *Watch over us.*

The draasin snorted.

Tan hurried to the spot where the pool of spirit had once flowed, before releasing the artifact. It had ebbed with the release, and Tan prayed some part of it still remained.

He sent out a sensing, listening for anyone in the cave. It came as a distant connection, but it was there, vibrating against his senses. There was someone in the shaped garden.

Can you slow them?

He sent Asboel an image of the shaped garden. The draasin sniffed in a breath of steam and swooped toward it. He struggled to get close; the shape of the stone made it difficult. Asboel snorted again, this time in frustration, and turned, swirling back into the air. He circled overhead.

I cannot.

Tan nodded. He would have to do it on his own.

He ran to where the pool once had been, clutching Amia against him. She remained still, the convulsions over for now. They would return unless he found some way to heal her.

Pressure pushed against him as he reached the remnants of the elemental pillars. Though only the nymid remained, upholding their part of the bargain, some memory of the barrier still stood, blocking easy access. Had he not worn the nymid armor, he didn't know if he would have managed to slide in.

Once inside, he turned to the depression in the ground where the silver liquid once flowed. Now, nothing remained.

Amia sighed.

He turned to her, pulling her away from his chest. "You need to reach the Mother. Only she can save you."

Amia blinked weakly. The convulsions had taken too much out of her. "It's too late. She is gone from this place."

Tan looked around and shook his head. "This is a place of convergence. She is never truly gone."

Amia smiled. "You think to know the will of the Mother?"

"No. I know the elementals," he said.

Here, he could reach the nymid, the draasin, and even ara. Likely golud was here. That meant spirit—the Mother—would be found here as well.

But how? Was there anything Tan could do to help her reach them?

"The Mother only comes…" Amia started, but another convulsion cut her short.

This one lasted longer. With it, she struck her head on the stone. Tan swept his arms beneath her, protectively.

What had she been about to say? When would the Mother come?

A sound came from behind him and he turned. Jishun the archivist stood at the edge of the shaped garden. Now Tan understood the other Amia mentioned.

He stared at Tan, studying him. A dark smile flickered across his face.

With him stood the fire shaper. She carried a small bowl of slick black obsidian, similar to the one he'd seen in the caravan wagons. They stared at Tan, watching him.

Tan noticed the long, silvery object in the Jishun's hand. The artifact.

Draasin! I need you!

He sent the thought with a sharp focus, directing Asboel where he needed him to go.

Asboel hesitated a moment. Tan understood why: what Tan asked meant returning to where he'd been trapped for centuries. But if Asboel didn't, the youngest would suffer. Incendin might reach the source. All of this, Tan sent through his connection to the draasin.

Asboel screamed down to the ground and landed at the edge of the barrier, touching his massive talons to the ground. Heat rose from his back, forming the barrier of fire.

Asboel fought against another attempt at shaping. Tan felt what the archivist tried, felt the soft push against Asboel's mind. He forced more of his focus through the connection with Asboel, wrapping tightly around his mind.

Asboel roared. The sound filled the mountain, echoing loudly.

The fire shaper sneered at him and narrowed her eyes. She set the obsidian bowl onto the ground. With a flash, she sliced her hand and blood dripped into the bowl. Steam rose where it touched. A bright flame erupted.

Tan didn't want to learn what she shaped. Dark energy radiated from the bowl, power he felt deep within his body. He shivered.

The pillars needed to be formed or they would reach the pool. And then… could they reach the Mother?

Tan could not allow that. Whatever else he did, he needed to protect the Mother so he could save Amia.

He sent another thought, this rolling from him like a wave.

Nymid! The pillar!

Nothing happened at first. Then water slowly burbled up, spilling over and forming the pillar.

Would ara hold as well?

Ara! Please help the son of Zephra again!

He let the thought go on a wispy breath of air.

Wind fluttered, slowly turning into a translucent pillar, once again holding.

That left only golud.

Tan had never spoken to golud, but to form the protection here, he would need golud to help hold it, give him time to somehow call the Mother to help Amia. But how?

Tan was able to speak to the other elementals. Would he be able to speak to golud? And if he could, how would he do it? Each elemental had a different way of speaking. With the draasin, it was harsh and hot. With the nymid and udilm, there was a sense of movement, like that of waves rolling. And with ara, it had been more like a plea to the subtle touch of the wind elemental. How would he speak to golud?

The archivist and the fire shaper pressed against the incomplete barrier. The barrier held, but Tan sensed it wouldn't last for long. If another shaper joined—or worse, a warrior—the barrier would fall.

And then lightning streaked into the mountain. Thunder chased it. A warrior came.

As the blinding effect of the lightning faded, Roine stood on the other side of the barrier, looking from Tan to Jishun. For a moment, Tan thought Roine might attack him. A shaping built quickly—a sharp jab of pressure behind his ears—and then a look of pain crossed Roine's face. In a flurry of shaping, he pressed an attack on the barrier, using a mixture of earth, wind, and water, joining with spirit and fire already attacking.

The archivist had shaped Roine. And now he attacked.

"Fight it, Roine! Protect yourself from what he does!"

Had he not needed to focus on reaching golud, he would have tried helping Roine as he'd shaped Asboel. Even that might not work. He had no connection to Roine, not as he did to the great elemental.

Roine opened his mouth. Anguish twisted his face.

"Theondar—" The archivist said his name with a heavy shaping.

Roine's eyes went flat, the resistance in his face disappearing.

The attack on the barrier intensified and it began to fall.

In desperation, Tan sent a call to golud.

He had been sensing since he was a child, learning how to sense earth from his father, a powerful earth shaper. The earth and sensing flowed through him more naturally than any of the other elementals, in spite of the fact that he spoke so easily to the draasin. And Tan *had* shaped earth, had seen it respond to his requests. Now he needed another response.

Would golud answer?

Please help, golud. Form the fourth pillar. Protect the Daughter.

It came out in a rumble, like the earth itself moving.

Slowly—almost too slowly—golud answered.

Tan sensed it more than heard it. The voice of golud shook him, vibrating through his bones. Golud did not speak like the draasin or nymid, did not move like ara, but there *was* a sense of movement, of great strength and focus.

As golud slid into place, the barrier formed in full.

Tan sighed. The barrier would hold. When they had come for the artifact, the draasin had already abandoned it. This had been the reason the nymid armor allowed him entry. Now, the pillars formed the barrier in full.

Even with all the elements pressing, the barrier would stand. Except Tan would not be able to escape. He needed the pool of liquid spirit to return to help heal Amia.

She convulsed again, and he held her. Thunder rolled, echoing loudly in the cavern.

Through his connection to Asboel, Tan felt the barrier straining against the force of the shaping. It could not hold forever. If another shaper appeared, it might upset the balance enough.

Thunder cracked loudly again. And lightning followed.

When it cleared, Lacertin stood on the other side of the barrier.

Tan's stomach sunk with the sudden knowledge that they were doomed.

CHAPTER 30

Finding the Mother

TAN COULDN'T MOVE. Lacertin's arrival meant another shaper, and one who might be stronger than Roine, stronger even than when he had called himself Theondar.

He carried a sword much like Roine's and wore pants of a deep red leather with a black jacket buttoned tight across his chest. The power of his shaping built as he stood looking around them.

Of course he would be here. He worked with Incendin, had aided the lisincend as they tried reaching the artifact. Roine had driven him back, but he hadn't been killed. Now that Incendin had the artifact, how would Lacertin use it?

Tan waited for his shaping to join the others in attacking the barrier.

Instead, Lacertin stood, looking from Roine and the fire shaper to Tan standing inside the pillars. He stared at the draasin the longest, shaking his head slowly.

And then he attacked.

Lacertin's shaping built sharply and with incredible strength. Tan grabbed his head, afraid Lacertin's shaping would simply destroy the pillars that were keeping him safe for now.

The fire shaper's dark smile deepened and the pain on Roine's face pulled his face into a tight mask. How violently must the archivist be shaping him?

Tan tried reaching through the pillars, pushing a shaping of water and air around Roine, as he had with Asboel to protect his mind, but the pillars blocked him. Tan could do nothing to help his friend. And if he couldn't, Roine would attack him as if *he* were the enemy.

Even the archivist leaned toward the pillars, eyes fixed on Tan. Then the shaping released in a rush.

Wind whipped suddenly, throwing Roine and the fire shaper off their feet. Lacertin shot into the air on a shaped cloud and sent lightning streaking toward Roine, who reacted, but almost a moment too late. He lifted his hands and diverted the lightning to the side, where it exploded behind him, and sent pieces of stone flying.

Lacertin glanced at Tan and nodded at Amia. "Do what you must. Save the girl, but keep *her* from reaching the source!" he said, pointing to indicate the Incendin fire shaper.

With a sudden shaping, he streaked into the sky.

Roine looked to Jishun, who nodded. Then he shot upward, after Lacertin.

Tan frowned, staring at where the two warriors had been. In the attack, Roine had lost his sword. Now it rested on the stone, runes catching the pale shaper's light.

Had Lacertin just *helped* him?

The idea seemed impossible, but what other explanations fit? How else to explain Lacertin attacking Roine and telling Tan to keep the Incendin shaper from the source?

Unless Lacertin had another motivation.

Fire pressed on the barrier, and Tan ignored it. With Roine gone, the barrier would hold longer. He had more time before the shapers would make it through, but he should hurry. How much time would he have before Roine or Lacertin returned?

Tan turned toward where the silvery liquid had once formed the pool. Now he had to somehow figure out a way to draw the Mother.

He didn't have to. Thick, silvery liquid bubbled from an opening in the ground, spilling around and filling the pool. Tan stood back, amazed at first, but then realized what Amia had been about to say.

The Mother only comes...

The elementals. That had been the key.

They formed more than only the barrier. The elementals *summoned* spirit.

Amia didn't move. The last convulsion had weakened her to the point where she now remained motionless and limp in his arms. Tan looked at the liquid, knowing he had to get her into it, but not certain how. He had seen what happened when anything other than a spirit shaper touched it. How could he get her into it safely?

The Daughter...

This came from the nymid, jarring him.

She must reach the Mother.

He nodded. *Will your armor protect me?*

It was the draasin who answered—with laughter that filled his head. *You are clever, Little Warrior, but you can be foolish.*

Tan frowned and looked over at the draasin, who blinked.

He quickly pulled Amia's clothes off, remembering how she had gone into the pool nude the last time. His breath caught when he saw bruises on her stomach and angry welts on her arms. What had they done to her?

There was only one way to get her into the pool, and had it not been Amia, he might not have tried.

Tan quickly tore off his clothes and set them to the side. If he survived, he wanted something to cover himself with.

And then he lifted Amia, girding himself as he stepped carefully into the silvery pool.

He gasped when it touched his legs, swirling around him.

Pain flooded through him, filling him. Tan staggered, almost falling. Seeing Amia, he pressed on. If he fell—if she didn't make it far enough into the pool—she might not survive.

He took another step. The liquid swirled around his thighs.

Pain ripped through his body, beating at his mind. The shaping made of water and air that he'd been holding in place crumbled. He felt his mind exposed and raw. That meant the archivist would be able to attack. Nevertheless, he took another step.

Now the pool was up to the middle of his chest. Pain burned through him one more time, washing over him like a wave, and then was gone.

He blinked and tilted Amia, slowly lowering her into the liquid. She didn't move, didn't make any sign that she knew what was happening. When the liquid reached her chin, she gasped and fell forward, sinking beneath the surface.

Tan dove after her. The liquid consumed him, rolling over him, and flashes of light and color swirled across his vision. For a moment, he thought he could sense everything in the world, that if he opened his mind, he could understand everything. His hand touched Amia's and he grabbed, pulling her back toward him.

She squeezed back.

In that moment, they were united in a way he'd never known. Different than the connection they had shared from their shaping, different than how he understood Asboel. Tan saw the shaping that caused her convulsions, a twisted film of darkness swirling through her mind, and gently removed it with a shaping that seemed guided by another presence. Once that shaping was gone, she gasped again, sucking in a mouthful of liquid. As she did, he sensed another source of pain from her and understood the headaches she'd been experiencing. They were not from shaping him, but from a twisting of the shaping worked on the youngest. The shaping had been changed, Amia's intent had been turned, twisted with a dark intent and used to control the youngest. With a thought, he untangled the twisting of the shaping, releasing the youngest from the pain of the dark shaping.

Go, Enya, he sent, knowing then her name. *Rejoin Asboel in the hunt.*

He felt the young draasin stir and rise, no differently than how he felt Asboel. She seemed to blink, realizing her release. With a flick of her tail and a quick beat of her wings, she took to the air. Through her eyes, Tan saw the mountains as they disappeared beneath her.

Through the thick, silvery liquid, he felt Amia. She turned to him, pressing her warmth against him. He could not see her but felt her presence, the sense of her as clearly in his mind as if she stood before him.

Tan held her for a moment. That moment could have been infinite. Within the pool, anything seemed possible.

He turned his attention to Asboel, knowing what he needed to do. *She is healed.*

Asboel roared appreciatively within his mind. *Perhaps not so foolish.*

Go. Join her in the hunt.

If I go, this protection will fall.

Tan sent a sense of reassurance. *If you stay, the Mother remains.*

He understood now. Before, the artifact held the pool in place even after the draasin were freed. If the archivist and the fire shaper reached the pool—if they returned the artifact here—they would have access to the Mother, to this source.

Asboel sent his frustration. *I will go. For now. You will survive and I will find you.*

Is that a command?

Asboel sent a sense of amusement tinged with worry. *Maelen.*

It was all he needed to say.

With a roar, Asboel took flight. He circled the inside of the massive cavern briefly before erupting into the sunlight, rising high into the sky and streaking after Enya.

Tan hesitated a moment more, enjoying the pressure of Amia against him, and then took a step forward.

The liquid pulled away from him. The level in the pool dropped as well, quickly disappearing back into whatever reservoir stored the source of the Mother.

Their heads emerged.

Tan looked at Amia. She blinked at him and then smiled. "How did you know?"

He shook his head. "I didn't know."

She pulled him toward her and wrapped her arms around him, unmindful of her nudity or the fact that shapers trying to harm them stood paces away. "You risked yourself for me?"

"Did I have a choice?"

Her eyes widened. "The shaping?"

Tan laughed and kissed her on the mouth. She kissed back. "Not the shaping. I would risk everything for you. I don't need a shaping to tell me that." He looked over toward Jishun. "Can you defend yourself?"

Her eyes narrowed and she nodded. "Now that I know I need to. I hadn't met another spirit shaper outside the Aeta. What are you going to do?"

Tan looked beyond the pillars. He saw the fire shaper first.

Her eyes stared at the fading pool of liquid. The fire burning in her obsidian bowl streaked upward. One hand pressed into the flames, pushing it outward so it encircled the pillars. Whatever strange power she worked pressed against the elementals and he felt their pain. They fought, but they would not last for long.

"The archivist shaped the kingdom shapers," Tan explained. "Roine…"

She nodded.

"Can you free them?"

Amia tilted her head. "I don't know. Possibly."

"We need to stop them first." He nodded toward the fire shaper and the archivist.

"How?"

Tan shook his head and grabbed his clothes, quickly pulling them on. Could the nymid armor help somehow? It might protect him long enough to stop the fire shaper, but that left the archivist. He'd already harmed Amia. She thought she could protect herself, but the archivist had more practice. If he managed to shape her again, now that Asboel was free, Tan didn't think he could summon the Mother again.

As Amia dressed, he looked at the elementals. Ara strained, flicking with agitation. Golud held but rumbled softly, leaving the ground trembling. And the nymid fought, but the force of the dark shaping was nearly more than they could bear.

They could not withstand the shaper, not with whatever darkness she used to augment her shaping. It would be up to him.

Tan looked over at Amia. "Be prepared for—"

He didn't get the chance to finish. Wind whistled into the cavern, coming in on a funnel. Thunder rolled somewhere nearby. An earth shaping pressed upon him. And fire burned. The kingdoms shapers had come.

Amia looked at him, eyes wide.

"Free them from the archivist's shaping," he said.

Amia focused, a shaping building. "It will take time."

"Release Ferran first."

She frowned and nodded. Her shaping built with a steady pressure behind his ears.

Tan let her work, turning to the elementals. He needed enough time for what Amia needed to do. If they could hold a little longer, he might have enough time to even the odds.

Please, hold on.

He sent the request three times, to each of the elementals. He felt a surge of steadying strength from each in reply.

Earth rumbled, rolling toward the archivist.

Amia had freed Ferran.

"We need a fire shaper too," he yelled.

Her shaping built.

The Incendin fire shaper glanced from Amia to the archivist. Her eyes twitched as understanding of what Tan and Amia attempted came to her. With a flash of a hidden obsidian blade, she slashed across the archivist's wrist. Blood spurted from him and his eyes went wide. She moved on a finger of flame, pulling the bowl toward him to catch his blood. Flames licked higher into the cavern as his blood joined hers in the bowl.

She grabbed the artifact from the archivist's hand.

Tan's heart stopped for a moment, catching as he stared at it.

The shaper plunged the artifact into the bowl. The archivist reached for it, but the fire shaper held his hand in place. Fire streamed *through* the artifact, drawing away from her shaping against the elementals. The archivist screamed. The fire shaper roared.

And a shaping built.

Tan felt it building unlike anything he'd ever felt before. Wind whistled into the cavern, growing louder and louder. Fire and earth mingled, pressing against the swirling chaos.

Protected by the barrier, Tan and Amia were kept safe, apart from whatever shaping happened on the other side.

"I can't find a focus," Amia said.

The shapers battled. Tan saw none of it; too much debris scattered around, but he felt the shaping worked by the Incendin fire shaper. Darkness worked within it. It mingled her fire and spirit from the archivist, somehow pulled through the artifact into a shaping she forced upon herself.

With a flash of understanding, Tan knew what she did.

There was only one reason an Incendin fire shaper would turn a shaping upon themselves. She wished to serve fire more intimately, twisting with it. She sought to become one of the lisincend.

"Tan—" Amia seemed to come to the same realization as him.

"Focus on Roine. If he returns, we will need to free him from the archivist's influence."

Amia stared at him with worried eyes. "What are you going to do?"

"What I must." With that, he sent a thought to each of the elementals. *Thank you.*

Ara slipped away on a flurry of wind. Golud rumbled, fading back into the earth. Only the nymid lingered.

Twisted Fire.

I will do what I can.

Twisted Fire used the Mother.

Tan frowned. *The artifact? What did she do?*

280

She seeks to become Fire, but she is Twisted. Careful, He Who is Tan.

Then the nymid disappeared, flowing away with the water, streaming toward the lake.

The barrier fell.

Tan ran toward Jishun first. He didn't want to risk a spirit shaping while trying to deal with the fire shaper.

He needn't have bothered. Jishun lay on the ground, pale and cold, as if all the blood had been drained from him. Eyes stared blankly. The silver ring, the mark of the Athan, circled one finger.

The artifact was gone.

Tan slipped the ring off Jishun's finger and stuffed it into his pockets. He turned from the dead archivist and looked for the fire shaper.

She stood only a few paces from him, transformed.

The shaping had burned the clothes from her, leaving her naked. Skin that once looked youthful and smooth was now leathery. Her eyes had peeled back and her lips thinned. Her arms had twisted. She roared, and leathery wings peeled from her back.

A satisfied smile stretched across her face, twisting her mutated features. She clutched the artifact in one hand.

Tan backed away and nearly tripped on something. Tan backed away and nearly tripped over something: Roine's sword. He grabbed it and held it in front of him. The runes along the blade glittered.

The fire shaper hissed.

He understood what she had done, but not *how* she had done it. The shaping had turned her into something like the draasin, leaving her even more twisted than the lisincend.

He understood what the nymid had said. The Incendin fire shaper sought to become fire and used the artifact—shaped out of spirit itself—to do so. The foulness of what she'd become burned at his senses. What would have happened had she reached the pool of spirit?

281

Heat pressed with rapid violence toward him. The pressure built, more quickly than he could react.

Without thinking, Tan pulled on the connection to Asboel and used his knowledge to absorb the shaping. The heat filled him, leaving him with a raw, pained sense.

The fire shaper—the lisincend or whatever she now was—roared at him again. Her voice filled the cavern, echoing off walls.

A blast of fire struck toward him.

Tan couldn't react in time. Even were he able to somehow absorb it like he had the last, he wouldn't be fast enough.

Stone rumbled and rose from the ground, deflecting the shaping.

Golud? Would it help without him asking?

Tan looked over to see Ferran facing the fire shaper and understood. Not golud, but a Master shaper, restored to himself.

Another section of the stone pushed up, rolling toward her.

Thick wings caught the wind and she lifted into the air.

She circled, testing out her new ability, and then fire shot from her mouth, scorching toward Tan and Master Ferran.

He looked over at Tan, a pained expression in his eyes. Tan didn't need for him to speak to understand that Ferran couldn't do anything against this type of fire.

Wind whistled through the cavern, catching the twisted lisincend and tossing her against the rock. A funnel of wind raced up from the ground, catching the fire and throwing it back toward the lisincend.

Tan looked over to see Alan sliding toward him on a cushion of air. His face twisted in concentration and sweat pressed from his brow. He was another shaper Amia had freed.

With more time, she could free the others. And then the odds would be even.

But the fire shaper turned her attention to Amia. She stood near where the pillar of water had formed. Some residual of the nymid still swirled through it, but not enough to protect her. The lisincend swooped toward her, fire coughing from her mouth.

Tan dove toward Amia, grabbing her and rolling her under him to protect her from the flames that pressed toward them. He pushed out with Roine's sword and screamed. A shaping surged *through* it, catching the fire.

The lisincend roared again.

If Tan needed any more proof he could be a warrior, holding— and *using*—a warrior's sword was it. He rolled, pulling Amia with him. Somehow, he needed to get free. If only he hadn't sent Asboel away, but the draasin had already done enough to help. Without the fire elemental, Tan would never have reached the place of convergence, would never have known what the archivists planned, and would never have saved Amia.

But with the fire shaper's transformation, they didn't have enough strength.

Tan tried a shaping, but he couldn't focus well enough to succeed. Wind wouldn't answer and there wasn't enough water for him to do anything useful. He did not think fire would succeed against a twisted fire shaper.

Lightning streaked into the cavern again, followed by a painful clap of thunder.

Tan hazarded a glance up. If Roine returned, Amia might not have enough time or strength to free him. And then the shapers would truly be outnumbered.

It was not Roine.

Lacertin hovered on a shaping of wind. Thin whips of wind and water streaked from his hands, catching the lisincend and twisting her in the air.

She shot fire at him, but Lacertin ducked it.

"You are a servant of Incendin!" she screamed.

Lacertin shook his head. "I serve no one but myself. I have never hidden that fact."

She shot a lance of flame at him. The heat pressed upon Tan, burning him as he rolled.

Lacertin somehow *trapped* the flame, and it extinguished. "I admit my time spent in Incendin had its uses. Not the least learning from your fire shapers. But they lack for creativity."

She snarled and dove toward him, her wings folding as she did.

Lacertin flipped his wrist and streaked toward the top of the cavern. The lisincend chased him.

And then another bolt of lightning streaked into the cavern with a thundering boom.

Roine stood before them. He stared at Tan, at the sword in his hands.

Tan pulled Amia behind him.

Stop him!

Her shaping built sharply. "Theondar!" The word came with a snap.

He blinked and looked at her with uncertainty. "I—"

A shaping built from him directed at Tan and Amia.

"*Theondar!*" she snapped again. Her shaping came with more power and urgency. It shook Tan's bones and washed out from her in a flood.

Roine fell to his knees. He trembled for a moment, looking much like Amia as the shaping had overwhelmed her mind. Then it faded. Roine collapsed.

Tan reached toward him, but Amia held him back.

"Careful. I can't tell if the shaping was successful. The archivist was more skilled than I realized."

Tan patted her hand. "I have to know. It's Roine."

Amia smiled tightly. "But he's also Theondar."

Tan swallowed and hurried over to Roine. The warrior's chest rose and fell slowly. Tan touched his arm lightly.

Roine's eyes opened and flickered over to him.

Tan stiffened, uncertain whether Amia had successfully shaped him or if he was still under the archivist's influence. "Roine?"

Roine took a deep breath and looked around. "Tannen." He turned and fixed his gaze on Amia. "Amia. You shaped me."

Amia nodded. Tan felt her building a shaping, as if preparing for the possibility that Roine hadn't fully been restored.

"Thank you."

Tan sighed, relieved. He reached a hand out to Roine and helped him to his feet. "The Incendin shaper used the archivist and the artifact."

"Used for what?"

Tan pointed toward the ceiling. Lacertin darted on his shapings, attacking the shaper. She flew, lunging, using her hands like claws to twist and bite at Lacertin.

"Lacertin helps," Tan said.

Roine frowned. "Lacertin helps only himself."

"Right now, that means helping us."

Roine sighed. "Then I need to help Lacertin." The disgusted tone of his voice told Tan everything about how he felt. "I'll need my sword."

Tan handed it to him and Roine frowned. He shook his head slightly. With a streak of lightning, he shot toward the ceiling. He joined Lacertin in attacking the Incendin shaper.

At first, she held them off, but they worked together, a memory of a time when warriors danced in the skies, keeping her focus divided. Each shaping pressed harder against her, inching closer to overwhelming the protections even her augmented shaping offered. Much longer and she would fall.

Amia laid her hand on Tan's arm. "We need to help the others."

He turned away, comforted that the two warriors could handle the twisted shaper.

Ferran and Alan battled the kingdom's shapers. Fire and water slapped against wind and earth. One shaper lay unmoving on the ground. Amia leaned over him and formed a quick shaping.

As she stood, a blast of fire shot at her from the shaped trees.

Tan jumped in front of it, the nymid armor absorbing the impact. Amia fell back, striking her head.

He turned, ignoring the others around him. Amia lay unmoving. Blood oozed from her scalp. Her eyes rolled back in her head. Tan's heart hammered, but she moaned softly.

He touched her hair, smoothing it back. "Amia?"

"I'll be fine. I can't shape like this." She swallowed and opened her eyes weakly. "I'm sorry, Tan."

Ferran and Alan pressed back. The kingdom's shapers still under the archivist's influence overwhelmed them.

"Don't worry. We'll be fine."

She grunted. "You can't lie to me."

He nodded. Even were she not a spirit shaper, she would probably know when he lied. Their spirit shaping only ensured it. "I'll do what I can."

She took his hand and squeezed. "You're blessed by the Great Mother too. You can use it to end this."

"But I'm not."

She started to shake her head and then winced. "I saw you when you joined me in the pool. You wouldn't have been able to do that without her blessing."

Tan started to argue again, but stopped. *Could* he be blessed by the Great Mother?

Asboel seemed to think so. Hadn't he claimed Tan shaped him during the attack with Enya? And he had managed to enter the pool of liquid spirit. Without spirit shaping, he wouldn't have been able to do it.

With the other shapings, he'd spoken to the elementals for guidance and used that experience to help his shaping. He'd never spoken to the spirit elemental.

Or had he? Wasn't that what he'd done when he stepped into the silvery pool? Wasn't that what he'd done when he felt joined to Amia? Could he do it again?

Tan knelt, one hand still holding Amia's. He closed his eyes, focusing, doing everything he could to remember what it had been like when he stood in the pool of spirit. Memories of it floated into his mind, filling him. Memories of knowledge and understanding, of the sense of being joined to Amia in a way he could never explain. Memories of strength.

Tan held onto all of this in his mind, and then he sent out a shaping.

"Stop!"

He infused the word with his shaping. It washed out of him, released with a burning energy, rolling from him so that it shook the stone, the cavern, *everything*. He realized he had formed this shaping before, only then, he hadn't understood what he was doing. It was the shaping that stopped Enya and Asboel as they fought.

Everything around him ceased moving, as if time itself stopped.

Lying next to him, Amia smiled.

Master Ferran stopped his earth shaping and stared ahead. The wind shaper, Alan, floated to the ground and stood waiting. Water shapers stood motionless. Fire shapers hidden in the trees no longer threw their angry heat.

Above him, even Lacertin and Roine hesitated.

Both threw shapings at the Incendin shaper but stalled, sinking toward the cavern floor. Lacertin resisted. In another moment or two, Tan suspected he would manage to free himself from the attack. Roine blinked, as if the additive effect of so many spirit shapings upon him overwhelmed his ability to resist.

Even the twisted fire shaper hesitated. But then, with an angry roar, she spewed flames from her mouth and shot out of the cavern, disappearing into the sky, taking the artifact with her.

EPILOGUE

A S THE TWISTED SHAPER DISAPPEARED from the cavern, Tan reached for his connection to Asboel and sent an image of the Incendin shaper.

Twisted Fire. They seek to displace the draasin.

The sending took much strength. Already, Asboel had flown far from the place of convergence, now flying alongside Enya and the other draasin. Through that vision, Tan saw the other draasin as she flew, two massive eggs clutched in her talons.

The draasin are not so easily displaced. I will hunt in time, Maelen.

Tan sighed. With the change, Incendin had just become more powerful. And if they could recreate the shaping now that they had the artifact, others would be in danger. Already, Incendin required Doma to send them shapers. How much longer would the barrier last now that Incendin attacked in full?

Whatever else, the battle with Incendin was not over. Not yet.

Lacertin landed next to him. Ash and dried blood caked his face. His dark hair hung by a twisted cord behind his head, but much had pulled free. His simple black jacket and pants looked made of a strange, familiar leather. Tan stared at it a moment before realizing where he'd seen it before. Lisincend skin.

"You have done well, Tan."

Tan looked at him, startled. "How do you know my name?"

He snorted. "There is much I know. Why do you think I left the kingdoms all those years ago?"

Tan tried remembering what his mother had told him about Lacertin. None of it made sense now. "You didn't sneak into the king's chambers?"

Lacertin sighed. "So much from that time was a mistake, but I cannot change it. Had I not learned what they planned... how they intended to use the artifact..."

"You learned of the archivists," Tan said, suddenly realizing.

Lacertin nodded. "And none believed. They came to this place to reach pure spirit. Had it not been for you, they would have succeeded."

"But why? Why did they help Incendin?" Tan wanted to know why Lacertin helped Incendin too, but now he wasn't sure he had.

"They never helped Incendin. They used each other. The archivists couldn't summon spirit, not without help. They needed shapers of other elements to draw the elementals here. And Incendin has been collecting shapers for years. When they learned of the draasin..."

It had been Tan's fault the archivists had learned how Amia had shaped the draasin. "They thought to shape the elementals?"

Lacertin's face clouded. "I'm not certain what they intended. As much as I've discovered over the years, much is still unknown."

"I still don't know why the archivists used the Aeta."

"Ask her," he said, nodding to Amia.

With a quick movement, he touched her head. The shaping he used happened in a flash.

Tan started toward her before realizing what he had done.

Amia sat up, touching her now-healed head. She blinked, looking up at Lacertin. "Thank you."

"Not me. Had it not been for Tan…"

"What about the archivists? What would Amia know?"

"Think of who shapes spirit."

She looked at him. Sadness filled her eyes. "They were Aeta once."

It made a twisted sort of sense. "But the spirit shapers of the Aeta are all female."

Amia shook her head. "Not all. Only women can lead. There have always been men with the ability to sense, and I'd never known one to be blessed by the Great Mother, but there is no reason they could not exist."

Lacertin shook his head in irritation. "Because they leave, sought out by the archivists. I still don't know what they intended here, but it seems Incendin got the upper hand. And Alisz finally got what she has wanted."

Tan thought of how the fire shaper had changed, twisting into something different than the lisincend. "They want to displace the draasin, don't they?"

Lacertin nodded. "That has always been Fur's plan. He has never understood why it hasn't worked. When he learned of the remaining draasin…"

Tan took a deep breath. It would not be the last time Incendin attacked. And Asboel would need help.

He took Amia's hand and met Lacertin's eyes. "How did you know to come here?"

Roine finally landed and stood near Master Ferran. He watched Lacertin with suspicious eyes. Alan came alongside them. All held a shaping ready.

"Your mother asked me to help."

"My mother?"

Lacertin nodded. "Once she learned I still lived, and once she realized why I had gone. Few shapers recognize the importance of my barrier as well as Zephra."

His? Had it been Lacertin who created the barrier?

"But she didn't know about you," Tan said. If she had, wouldn't she have warned him?

Lacertin smiled and leaned toward Tan. "She does."

Does. Not did.

Lacertin nodded. "Yes, Tan. Zephra still lives."

DK HOLMBERG currently lives in rural Minnesota where the winter cold and the summer mosquitoes keep him inside and writing.

To see other books and read more, please go to www.dkholmberg.com

Follow me on twitter: @dkholmberg

Word-of-mouth is crucial for any author to succeed and how books are discovered. If you enjoyed the book, please consider leaving a review online at your favorite bookseller or Goodreads, even if it's only a line or two; it would make all the difference and would be very much appreciated.